THE PLAY
A CHICAGO NIGHTS NOVEL

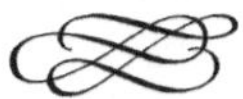

NATALIE WRYE

ABOUT THE PLAY

Becoming enemies with your neighbor is never a good idea.

What's even worse is when the neighbor is an incredibly hot client.

Baseball god Sevin Smith is no longer just the noisy bachelor living above me. Now he's the MVP client I have to protect from a paternity scandal, and I'm not thrilled that my boss has me on the case.

That's fine. I can pretend and work with a man who's become my enemy.

But what I can't pretend is not to be attracted to him.

Not to fall for his sexy laugh and easy smile. And I definitely can't pretend I'm not falling for the spunky eight year old kid that may or may not be his.

Yes, I admit it: Becoming enemies with your neighbor—the sexy sports star—is never a good idea.

But falling in love with him might be the worst idea of all...

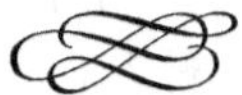

CHAPTER 1

MILY

CHICAGO, ILLINOIS

Thursday night

Was there anything sadder than wearing sexy lingerie under your Armani skirt suit, knowing no one would see it?

I wasn't sure, but if I had to take a poll, I'm sure the answer would be right up there with crushing on your sister's boyfriend or falling over your discarded shoes on your two AM trip to the bathroom.

Thirty minutes ago, when I realized Jason wasn't showing up for our date, I couldn't have imagined that my night could get worse than that typical two AM bathroom trip.

Maybe… I was wrong. *So very wrong.*

Heading home to slip quickly out of my little black dress and into a business suit wasn't exactly what I had in mind when this night started out either, but I throw my shoulders back anyway, tying the belt around my trench coat tighter.

Because when you get a call from your boss, you can't say no. Even late at night.

The early March Chicago weather is cold this year, made

chillier by my lack of love life, and the second I march up to that familiar brick building, I swipe my key card at a sensor most people rarely take the time to see, trying not to be upset at another start to a weekend…

Alone.

The inside of the lobby when I enter is quiet, cold. At this hour, it's dark, and with nothing but the sound of my high heels clicking to keep me company, I reach the end of the hall, my finger poised to the elevator button.

Somebody's finger makes it there first. I jump at the touch.

"So," the owner of the finger presses without preamble. "Did you do it? Did you bring Jason home?" My favorite colleague's voice lowers. "Are you wearing the lingerie we picked out? Did you puff, powder and primp your nether regions just like I told you?"

I sigh, stepping into the elevator alongside him. My eyes focus on the ceiling.

"Fuck Jason."

Ben chuckles. "That's exactly what I thought you were going to do."

"Sorry to disappoint you, but not a thing is going on with my nether regions tonight. Jason… He's a jackass."

"Well, damn… I helped you pick out La Perla for tonight, and it was all for a jackass. What the hell happened? I thought that tonight was going to be *the* night."

"You know," I finally look over. "For a communications consultant, you're sure not picking up on my non-verbal cues."

"That's because they're all pointing to signs that you didn't get laid. And I'm not accepting that."

"Accept it, please. And never mention it again." I huff. "Besides, I didn't say that I was definitely going to sleep with him," I correct slowly, "I said it was a *possibility* that tonight was going to be the night. *Possibly.* And that was true, until I sat there for *an hour* at the restaurant, stood-up and sadly sipping my wine like an All American Reject. Wasn't exactly my idea of a good date night."

Ben exhales, his chin dipping to his collar. He throws his hands on his hips. "That sucks."

"I know."

"Almost as much as being called in for a work meeting at nine o'clock on a Thursday night." He smirks. Just as the elevator stops. The doors part.

"If Stephan hears you say that, he'll have your balls." I walk out, heading towards the conference room with Ben trailing a foot behind me. He leans in to whisper.

"He *already* has my balls. And since our boss is *the* sexiest man in Chicago, I say he can keep them. My balls look better in Stephan's hands than they do on my body, I'm sure."

"What's this about me having your balls in my hand?"

A pair of footsteps turns the corner and Stephan Knight, walking shadow that he is, steps right into sight, making Ben and I stop.

My gaze trails over him.

Over the salt and peppered hair. The broad shoulders. *That jaw.*

His midnight blue eyes are the color of his collared shirt, and each smoky iris is fixed on us as he welcomes us inside. "Glad you guys could make it."

As if we had a choice.

Ben is certainly not lying; Stephan Knight might be the sexiest man in Chicago. But he also might be the scariest.

The former Chicago District Attorney is anything if not surprising, and with this spur-of-the-moment meeting, I'm certain of only one other thing tonight besides that fact that I'm not getting laid.

We have a new client.

The almost-midnight meeting tells me so.

The offices of The Firm Crisis and Emergency Management

are half-lit, and so are my senses, each part of my body thrumming in anticipation of tonight's news.

In the conference room, I take a seat at the long, rounded table next to Ben. Stephan, of course, sits at the head, his eyes alert as additional sets of footsteps join us.

Kayla, Bowen and Sabrina make six, and so the meeting begins. Stephan cuts to the chase.

"We have an assignment, people." He steeples his long elegant fingers. "And it's a good one."

I can see the excitement in his eyes as he stands to his feet.

Wow, this really must be good.

Stephan walks to the whiteboard on the wall, turning to face us all.

"This is an in-house job, guys, so I want everyone to pay attention. Kayla, take out the file. Ben, get the lights. Emily?"

My ears perk up. "Yes?"

"I want you taking notes." Stephan glares at me. "This case has a lot of entertainment law in it. And since that's your specialty as of late, I'm going to need you on this assignment like bread on butter. Am I making myself clear?"

"Crystal." I'm already taking out a pen and paper, my hand poised. Electricity skims over the surface of my skin.

Here we go.

Waiting for a night like this has been a long time in the making, and fortunately the wait has nothing to do with that asshole Jason but my own career.

I was barely skimming by when I joined The Firm hardly making rent. My entire client list was friends and family—referral-only, and though my fees were not cheap, I'd come to discover that unfortunately nothing about living in downtown Chicago was cheap either.

Especially my rent.

Six months ago, I was nowhere near being on the street but funds were dwindling. Add student loans, the cost of running my own law operations and ailing grandparents, and I was practically bleeding dollar bills, the short-term success I was starting to enjoy ripping away at the seams.

I'd been a secretary in New York, for God's sake. A naive law grad with little money.

Funny how life could humble you in half a year, and at my new job, that was still the case.

I was the new girl, Stephan Knight's most recent employee. And he hadn't so much as looked at me until tonight.

I'm practically vibrating as he rattles off this assignment, his blue eyes on fire. I watch him.

"Kayla," he shoots towards the PR agent as Ben flicks on more lights. "Can you read the file to the room, please?"

One of my closest friends clears her throat, her dark hair bobbing as she brings the folder closer to her nose. She starts.

"I had a client—excuse me—almost had a client. And he's close to The Firm family. About eight months ago, I was set to becoming Sevin Smith's PR agent. But," she sighs loudly, "when my fiancé and Sevin went into business together, I resigned because of a conflict of interest. And Sevin has yet to hire a new PR agent."

"Which, I'm guessing, leaves little Mr. MVP open to all types of public scrutiny with no protection?" Ben leans forward.

"Exactly. And he needs it more than ever..." Kayla huffs out soundly. "Because he's being blackmailed for a million dollars."

The room falls still.

"An old fling is claiming that Sevin's the father of her child, and she wants to be paid to go away. She saw me on the news with Sevin a few months ago, and now she's contacted me, threatening to go public. To tell everyone that Chicago's shiniest new import is 'nothing but a deadbeat dad.'" Kayla closes the folder, lancing us with those sharp oceanic blue eyes. Her lips are pressed shut. "End quote."

And the air grows thick. Made thicker by the fact that I have no idea who this Sevin guy is, and everyone else does.

There's a new gloom added to the room. A moment of silence.

We always have a moment of silence.

Probably for the possible death of our clients' reputations. If we were to ever lose a case. Because we don't.

Stephan's stare reminds us as he claps his hands.

"So, is that clear? Emily…" His eyes go to me. "I want you as primary on this case. This is your area of expertise and I want you working beside Kayla and Ben as we figure out how to keep this out of the press and deal with the legal demands of this ex-groupie's sudden paternity claims, if any. Until we prove that Sevin is the father, or likely isn't, *I don't want a word of this breathed to the outside world*. Bowen." He glances at the tall chiseled man on the other side of the room. "You make sure this groupie knows the meaning of silence. We begin work tonight. Everyone understand?"

The rest of the room nods. I stay still.

Stephan starts rattling off a set of new instructions, and his five employees go flying.

I'm already logging into my "Family Law" files on my phone as another cog in The Firm's wheel when Ben sidles up to me. Face flushed, his manicured hands high, he taps his handsome cleft chin, checking my face, a small smile framing his full lips. He watches me closely.

"So…this is big, isn't it?"

"Your ego. Why, yes, it is. And admitting it is the first step." I flash him a grin for a second, and he grins back, the epitome of arrogant composure. He crosses his arms.

"Stephan has you leading one of his cases. This is huge. Six months at The Firm and you've already earned his confidence. That has to mean something."

"Yes, it means that I can pay next month's rent. And I hope that's all you're implying…"

"I'm a Communications Consultant. I don't imply. I say things outright. And I'm saying that if Jason doesn't bite, then you might want to put that Jason-La Perla lingerie to good use. Preferably with someone else who could appreciate it. Someone single. Someone handsome. Someone like…"

"If you say Stephan, I will literally go 2007 Britney Spears on you."

Ben shudders, one hand flying to his chest. He gapes. "Excuse you very much. I would never say Stephan." His voice lowers. *"Especially when I plan on saving him for myself."*

I frown. "So who are you talking about then?"

"I'm talking about Sevin Smith."

"Jesus, Ben. The client? I'm a lot of things, but dumb and desperate aren't any of them. And I don't get it… Sevin Smith?" I ask, genuinely perplexed. "Who is he anyway? Is he an actor?"

"Actor?" His clean-shaven chin cocks. "Oh honey, you've got to read a blog at least once in a while." He reaches for his cell phone, typing a few words before showing me the screen, his face serious as I lean in to look.

What I see takes my breath away. *This Sevin guy is gorgeous.* No doubt about that.

A headline flashes before my eyes—some campy title about championships and franchise legacies but I'm too busy staring at the featured man's face, rugged and stubbled beneath a Chicago Cougars baseball cap.

Ben has to remove the phone for me to stop staring. He winks down at me. "A complete dish, isn't he?"

I nod, not knowing what to say. "Sure. He's a…whole meal, I guess."

"A shame you two didn't hit it off." Ben tucks his phone away. "If you had," he whispers between tightened lips, "you might have had a chance at sampling some of that hunk. Well, if I don't get to him first."

I can't hold back the scowl that decorates my face. I incline closer to Ben. "What are you talking about? I don't even know the guy."

"Oh, but you do. I'd say you know him rather…intimately."

The air tenses with his suggestion, and suddenly I have to struggle to breathe. That can only mean…

I exhale. "You mean this Sevin guy's my…?"

"Late night bedroom scream-fest a floor above? Yup." He announces with a *pop*. "And I can't wait to *accidentally* bump into him on the elevator in the next few days. It's already been confirmed. Emily," he breathes, "*Sevin's your new neighbor. At least that's what I overheard Stephan telling Bowen. Since that sexy bastard knows everything.*"

And the minute Ben says it, I know it's true. Because Stephan does know everything.

The air gains an extra thousand ounces of weight. And suddenly I can't breathe.

Having to prove myself at this job is one thing; proving it while holding a stick of dynamite is another.

And this neighbor is a stick of dynamite, one that's already exploding.

The tension in my apartment building was already teeming between the two of us, the anger palpable. I'd already called the cops on the "Noise Nuisance" more times than I could count, and not once—but twice—he'd left little notes on the building's bulletin board, taunting me like a child, dangling his sex life and my obvious lack-thereof like a proverbial carrot in front of my face.

It was like middle school all over again. Only with high-priced apartments.

And suddenly I feel sick.

My discreet new boss just gave me an assignment for my not-so-discreet enemy of a neighbor. *And I have to take it.*

Makes me wonder if the almighty Stephan can hear my

thoughts now. Or if he knows about the La Perla lingerie I'm hiding.

Whatever my rich attractive Ben-stalked boss does know, I hope it has nothing to do with how much I hate our new client. And how I'm considering killing him before this case is all over...

I bite the inside of my cheek, leaving the conference room, wishing that my worries were only as small as a bathroom trip at two A.M.

Because I now have the answer for which is worse.

CHAPTER 2

*E*MILY

Friday - midnight

An entire day doesn't erase the bad taste from last night's meeting. And neither does this Kung Pao chicken I'm eating in bed.

Instead of writing notes like I'm supposed to, I've been writing the words, *Sevin Smith is my client. Sevin Smith is my client,* over and over, but the doodling is no catharsis for my trouble.

Because my asshole neighbor is my client. And there's absolutely nothing I can do about it.

I figure if I say the sentence more, it'll start to make sense.

The twenty-four hours after Stephan's secret meeting is stuffed with nothing but research on our new case, and with my head stuffed in my laptop and takeout in my lap, I do my absolute best to avoid the possibility of ever running into Sevin Smith in my apartment building.

But the time marks eleven o'clock, a full day after the new news.

I find myself shiftless, looking up paternity statues for the state of Illinois, my eyes tired from the effort.

Headphones in, Fiona Apple music on, I try not to stare—weary and dry-eyed—at the pile of laundry in the corner of my bedroom where, if everything had gone according to plan last night, Jason might have set up a bottle of wine.

The La Perla lingerie (the ones Jason once hinted he liked) sits lonely on top of the laundry pile, and I pretend I'm okay with China Taste being my date for the night.

That I'm okay with being rejected by another guy in an online world where even a man you've been dating for two months might ditch you for other options. That I'm okay with going back to wearing my bikini-cut panties with the cartoon characters on them instead of the high-priced, hoping-to-get-laid lingerie.

Fiona's still singing to me, lovely lyrics that tell me I'm criminal as I sit on the edge of my bed in my *Hey Arnold!* cartoon undies, and with redemption on my mind, I finally get up, grabbing the dirty clothes from that sad little corner.

Slapping on a pair of sweats, I grab the overflowing hamper. Music at last on pause, I prepare to take the long elevator trek down to the fourteenth floor, dragging the dirty laundry behind me, checking my phone for the fortieth time.

Midnight.

On a Friday night. Alone with nothing but unclean drawers.

Pathetic.

Pressing the elevator button for the communal laundry room many levels below, I get in and pray that none of my neighbors see me.

Standing there. Makeupless in a t-shirt and sweats, mouthing the words to nineties music with Chinese "special sauce" decorating the corner of my lips.

But my prayer for a quick trip is wasted somewhere around the twenty-seventh floor as the empty elevator slows.

I wait for the doors to part.

And as soon as they do, a pair of green eyes peer out beyond the tiny elevator space, snatching the already-shallow breath from my body.

My heart kicks into high-gear, pulse pounding as the silver car opens to reveal my upstairs neighbor standing just outside of it.

The man living right above me. Mr. Makes-Too-Much-Noise.

Mr. Makes-The-Women-He's-With-Scream-Bloody-Murder-in-Bed.

Sevin Smith is my client all right.

But not just that. Right now, Sevin Smith is in my elevator.

And he's looking right at me.

My breath seizes in my throat, forgetting how to make it to my mouth.

Fuck.

Sevin Smith is in my elevator. Seven Smith is in my elevator.

My asshole neighbor is in my elevator.

Hell, we may have taken this elevator a million times together since he's moved in. But I guess I've always been too busy, too buried in some new client brief to notice the serious-faced Adonis riding a few feet away from me.

Every day.

He says nothing as I shift on my feet, a strange glint playing in his irises as his hardened stare clashes with mine.

I can't move. Or talk. Or think in those few seconds that pass between us.

In that moment he takes his first step towards me, I don't know how...but I know that he knows. Knows that I'm the neighbor, the one who's called the cops. Or even the one who's taken him on a client.

But he doesn't speak.

Not one word.

The gorgeous real-life version of the man from the magazine just stands there, a human statute in low-slung jeans.

And to make matters worse, as if to confirm he knows my

little secret, he lifts his chiseled chin towards me, raises one eyebrow…and smiles.

Smelling of smoky musk and pure man, he sucks the very air out of the small lift as he walks inside to stand, a package in his hands, his muscular body taking up half the space.

At the vision of him coming to stand beside me, my heart leaps into my throat and decides to dance.

The double doors close, locking us inside, and I'm seconds away from melting into the floor—anything to escape this pure Hell I'm in.

I curse myself in every word in English…and a few that aren't when suddenly the chiseled granite of a man beside me speaks, his husky deep voice filling the elevator with its warmth.

"Hm." He grunts, a small gravelly sound. His face doesn't move much.

"You know, I've never seen anyone use the elevator this late but me…"

"Excuse me?" I'm not sure I hear him right.

"The elevator. This late." He doesn't look at me. "I've never seen anyone past, hell, ten. I've only ridden it about three times or so, because it's always stockpiled with people. It's almost like they're waiting for me to get on so they can stack up like Legos."

I tilt my face towards him, my voice breathless as I respond. "I think the majority of the people in this building wait until I'm late before they decide to make a go for the elevator. I'm convinced they're having meetings on how to fuck up my life."

Out of the corner of my eye, I notice a smile spread across the stubble on his chiseled face. I try not to stare at his lips as he talks. "Don't think anyone needs to have meetings on how to fuck up *my* life. I'm doing a pretty grand job of fucking it up quite well by myself these days."

I bite my lip, the skin rolling between my teeth as my mouth starts speaking on its own. "And maybe screwing up mine in the process?" I lift a brow, never looking at him. "I was under the impression that I had dibs on this elevator at this hour."

He grins, a small gesture I see from the corner of my eye. "Maybe we need a reservation system, you know. A way of booking this damn thing." He smiles wider. "How would that work exactly? Would I walk right up to the doorman downstairs? Say 'I have a reservation for the elevator. Name's Sevin Smith. Asshole. Party of one, please'?"

I can't fight the smirk curling upwards on my face. "Pretty sure he'd turn down your reservation if you worded it like that."

"Damn, you think?" He glances at me for the first time since he's entered the elevator, and I have to fight to keep my knees from faltering. "We've gotta work out some type of system then."

We. The casual way he throws out the word has me imagining inexplicably dirty things with this man—this client that I'm now standing with. I clear my throat.

"Well, there is the MyNeighbor app..."

"MyNeighbor app?" He looks sincerely confused. "Sounds very "Mr. Rogers"-like. Does the app come with the Mr. Roger's hand puppets too or am I expecting too much?"

"Trust me." I hold up a hand, letting myself laugh. "It's nothing like Mr. Rogers or his neighborhood. Just a bunch of neighbors bitching about garbage disposal processes, juicy gossip and which tenant didn't take his or her trash out on time."

He lifts his chin towards me. "Sounds invigorating."

"It absolutely...is not." I chance a glance at him, and my pulse beats double time. "But it helps you stay on top of local news, ongoings in the building."

"Ongoings like stalkers, creeps or the occasional elevator reservation talk?"

"Something like that." I catch his eye and keep it this time.

He's absolutely mouthwatering, standing there like that in a simple t-shirt and jeans, and for a blissful sixty seconds, I forget...

Forget that I secretly hate this man. Forget that he's my client. Forget the havoc he's wreaked in my life.

I'm not even supposed to meet with him. Not yet.

I'm supposed to meet him with Stephan in The Firm's offices. Where there's much more feet—*and maybe even mace*—between us.

I purse my lips to keep from saying anything further, and the elevator stops, signaling my floor.

I close my eyes slowly as I leave the elevator and still Sevin stands there. He stares after me, his eyes burning a path of heat down my back.

I turn to him from the hallway, my stare finding his.

"Well, it was…nice. Nice to meet you, Sevin."

It really was. Despite every ounce of blood in my body that says to avoid this man like the plague. I inhale deeply as he says nothing for a full second, his green eyes sparking with something sensual buried deep inside.

He opens his mouth. "It was nice to meet you, too…Emily."

My lips fall open, shocking sucking the breath from my lungs.

Shit, he does know that I'm…well, me.

The shock morphs into relief when he points downwards at my personalized law school grad t-shirt, and before I can utter another word, the doors shut, leaving me more flustered about my new client than I've felt about a man in years, my pulse playing the congas for hours even after his distinct scent leaves my skin.

* * *

SEVIN

My Friday night had been off to a bad start. *Until now.*

Minutes after the pretty brunette leaves the elevator, I'm still thinking about her. The only thing that stops me from thinking about her even more is my ringing cell phone, and by the time I step out of the elevator onto my penthouse floor, my cell phone rings again, and I realize I missed my chance.

My chance to give her my number.

Damn.

I've only been back in town for the day since the Cougars had it off, but already so much has happened.

A quick check-in with my doctor on my recently-rehabbed knee, a session with my trainer that damn near killed me, a quick clean-up of the women's underwear in my guest bedroom—*that was fun...*

Oh, and picking up a package delivered to the wrong floor right before meeting the most sexily dressed-down woman I've ever seen.

On top of all of that, my assistant won't stop calling me non-stop.

I press the "Ignore" button on my cell as Naomi's name flashes there, twisting my penthouse key into the lock.

I feel it click.

But when I open the door, she's already standing there behind it, her brown eyes piercing me from behind the kitchen counter as she turns. Her arms cross under her ample chest, pressing tight.

"Thanks for hitting the 'Screw you' button on me, you asshole."

Asshole. Since it's technically past midnight, I guess that's the first for the day.

I am sure there will be many more.

Naomi holds up her phone. "I thought you might ignore me, so I decided to drop by." She tilts her head. "And I was right."

"No offense, Nome. But I'm tired from these spring training games all week, and I needed a break. So sue me." I walk to the fridge. "What do you want to get on me about this time? That I should be ashamed of having a social life? That my sexual history is going to prevent a future in hosting Good Morning America? Because if that's what you're getting at it, then it would help if you actually said it. I gave up that dream a million orgasms ago."

Behind her bulky glasses, my assistant's eyes widen at me with growing sympathy. The air in my penthouse is the opposite—cold from lack of regular use, while she paces the length of my living room, her fingers tapping lightly against her arm.

She bites the edge of one red nail.

"It's not quite that simple, Sevin."

"Hate to be a little rough here, Naomi. But I'm running off about three hours of sleep, and it's not exactly how I want to spend the next three weeks getting ready for the regular season." Her eyebrows knit together, and I shrug. "That damned downstairs neighbor of mine again. Apparently instead of getting laid like a normal human being, she gets off on calling the cops on me, so the neurons are firing a little slow today."

"You mean that Cold War of yours is still going on? And how exactly do you know that Mr. Telephone Man living below is a woman instead?"

"Because I heard Sarah McLachlan playing beneath my floorboards and any sane man listening to that would have killed himself by now." I inhale deeply. "So while my three brain cells are still firing, Nome, by all means, paint a picture for me here of this new tabloid story. Create a sketch. Use a crayon. I'm flexible."

She sighs, ruffling her curly brown bob. She walks slower. "I know I'm taking a long time to get this out, but I need you to *promise* not to freak. Trust me: I wouldn't bother you this late, if it wasn't freak-out-worthy."

"Meaning?" I lean forward on the couch, hearing it squeak.

"Meaning…it would be different if this new tabloid story was going after your purported bevy of bedmates. Or your stats at shortstop. Or even that fight you had with that St. Louis pitcher from last week."

"Guy's a tool. Not my fault he didn't have the arm he claimed to have to back up that mouth of his."

Naomi cocks her head. "And yet you nearly succeeded in *breaking* that arm. Not so expected from a man whose teammates previously nicknamed 'Mr. Cucumber.'. She pauses. "You're different these last few weeks. You've *been* different."

"I'm not different because I had a moment. Aren't people allowed to have moments?" The silence thickens between us, as I grip my hair, a headache starting to form behind my eyes. I have to stop my fingers from shaking. "So, are you sure that asshole pitcher didn't give an interview about me? Call me nasty names? Nome…" I try to reason with her. "If so, I can deal with it."

Naomi goes to town on that nail, chewing it to shreds—a tell-tale sign of her nerves. "Uh, no." She exhales. "This is so much worse than that."

"Nome, seriously, the theatrics are killing me. And I gotta be honest with you: My acting skills are not exactly up to snuff." I blurt out, frustration making the top of my head heat under my baseball cap. "I'll have a pack of Crayola™ delivered to your place, if it will make things easier. I need you to spell. This. Out."

Picking up her pace again, I watch Naomi cross the hardwood floors again, that nail of hers wearing thin.

"Okay, so it's like this: How good are you at keeping track of the women you've been with?"

"And by 'been with,'" I motion, "you mean like…?"

"Played a game of 'Hide the Salami'? Yup, that one."

I frown. "I don't keep a running number."

"Names?"

I cock an eyebrow. "You're kidding, right?"

My assistant's lips wear thin. "Would you remember a woman by the name of Deborah Jett by any chance?"

I think. *Deborah. Deborah. Deborah.*

Rings a bell. Not one that tinkles too loudly, though.

I do remember a couple of Deborah's. Maybe a Debbie. Or two.

I haven't been the *most* sexually active player in the League, by any chance. Far from it. But the women I've been with…especially recently.

Ever since the MCL tear and prognosis several weeks ago, my penthouse *has* seen more guests than usual, a fact made more clear by the easily irritable neighbor below me who hasn't taken too kindly to the sex marathons.

Maybe this neighbor is the Deborah Naomi's talking about. Could be.

Miss Bane of my Existence living below tends to play the type of Angry Girl music that I thought upped and died in the nineties, and it occurs to me that maybe she is this Deborah person, calling in whatever tabloid story Naomi is so against telling me about.

I run a palm across my face.

"Is it her? The woman downstairs? Because if it is, then feel free to schedule a sit-down with Miss Uptight. It's about time we meet face-to-face…"

"Sev!" Naomi interjects. "That's not it!"

I blink, frustration making my brow furrow further. I stand. "Then what the hell is it?"

Naomi sighs. "Deborah." Her breath is heavy. "This woman Deborah is saying that you have a child. That she has a child." She swallows. "That your child is her child."

My blood grows cold. Every piece of my body including the bum knee locks up, and I lean closer to Naomi, not wanting to miss a word.

"Excuse me?"

Naomi closes her eyes, opening them just as fast. "Deborah Jett. A single mother living in New York. She has a child. An eight-year old girl. She says you're the father of her child."

I won't believe it. "Bullshit. That can't be right."

"Are you sure, Sevin?"

"Yes, I'm sure." I start to pace. "I never sleep with a woman without a condom. Never."

"Never?"

"*Never.*"

But even as I say the word, it shakes.

An eight-year old. That would mean that me and this Deborah met nine years ago.

Right before I joined the League.

I was a mess back then. Screwed up.

It was the year I'd broken up with Kimmy, and as a nineteen-year old entering the Major Leagues, I'd done what most healthy red-blooded American men would do when exposed to a new world of wealth and women.

Except I was worse. *Much worse.*

The entire year between leaving college and entering the draft was only a blur. A blur of bedroom sheets, sweaty nights and booze.

And I can feel the color drain from my face as I remember it all. Naomi looks at me harder, her almond eyes rounding. She licks her lips.

"So, I'm guessing that 'never' isn't as rock-solid as we thought?"

I swallow, nodding, barely able to look at her. "Fuck, I don't know. That would be nine years ago…and I just don't know." I glance at her, finally meeting her stare, holding onto the edge of my baseball cap—my only calm in the rising storm. "The season starts in two weeks, Nome. Two damn weeks. I don't need this shit right now…if isn't true."

"I know. And normally, I wouldn't even tell you about something like this. Especially because this type of thing happens to sports stars all the time." She blows out a breath. "But this really has me freaked out." She nods, her irises holding onto some resilience. "And this Deborah woman says…well, she wants…" She hesitates, licking her lips. "Sev, she wants a million dollars to keep quiet about it."

"A million *what*?"

"A million dollars. Enough to buy a shit-ton of those crayons you love so much." She grins, but it falls. "It's a good thing Kayla told us about this woman before she officially started shopping it out to the blogs."

I glare at her, my blood gone cold at the thought. Doesn't take a million dollars of crayons to realize what's going on.

I'm being blackmailed. I'll never look at a pack of Crayola™ the same again. *Fuck.*

I exhale. "And what does our PR extraordinaire think about our chances of making this bullshit story disappear?"

Naomi starts biting on the edge of the damn nail again, and I already know I'm not going to like the answer.

Goddammit. And just when I thought the Good Morning America news was the worst of the day...

CHAPTER 3

SEVIN
Saturday afternoon

My body is still on Chicago time.

This morning's early morning flight back to Arizona took a lot out of me, and even after I'd slipped on that now-familiar white Chicago Cougars uniform, stepped onto the field out into that Arizona sun, everything felt, well, off.

My ex-PR agent Kayla was on the case of my alleged paternity, but that wasn't enough.

I had a feeling I was being suckered, summoned into some Hell dimension by a potential one-night-stand out for money. And it didn't help that, on Kayla's advice, I was using her current crisis management firm to represent me—some shadowy organization only known in certain celebrity circles to make media scandals basically disappear.

And now I was one of them. One of those scandals.

I tried my best to focus on this hot afternoon's game. I did.

But a line drive in the sixth inning had me beat. My busted knee twitched in ways it shouldn't have in a base run in the seventh, and by the eighth, I was in sloppy form.

I'd avoided an ass-chewing by Coach when all was said. But barely.

Ten minutes after the Milwaukee Bruisers sent us slumping back to the locker room with a score of 5-4, I peel off that sticky uniform, wishing I could peel off the rest.

Peel off this paternity bullshit. Peel off the niggling thought somewhere in the back of my mind that maybe it isn't bullshit at all…

I slap my baseball cap into my locker, listening to it crash.

"What's shaking, Sterling?" The nickname is almost like a taunt today. "Still bummed about the sixth inning?"

The disappointment must be all over my face. I barely glance up.

"What's up, Saw?"

"Other than my cock?" My old college teammate and current Cougars second baseman chuckles. "Nothing much. Just wanted to check on you. See how you're handling everything since the injury."

"Basically eating *shit* for breakfast, lunch and dinner. But that's nothing new." I pray that my teammate can't see the tension that's been racking my body for the last day and a half. I exhale. "Hey, man. In case I didn't tell you enough before the game, I'm sorry. About your foot, I mean."

"Eh." Sawyer brushes it off, unruffled as ever. "I only need it to walk. Or run. Or punt that baseman who broke it into oblivion. At least one of us is going to win that pennant this year. *Because you are going to win it, you know.*"

Am I? Every part of my life feels uncertain these days, especially my baseball career. I close my eyes, thinking of the problems waiting for me back in Chicago.

Me. A father.

The two words don't even go together. Luckily, Sawyer saves me from my thoughts.

"Tell me that you're not going to let a little knee twinge keep you from taking the Cougars to the playoffs."

I smile. "Like hell I will. Especially after the beating I want to give the Bruisers this season."

"Yeah." He shrugs, rubbing his shoulder. "They really had our number today. They squeezed by with a win. One or two runs. Every damn time." He hesitates as if thinking about today's loss. "I figured you might want to celebrate."

I feel my brows scrunch. "Celebrate? A loss? And…tonight?"

"Hell no. Thursday. Or Wednesday night, if you prefer. Either way, we have plenty of time to head back to Chicago and put that new penthouse of yours to good use."

Chicago. Back to arranging a sit-down with this "agency" or whatever. These fixers.

Back to getting to the bottom of what is quickly becoming the biggest pain in my ass.

"Jesus Christ," I grunt at Sawyer. "Do I even want to know what kind of 'celebration' is going through that thick head of yours?"

"Depends on which head you're referring to." A wicked tinge enters his rough tone. "Just thought we might throw a little shindig while we can, to commemorate you being back in action. For a minute, we all thought you might not even make it to spring training season."

I scoff. "For one, Saw: I didn't become the number one draft pick my rookie year, last year's Golden Glove recipient, and a two-time MVP of the National League to let a banged-up knee keep the Cougars from the season we deserve. And for two: Shindig? You? You've never thrown something as small as a shin-dig in your life, Sawyer."

"Okay, okay," he corrects. "It's a full on fucking rager. But you don't understand, Sev. The Playboy Anniversary Party is downtown at the Century Club next weekend."

"And?"

"And I've convinced three out of four attending playmates to attend our party first." I hear the grin in his voice.

I shake my head, my eyes closing as I listen to the music, losing myself in it. "Technically, I had no knowledge of it, so it isn't 'our' party. And if we were to even try, then I'm sure my spinster of a downstairs neighbor who sees fit to block any cock within in a five-mile radius might have something to say about that." I grunt. "Guess I have you to blame for her wrath with your regular *house-guests*, huh, Sawyer?"

"Who, me?" My old friend blinks innocently. "It's not my fault, Sterling. I didn't choose the bachelor life; the bachelor life chose me. And apparently *no one* is choosing that irritable downstairs neighbor of yours. Or she wouldn't be so damn cranky all the time because someone else is getting some." He pauses. "I have an idea: Why don't you knock on the old bird's door then? Introduce her to your famous Sterling—"

"'Silver Cock'?" Can't believe the nickname, nine years old, is still with me. Only today, the moniker seems more mocking than anything.

Sawyer laughs out loud again, his chuckle long and raspy this time. "I was going to say 'smile.' But since we're on the subject…" He trails off, his voice lowering with mischief. "What if she's hot?"

"What if she's old?"

"That's why they invented the term 'cougars,' Sevin. She could be both."

"I highly doubt it. The woman's anus is tighter than the banana hammocks you used to wear in college."

"Hey," he counters, indignation swirling in his tone. "Don't knock the Speedos until you try them. And the old girl might not be so uptight if she met you. Hell, the fact that her anus is so tight could be a plus, if you know what I mean."

He laughs again, and I remember what it was like when I still attended parties, had friends. When baseball hadn't consumed what was left of my life.

I shut my locker, noticing that we're some of the last players left. I grab my towel. "Hell no, Saw. Not this week. Not yet. I'm not in the mood for any parties. Any police. Any bunnies."

My hardheaded teammate starts to protest, but I've already ended the conversation. Stripping to my naked skin, I wrap the towel around my waist, heading for the showers.

The long hallway there is quiet, almost eerily so.

The sensation of being watched slivers up my spine, and I spin slowly on my heel, glancing over my shoulder at the emptying space around me, half-expecting some paparazzo to shove a camera in my face.

Because fuck, I can't stand living like this.

I'm paranoid. About this whole paternity deal.

The fluorescent lights beating down over the tiled floor only heighten my awareness, and I try to rein in the adrenaline still beating through my pumping heart.

Now alone inside the tiled shower, I twist the overhead faucet on, turning the heat on as hot as I can stand it. My head falls under the faucet's spray, my dark hair splaying across my forehead, and I slam a hand to the wall, bracing myself.

The pent-up frustration inside my body still has found no relief, even after the game, and soon I find my thoughts on the beautiful brunette from the elevator.

Hazel eyes. Dark hair. Full and kissable mouth.

It was a deep, dark pleasure to watch that mouth fall slightly open when she first saw me, to watch the corners tug upwards when I made her laugh.

A set of lush bangs tickled across her long, thick eyelashes, and I battled my impulse to brush the strands aside and feel those lashes flutter under my kiss.

If she recognized me from those dumb magazines, she never let on. But for the first time in a long time, I longed for someone to notice me, to look at me in all the ways I've avoided since the pressure of this trade to Chicago started breathing down my neck.

Maybe chatting up a neighbor in the elevator wasn't exactly my brightest idea, but I couldn't help it.

Seeing that soft cotton cling to the elevator brunette's tanned, smooth skin was enough to send my synapses spiraling into 'stupid-dom.'

Her hair smelled of honeysuckle and sin. Her tiny body was tight and curvy in all the right places. For an agonizing second under the shower, I wonder how curvy that body is underneath the warm fabric.

Naked, my body still shredded from the game, I somehow muster up the strength to reach for my now-hardening cock. It only takes a few slick strokes of the damned thing before its certified steel, and soon I am pumping myself to the thought of finding out just how soft this elevator Emily woman is, of discovering all the sensuality hidden in those shy hazel eyes.

Goddammit, I can't remember the last time I've been this hard. And I've had many opportunities over the past few weeks.

Thoughts of trapping my elevator co-conspirator between those steel double doors, of sinking my hand into her silky hair as I lower my head to suck on the skin beneath it, I am panting hard, almost to the brink of orgasm.

I stop myself before it's too late, my body tense and tingling from holding in my release. I barely manage.

Jacking off in locker room showers isn't exactly my style, and I sure as hell don't want to make it a bad habit.

I don't need more reasons to despise myself. God knows I have enough of those already, and strangely, the only thought that helps me forget right now is *her*.

* * *

EMILY
Saturday night

I can't get Sevin out of my head. And no pair of mental pliers will do the trick.

I should recuse myself from his case, I know. The conflict of interest is too great.

But the thought that Stephan is letting me lead this case, the thought that he's giving me the opportunity to prove myself, is enough to stop me from ruining yet another weekend night, and instead of reaching out to my current (rather intimidating) boss, I type a text to my old one, hoping Violet Keats, New York's most ambitious attorney, will tell me what to do.

Or at least give me a hint of advice.

I've never needed it so badly.

If Ben was right, then I do have Stephan's confidence. But I'm not so sure that I should.

Especially after everything.

Knowing where Sevin lives, that he's my neighbor, is bad enough. But how would the ex-district attorney feel if he knew that Sevin and I secretly hate each other? And if he knew the reasons why?

Would he balk, knowing we had met? Would he consider it a victory?

Would he chalk my hesitation up to some sexist idea of womanly wiles? Or he would chastise me for interacting with Sevin enough to soak my Bugs Bunny-patterned underwear?

Maybe so.

Maybe it's best to keep the tiff between Sevin and I a secret.

Cross-legged on my couch in a simple tank shirt and shorts, I try to pry the thoughts of Sevin, secrets and either one of our underwear out of my mind, even as I type on my laptop, knocking out another late night of work on Sevin's case.

I wish I could keep my mind on just that: *the case*…instead of the man the case surrounds.

Interestingly enough, these days, he is the only man on my mind. Especially after ending my fling with Jason.

Tonight's text to the flakiest asshole in the Midwest, breaking our "situationship" off, was well-deserved, and even though, I know dumping Jason is the best decision I've made in weeks, there's still this annoying thought that maybe—*just maybe*—I'm still in over my head.

With work. And with the newest man in my life.

My client.

Despite a year in of hard work, family law, in some ways, is still foreign to me. Knee-deep in paternal rights statutes, I somehow manage to find my stride by the time midnight rings around.

When my phone pings beside me, I barely hear it.

I figure it's just another MyNeighbor message from Nina, my neighbor bragging about securing a new parking space when I get a message—a private one—from the tenant of Penthouse 1A.

There's no picture, only a name. The same name I've been secretly trying to put out of my mind for the past day and a half.

My breath catches in my throat.

SEVIN:

So, this is how you use this app, huh?

I WAIT several seconds before responding, hating how excited I feel.

EMILY:

Yup. Pretty much. Told you it's pretty boring.

HIS RESPONSE IS JUST as quick, leaving no doubt that he's writing back just as fast as I am. I squirm on the couch, uncrossing my legs.

SEVIN:

Not now, it isn't.

HE WAITS a second before writing more.

So, when does this trash talk begin?

EMILY:

What trash talk?

SEVIN:

You know what trash talk. Who's taking theirs out on time. Who isn't. Which person is letting their pup shit all over the hallway carpet.

EMILY:

I can save you time on figuring out that one out. It's mean old Mrs. Headley.

SEVIN:

Ahhh, I guess she's the one who's been calling the cops on me, then.

. . .

I SWEAR on everything I love my heart stops in my chest. I hesitate writing the next words.

EMILY:

Calling the cops? Mrs. Headley?

SEVIN:

Yeah, I mean, you're on the floor beneath me, aren't you?

HE KEEPS WRITING, and I read in horror, my pulse ticking up by a more hectic beat.

I DON'T KNOW **how these damn apartments are numbered. But I do know there are two 'penthouses' on my floor and whoever lives beneath me doesn't exactly think of me as Mr. Rogers. And to think, I've even been helping take care of that damn hallway cat.**

I LAUGH OUT LOUD, typing back doubly fast, relishing the small flutter in my belly. I clutch my phone closer.

EMILY:

You must be talking about Felix.

SEVIN:

Felix??? What kind of a name is Felix for an animal??

. . .

EMILY:

Felix. Felix the Cat. He's a cartoon. And that cat that hangs out in our hallways looks JUST like him. All black fur. Big eyes. Don't tell me you've never heard of Felix the Cat?

SEVIN:

If it ain't Garfield or a guitar-playing feline named Josie, I don't know him. Or her.

EMILY:

Come on. There are so many good cartoon cats out there. You've gotta know a few...

There's Tom from 'Tom and Jerry.' Sylvester the Cat. Garfield, of course. The Cheshire Cat. Pretty sure I can name a dozen others.

SEVIN:

Excuse me for not being a cartoon freak.

EMILY:

Are you calling me a freak, Mr. Elevator Reservation?

SEVIN:

If the fur fits...

EMILY:

I'll have you know that it took years of watching mindless

television to get this good at trivia that only six-year olds care about.

SEVIN:

Fair enough. When I was a kid, music was mine. I thought I'd grow up to be the next Jimi Hendrix-incarnate. Turned out I can't play guitar well enough to lick the bottom of Jimi's guitar pick.

EMILY:

Jimi Hendrix? Aren't you a little young to be listening to Jimi Hendrix?

SEVIN:

You're never too young for the classics. Jim Morrison. Janis Joplin. The Beatles. Pink Floyd. The Who. I have their entire catalogs on vinyl.

EMILY:

My, aren't we stuck in the sixties.

SEVIN:

Name a better decade.

EMILY:

The nineties. Gave us alternative rock gold.

. . .

SEVIN:

Or, as I like to call the nineties—a thinly disguised crude attempt at copying the sixties' classics. And I'm happy to show you the error of your ways... If you can brave the elevator long enough to come up and take a listen sometimes.

MY HEART LEAPS in my throat, forgetting where it belongs. I start typing back.

EMILY:

I'd need a key to access the elevator button to go to the penthouse.

SEVIN:

Well, what do you know? I happen to have one...
I have spring training games all this week, but Wednesday night's an entirely different story. If you're free, of course.

SEVERAL SECONDS PASS AS he writes another response, making my body prickle all over.

SEVIN:

What do you say?

THE SMILE ON MY FACE—THE one I force with my neighbors like Nina—is real this time, and it spreads with abandon as I start to type back to the man I told myself I'd stay away from.
But as I begin tap-tapping on the keyboard, the damn square

phone starts vibrating beneath my fingers, revealing a name I never see on the screen.

Stephan.

I can't pick up fast enough. I force a cough. "Stephan? Hello?"

"Emily." It's a statement, not a question. "How are you?"

I know he doesn't even want to know the answer, but I tell him, anyway.

"I'm fine. Great, actually. Working hard on the Sevin Smith case."

"Great." His voice is silk over steel. Soft, yet deceivingly hard. "Because Sevin Smith is now one of our premier clients. The Cougars organization is one of our best customers."

"Of course it is." "And we want to make sure they have access to our best resources."

"You are one of our best resources, Emily. Or you could be…if all goes well with Sevin."

There's a warning beneath his words, an unspoken threat.

The thought that Stephan Knight, my boss and one of the most well-connected men in Chicago, is calling me at midnight on a weekend makes the threat even more vivid.

And for the hundredth time, I remind myself that I asked for this. Wanted this. Worked for this.

My career is everything to me. Especially now.

My heart skips a dangerous beat as I remind myself that my boss is a walking, talking crystal ball, and even now he was probably watching me somehow, having snuck cameras inside my apartment to mock me—the new girl alone on a Saturday night, sipping ramen in a tattered t-shirt in her living room.

He answers my unspoken speculation.

"We're making Sevin priority number one. I want you by his side every step through this."

"Of course, Stephan. Whatever it takes."

"I'm counting on you."

The vote of confidence feels false. But I'll take it.

Because career rule number one…

Don't piss your boss off.

So, instead of telling him to eat a Chicago hot-dog sized dick for calling me at an ungodly hour, I simply smile and put my practiced corporate face on.

The knowledge that this—the late nights, the lonely meals, my couch, some nineties Meredith Brook music and noodles—has become my life makes my chest tighten for the smallest of seconds, and I pull my back straight, glancing over the shiny steel and silver of Chicago's Millennium Park, outside my windows, reminding myself…that isn't this what I once wanted?

A career that was shiny? Sterling?

I swallow my pride and the remnants of ramen still in my mouth.

"I appreciate your faith in me, Stephan," I, at last, utter. "I won't let you down."

"I'm sure you won't, Miss Armand. We take care of our clients. Professionally, of course. You'll do well here at The Firm. As long as you remember that."

The March Chicago weather outside of my living room window is still cold, I know. But Stephan's last statement is colder.

By the time he hangs up, my apartment feels hotter than one of the Hemsworth brothers sun-bathing in Hell.

And I'm still staring at Sevin's most recent message. My newest client. A man who could make or break my shiny, sterling corporate career.

A man I absolutely, definitely, undoubtedly need to stay away from.

CHAPTER 4

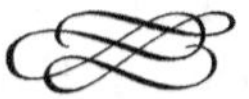

S EVIN
Wednesday night

I check the messages on my phone, pretending I'm not searching for Emily's reply.

Unfortunately, I'm not the world's greatest actor.

My phone has been unnaturally busy today.

A "touching base" text from my trainer. A quick call from my batting coach.

Ten messages from Kayla since this morning. Another two unanswered calls from Sawyer. And five texts from a New York-bound Naomi.

As for my hazel-eyed elevator buddy?

Exactly none.

Not that I've been searching for one.

I stare at her picture on the MyNeighbor app like a loser, hating how just the sight of her has my stomach tying in knots. I toss my phone as far as it can go, letting it land on my couch.

"Fuck. Fuck, fuck, fuck, fuck. *Fuck.*"

"Note to Sevin..." Sawyer mutters from the corner of my living room as I walk towards the bar, suddenly in need of another drink. "Once you finish one of those gin bottles, use it as a 'Swear Jar.' You're completely on edge."

"Fuck being *on edge*. I'm *over* the edge at this point," I grind out between gritted teeth, fingers closing around the gin. "Because Naomi's flight has already been delayed. *Twice*. She's locked on the island of Manhattan after spending a couple of days to see family. And while it's finally starting to warm up in Chicago, in New York? It's *Game of Thrones* weather. Full-on Winterfell."

Sawyer arches a brow. "Well, Ned Stark did say 'Winter is Coming.'"

"Which means she won't be there for an important meeting I'm having tomorrow with my lawyers. I'm totally fucked."

"My least favorite way to use the f-word."

I rub a hand through my hair. "I should have had the meeting with my lawyers when I still had the chance."

"And risk being late for Friday's game? Coach could barely take that loss against the Bruisers. The Serpents are the second best team in the conference. Hell, he won't tolerate any of us wiping our asses the wrong way. Especially you."

Damn. Sawyer's right. As much as I hate to admit it.

Coach had already called me this morning, checking on the status of my knee. His voice was gruff.

Even with every certainty that I was ready for the regular season, even with all the assurances from my doctor, trainer and physical therapist, I could see the old man still had his doubts.

I was a former New York Fever player, an MVP. But I hadn't yet proven myself with the Cougars, and the fleshy jowled curmudgeon was never going to let me forget it.

The urge to flip to the sports news articles about my status as a Cougar is stronger than ever, as Sawyer pokes and prods at my sanity in the living room of my apartment.

We're only supposed to be in Chicago for the next thirty-six hours, but I'm already exhausted from the back-and-forth of not just the travel, but of mentally skimming the sports pages again and again, the potential headlines about me burned into my brain every time I close my eyes.

"*Sevin Smith: A hidden love-child in his secret past?*"

"*Sevin Smith: Sports star. Famous face. Father?*"

"*Sevin Smith: A Different Type of 'Daddy' than You'd Think!*"

I close my eyes and see each one, even now.

Sawyer sits forward from the armchair he's perched in, his stare full of mischief as he glances up at me. He rubs his large palms together, a smile forming on his face.

"You might want to look on the bright side to having that babysitting Naomi sidelined for a bit."

I find myself sighing. "What's the bright side?"

"We can finally have that Playboy party we talked about. There's nothing like a little 'rabbit action' to make a man forget all his woes."

I spin on my heel. "Is your mind permanently in the gutter or does it sit and fester there all day? I'm genuinely curious."

He closes the magazine in his lap, standing to his feet. He shoves one hand in his jeans pocket. "Look, Sev, you don't have to tell me..." His voice trails off. "I'm an asshole for trying to make light of everything, and I apologize. But if I didn't make jokes, you'd slip back into that scary place you'd been right after we got drafted. And I never want to see you in that place again."

My shoulders slump as I stare at him. "It wasn't that bad."

"Wasn't that bad?" His blue eyes round. "In what was supposed to be the happiest times of our lives, you were stomping around as if someone had kicked your puppy. For an entire month, you had the patience of a disgruntled grizzly bear." He points at my lightly bearded face. "And the shaving habits to match. Guess you never outgrew that part, huh?"

"I'm just...stressed, that's all."

"Okay," my old friend sighs. "Then be stressed. But remember it's only baseball, Sterling."

A thought that turns me into ice.

Because baseball was part of my fucked-up, wanting-to-get-drunk soul. Always had been.

Any time that little round sphere full of leather and yarn was tossed in front of my face, my fingers itched to wrap their scrapped lengths around a bat.

That feeling when I stepped on a diamond. That damned rush.

It was silly, really. I was a goddamned adult in love with a kid's game.

But there was something about the game that had inked itself into my skin like a tattoo.

A childhood game, for fuck's sake, was undoubtedly my biggest reason for breathing, and sending that little white ball over a home run fence was as natural to me as existing.

"Only baseball"?

Never.

Telling me, a man who dreamed of being a shortstop since he was old enough to hold a bat, that baseball was a game—only a game—was like telling me not to wake up every morning. Like telling the jungle cat not to hunt and feed.

As if a code hadn't already been in the cat's DNA; baseball sure as hell was in mine.

Sawyer sighs as I stay silent. "I'm just saying, Sterling: You've got a bit of a dark cloud hanging over you, and I think the damn thing is starting to drift over me too. A party might help, I don't know, poke a few holes in it to let in some light. The damn post-draft day beard you once had is back. You seem to have developed a special relationship with that bottle of gin, something I've never seen you do. And your attitude is hella on ice. You might want to look into thawing it a little bit."

But I can't thaw my attitude. Not now.

There's too much uncertainty in the air.

Sawyer isn't wrong. The problem is…the only cracks I've seen in the ice forming have come from the few times I've talked to Emily, the sexy hazel-eyed beauty from the elevator.

I can't get the brunette out of my mind.

Her light, feathery laughter. Her small smile.

Her witty quips and sharp tongue were enough to interest me, draw me into her, not to mention those round, saucer-like eyes staring back at me.

Gold, brown and green in the most gorgeous way, those hypnotic irises waylaid me with a single stare. I'd thought about ripping those doors apart in those moments that she exited the tiny steel cage, pressing and holding her against the wall, letting her feel just how crazy she made me.

God knows I would have, if sense hadn't grabbed ahold of me first. Unluckily for me, however, I'm starting to think that maybe I should have said to hell with sense. Insanity was much better anyway.

Because it's been four entire days since I've messaged her on the MyNeighbor app, and, unlike any other woman I've interacted with, she doesn't give a shit. Because she still hasn't replied.

I'm starting to think I came off too strong. Or maybe not strong enough.

Either way, her obvious lack of reply has left me twisting in doubt, and dammit if I'm not used to doubt in my life anymore as Sterling Sevin Smith. I haven't had to worry about doubt in over nine years.

I turn to the devil on my shoulder AKA Sawyer, deciding that maybe he's right. Maybe a distraction is just what I need.

I know no rock record I have on vinyl will cut it for the type of night I need.

I cross my arms. "Forget tomorrow. How many Playboy bunnies can you get to my apartment in an hour?"

The sandy-haired devil grins, a sloppy smile spreading over his lips. He leans over to slap my shoulder, the hit sharp.

"Now we're talking…" He nods. "Just leave the rest up to me."

And I do. Every single detail.

Less than forty minutes later, we shake off the Arizona jet-lag and the exhaustion of the week to tidy up my apartment, and in that time, Sawyer has managed to call every centerfold in the city, racking up a crowd worthy of filling Chicago stadium…with half the clothing.

My penthouse fills with every size F bra in the state, as if somehow the double D's are out of style.

Cheesy strobe lights dancing around the ceiling, the sounds of sixties band Spirit's song "Animal Zoo" beating against the wall, Sawyer's little "shin-dig," as promised, blossoms into a full-on rager.

There's enough silicone in my living room to fill a rubber factory, and with a full glass of vodka and cranberry in my hand, I roam through the expansive penthouse, letting my gaze bounce around the rooms and halls.

Bunnies and 'Baseball Annies' line the kitchen and living room walls, making it nearly impossible to move through. A few of our current teammates and some of our old ones—those playing for the city's second team—stand at the center of a few female circles, smiles wide, eyes glazed from all the alcohol that continues to flow from hand to hand.

It's like the night before the draft all over again.

There's me—pretending not to care about a woman. And there's Sawyer, lavishing in all of the cleat chasers' attention.

Even Lenny's here, my old teammate from college in New York.

Fresh in from Milwaukee, the grizzly bear of a man comes lugging my way, one side of his wide mouth curving up into a smile that reminds me of how carefree I'd been just nine years ago.

He leans in beside me, his big body nudging mine near the kitchen counter. He nods to my drink.

"Question…" he starts. "I just need to know: Have you magically transformed into a fourteen-year old girl in the last few years, Smith?"

I frown. "Why do you ask?"

"Because you're babysitting the hell out of that drink."

I fight the urge to snort, nudging him back. "I forget how utterly lame you can be."

He motions to the rest of the room. "It's like Baskin Robbins in here. Thirty-one flavors of everything you could ever need."

I raise my eyebrows, glancing down in my own drink. "I'm on a diet."

"From what? Beautiful women?"

I shrug. "You could say that."

"If you truly mean that, then you're more anti-fun than I thought, Smith. Jesus, what happened to you?" His eyes narrow on my face, his long curly hair drooping near enough to brush me. I shove him back. "It's not Draft Day or anything. You can have a drink, you know."

He doesn't get how much I know. Unlike Naomi, a witness to the wreck I've been these last two weeks, no one knows how badly I want to drink right now, how badly I want to make impending thoughts of my career's end go away.

But the thought of me drinking myself into oblivion right now, of being too tipsy and missing one of Emily's messages is enough to make me want to take it slow.

Lenny takes a slurp of his own drink, downing half a glass in one gulp. I watch him swallow. "And no one's saying you have to gorge yourself on this..." He glances appreciatively over the penthouse. "Buffet in front of us. But would it hurt you to have a sample?"

I want to tell Lenny that I haven't sampled anything from a buffet like this in over six months, but I don't want to give the big man a heart attack. Instead I tilt my vodka glass towards my lips, taking a healthy sip.

The clear-ish pink liquid slides smoothly down my tongue—a bit tart with a bite.

Lenny slaps me on the shoulder. "There you go, Smith. Live a little. Welcome to, what we like to call, fun."

As if my entire career teetering on edge isn't *enough fun* for one lifetime.

But after glancing down at my digital itinerary for the seventh time tonight, I realize that Naomi isn't going to make it to Chicago for this meeting with "my lawyers" AKA The Firm.

I'm monumentally screwed. And alone.

While the Northeast is getting slammed with snow, preventing any travel in and out of the city, I know that by the time the damn unexpected storm lets up, I'll be knee-deep in shit.

I take another sip of my drink, swallowing harder this time, and more liquid sloshes down my throat.

Sixty minutes later, the liquid isn't just sloshing; it's 'water-falling.'

I'm on my third glass of vodka and the drinks just keep on coming.

Good ol' Sawyer and Lenny only encourage my encroaching debauchery and with several ounces of alcohol in my system, I find myself chatting up a busty blonde with sizable cleavage. Her golden skin practically glistens underneath the blue-white strobe lights, and I struggle to maintain conversation as she launches into the subject of the voting for 'Bunny of the Year.'

The room swirls for a second as I listen, coming back into focus just as quickly. I straighten against the wall, regrouping mentally as our talk meanders.

"So, is it trueee?" The bunny drawls.

"Is what true?"

"Are you as good on the baseball field as they say?"

"Better," I say, grinning, the alcohol making my ease with talking grow. I lift my glass to my lips again, just as the bunny grabs it. She wraps her fingers around mine.

"That isn't the only place I hear you're really really good."

The bunny's intentions are clear, as see-through as the shirt on her busty frame.

If only she were the flavor I really wanted.

The thought of my elevator ride-buddy Emily has me lowering the glass in my hand, the memory of stroking myself to thoughts of kissing the quick-tongued brunette making every muscle in my body freeze from the unexplored tension twisting through it.

She's the one I'd rather sample tonight. Not this 'Bunny of the Month.'

Not used to having liquid courage like this, I hand off the drink to the buxom blondie, making my way for the door.

CHAPTER 5

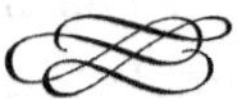

*S*EVIN
Wednesday night

Phone in hand, the MyNeighbor app now on the screen, I scroll to Emily's profile, noting the apartment number under her account. I take the elevator the single floor down, my pulse pumping.

I'm a wreck without some Jim Morrison or Zeppelin to calm me down, my mind racing a million miles a minute. I stare at my cell phone screen hard enough to break the glass.

Sweating beneath my t-shirt collar, my fingers are tingling, hair wrung and disheveled as I run one hand through my dark strands and use the other hand to pound on her door, my ears straining to listen for any noise inside.

I wait.

Nothing.

I knock two more times, fighting my need to break the damn door, when I hear the sounds of shuffling footsteps from behind me.

Like in the locker room at the fitness center.

Only this time, I swivel fast enough to catch the person

lurking over my shoulder, and I grab for the throat immediately, my grip hard—almost bruising as I squeeze.

A small voice yelps as I clamp down. The woman in my hand barely manages to cough.

"Don't." Kayla croaks, her brown eyes wide. "Didn't mean to…"

"Fuck." I swear, thinking of Sawyer and that damn cursing jar of his. "I didn't… I thought you were…"

"I'm so sorry, Kay. I didn't know it was you."

My alcohol-tinged thoughts are scrambled and I work hard to put them back together. I snatch my hand away from her neck. "God, I thought you were, I don't know, someone else."

"It's okay. It's fine," she wheezes. "What's a little choking between friends?"

I snort, patting her back. "I think the choking part is exactly how you and Deacon ended up as *more* than friends." I stand straighter. "How is our boy handling himself these days?"

"Good. Great, actually. Both bars have been bringing in business." My ex-publicist eyes me with intrigue. "You would know that if you stopped by once in a while."

"Just because a man is part owner of a bar doesn't mean he has to act like it, does he?" I let myself laugh. "Besides, The Alchemist is his baby. And we all know I'm not exactly father material."

Kayla's face turns serious, her blue eyes burning right through me. "You know that's exactly why I'm here, Sevin." Her dark hair falls over her face as her brown brows knit in front of me. "Deborah is here."

"Deborah? You mean…" I can barely get the words out. "She's here?" My eyes grow ten times wider. "As in Chicago?"

"As in right next door." She shifts on her feet, almost squirming. "I set her up in the hotel across the street."

"From my apartment?" My alcohol-tinged thoughts are scrambled and I work hard to put them back together. I squeeze my fingers into fists as I stare. "No offense, Kay, but I may have stopped choking you a minute too soon." I rub a hand across my nape, my eyes lowering. "What does the blackmailing leech want this time? My sanity not good enough? She need my soul this time?"

Kayla warns. "Sevin…"

"The woman is blackmailing me for a million dollars, Kay." I interrupt, my skin prickling all over. "And to be honest, I'm as likely the father of her child as Pee-wee Herman."

"I'll be sure to give Pee-wee my congratulations. But for the time being, I need to talk to Emily right now so we can get this sorted. *Shit.* I don't want to use my spare key, but…" The pretty brunette checks her cell. "Tried calling her, but I think her phone died."

"Wait, Emily? What does this have to do with her?" The words are out of my mouth before I can stop them.

My ex-publicist sighs, sagging against the apartment door in front of her. "Oh God, please tell me you guys are not still holding a grudge against each other?"

I gape, but Kay keeps going. "Yes, I know all about it. I know everything." Her shoulders slump. "I hope you know I don't give two shits about whatever little neighborly feud you guys are having. And I certainly don't care about your little hate letters to each other or calling the cops or whatever the both of you have done because we have bigger issues, Sev."

But I can't hear anything else. Not over the roar in my head, with Emily's name ringing in my ears.

My mouth goes dry, my tongue numbed.

Because just the thought that Emily—*my* Emily…

The sweet, irresistible, sexy-as-hell-in-just-a-t-shirt-and-sweats Emily might be my arch-nemesis is enough to make me sick, and God knows the amount of alcohol I've had to drink to talk to that Bunny has made me sick enough already.

I want to get Kayla to clarify. To answer the many questions circling in my head.

But my curiosity soon becomes buried under my rage, as I realize it's useless.

There's no doubt that Emily's the one, the neighbor.

She lives exactly one floor below.

Not to mention, the quick-tongued brunette practically told me so with her confession of her music choices.

I'd simply chosen not to see that the irritating tenant blasting Sarah McLachlan just one floor below would be the woman I'd been dying to bed.

And all the while she'd been making my life a living hell, sending what little sanity I have to brand new lows.

The thought is enough to sober me completely.

And fast.

My mind finally clearing, Kayla's voice calling after me, I make a beeline back to the elevator bank, the surface of my skin practically steaming.

I enter the elevator, swiping my key card to the Penthouse floor. The second the doors part, I'm marching out, my vision blind with barely contained rage.

Teeth tightened, fists cramping, I turn the corner, heading back to my penthouse as fast as my legs will carry me, every inch of my body on fire.

But I don't expect what I find around the bend when I do.

A wall. A living breathing wall.

A mass of blue uniforms stops me mid-storm, and I glance up to find another slew of Chicago's finest standing outside my door, their glances finding me in my rage.

I fixate my anger on them, my brow furrowing with every step I take closer.

"Jesus Christ, Emily sure made sure you boys have a hard-on for knocking on my door... What, another noise ordinance? That's fine." I reach in my jeans pocket for my wallet. "Just tell me how much I have to pay for another 'Disturbing the Peace' ticket so that you gentlemen can be on your merry way. I've got shit to do."

"Mr. Smith?" One of the officers steps forward.

I lift my chin. "Yeah, that's me...Or, if you prefer, you can call me the 'idiot dickhead who can't see past his own cock.' Either one works."

The officer frowns. "We're not here for a noise ordinance. We're here providing an escort. Your doorman called us, and we can't exactly leave abandoned minors unattended."

"Hank called you?" I shake my head, scoffing as I reach for my front door, the bass of music blasting behind it. I start to open it. "Remind me not to tip him for a few days. I'm in no fucking mood for any more guests."

And suddenly I can't turn my own knob.

What the officer's said is still processing through my half-drunk mind, and with a single second of clarity, I turn, body tense, a line of sweat circling fresh around my collar. I stare at his face.

"Wait, what did you say?"

"I said we can't leave a minor unattended, so we're bringing her to you." He steps aside. "This little lady belong with you? She says she does. Apparently, her mother dropped her off in your lobby, and the first thing she told us was your name."

But then I see it. Or rather, I see *her*.

The reason for the police escort.

A heart-shaped face framed by sandy hair peeks out from beneath the wall of blue, and I stare back into a face I've never seen before. A face exactly like mine.

My heart drops to the floor, and fate kicks the fuck out of it for good measure.

A knot the size of a baseball climbs into my throat as a new reality forms in my brain against my will.

Sawyer was right... Tonight, I am getting so screwed.

I swallow thickly.

CHAPTER 6

$\mathcal{E}$mily
Wednesday night

Liquid courage pushes me to fear's edge and plunges me over. Before I can back out, I am already writing a response message to Sevin's last, my fingers shaking as I type, glancing at Sevin's final message, eyes blurred from salty Chicago rain.

Sevin:

So, what do you say?

The message stares back at me like a neon sign, and I take a deep breath, exhaling doubt.

Emily:

I say yes... I can be there in about an hour and a half, if that's okay. I would like to talk to you.

. . .

AND ONLY TALK. At least that's what I tell myself.

Because I know I need to explain to Sevin exactly who I am.

The message is bold. It doesn't make any sense. And it's several days late, but it doesn't stop me from sending it, a butterfly fluttering in the pit of my stomach as I squirm on the cushiony bar stool.

Anxiety sticks itself in my throat, blocking all oxygen.

That is, until a message pings back, flashing across my cell's phone screen from none other than Mr. Elevator Man himself. My heart squeezes inside my chest as I read it. Right before my phone shuts completely down, its battery giving a final bleep of death.

SEVIN:

No need. I'm heading to your front door right now.

CLEARLY, Happy Hour isn't getting me drunk enough to deal with my now-dead phone and raging hormones, and after moving through the motions of the day like a zombie in a business skirt, I sit beside Ben at the bar, pretending I'm not terrified by Sevin's last message, pretending I don't want to dunk my head in a vat of alcohol.

I glance into my third glass of Riesling, wishing I'd ordered the gin instead.

Because after confessing to him about my not-so-small flirtation with Sevin, I'm a fumbling, bumbling mess of emotions.

Planting an elbow on the bar's oak surface, my best friend's bottom lip hangs low enough to catch flies as he gazes at me across the beautifully rustic bar known as the The Alchemist that he's dragged me into.

He doesn't blink as his eyes roam my face. "So you met…"

"Yup." I answer for the third time, staring into my glass.

"And the two of you have been…"

"No."

"But he invited you over his place tonight, so you could…"

"Maybe."

"I can't believe it." My good friend takes another swig of his drink, running a hand through his perfectly coiffed hair.

I shake my head, letting dark strands of my hair fly. "I know. Me neither."

"I'm talking about you." He inches closer on his stool, his tailored suit unwrinkled on his lean frame. "I can't believe *you*, Ems. I mean, seriously. You're the luckiest woman in this freaking city."

Licking his bottom lip, he leans in, excitement making his blue eyes light up. Strands of his blond hair fall forward, released from their gel prison. "You've been asked to *potentially* spend a night with the hottest man in Chicago. A man whose *muscles* have muscles. A man with the face of Adonis, biceps the size of oranges and an ass like two scoops of butter pecan ice cream…"

"Yes, I've got the picture, Ben, thank you very much."

I twirl my glass, finally feeling the alcohol in my system. I glance down at my dead cell phone screen, wishing it were a crystal ball.

Because Ben's not wrong.

Sevin *is* every bit as good-looking as the magazines have made him out to be. Which makes him all the more dangerous to be around.

There's something about the man. Something that scares the hell out of me.

Crisis management law is hard. Working with our type of clientele? Even harder.

But joking with Sevin, talking with him, laughing with him, hasn't been hard. In fact…it's as easy as breathing, which—shockingly enough—is hard to do around that man.

Around him, I feel that sort of seductive pull of throwing

caution to the wind, an act, I'm sure, my area of legality banned in forty-nine states.

There's something about his reckless confidence, the casual confidence in the way he talks, walks—and from the things I've heard in my apartment, *fucks*—that pushes at my professional and personal boundaries.

Which is exactly why taking him on as a client is a million times harder than I ever thought possible.

But I can't turn down my closest chance at proving myself in my new position; I can't do it. *Not when I'm this close.*

Even though I'm currently wondering what the color of my new client's boxer briefs currently are.

Ben nudges my arm, knocking me out of my own head. His stare is narrowed. "Penny for your thoughts?"

I don't want to tell him that my thoughts are currently on Sevin's butter pecan-like ass. Not yet, at least.

But I do need to talk to Sevin, and if it's one thing Ben is good at, it's knowing how to get a guy alone. And that's what I exactly need to do with Sevin.

To talk…of course.

Shaking my head, I straighten on my stool, my fingers fiddling with the edge of my skirt.

"You had a lot to say about Sevin when you first found out we were taking him on a client."

"Of course." Ben grins as he takes another gulp of his drink. "Sevin's *a lot of man* to talk about."

I suppress a smile. "What do you know about him?"

"Me?" He points at his chest. "Know about Sevin?"

"Well, you are the biggest mouth in Chicago, aren't you?"

He laughs. "I'm going to try to take that comment in the non-sexual sense, so go ahead."

"I know you've gotta have heard all the best whisperings and gossip about him."

"Well, he's new to Chicago, so there hasn't been much…" Ben

quirks one perfect eyebrow. "I mean, besides his sex life, of course."

I feel my stomach tumble. "Wait, what do *you* know about Sevin's sex life?"

Ben peers at me over his glass. "Do you really want to know?"

My chin tilts towards him. "Only with the fire of a thousand Persian suns."

"Well, it's just rumors…maybe. Sevin just joined the Cougars. And every woman in the city, of course, wants a piece of him. So far, it seems the only person who has ever managed that difficult task was Kimmy Wallace." He lifts his eyebrows, and my face falls blank as I stare at him.

"I'm sorry, and Kimmy Wallace is who?"

Ben huffs. "Say it with me, Ems. Blog. B-L-O-G. It's not that hard to find one."

I slap his arm. "Just tell me."

"She's only one of the most popular billionaire socialites in the entire world. Think Kim Kardashian…with blonde hair and better shoes. Kimmy is part-model, part-mogul, *all* media darling. American tabloid royalty. Oh, and her family only owns about half of New York."

I press harder. "And you're telling me Sevin was engaged to her?"

"Supposedly. Henry Wallace was a huge college coach at the time in New York. *Sevin's college coach, actually.* Which explains the rumors about the affair. And it gets even better."

Ben leans in. "Apparently, there was some sort of love-triangle between Sevin, Kimmy and the infamously handsome pitcher, Finley Sparks. *His roommate.*"

Ben rubs his hands together, enjoying every bit of the juicy gossip. And I have to admit: I'm enthralled. I'm practically shaking on my stool as he keeps going.

"I'm talking fights in the dug-outs. Full-on brawls on the field.

Everyone assumed it was just a 'Roommate, Baseball Bros-type of feud'. Turns out it was much deeper than that."

I take another sip of my Riesling, hanging on my best friend's every word. Damn my lack of knowledge about blogs. "And then what?"

"Well, someone had to win Kimmy, right? And let's just say it wasn't our neighbor."

The realization hits me like a punch to the gut.

She chose the roommate? This Finley pitcher guy, whoever the hell he was?

Who the hell was this Kimmy Wallace chick? And how had she managed to hide the massive brain injury she must have suffered?

What woman could pass on a man like Sevin Smith? But then again, maybe I didn't know the Demi-god as well as I was beginning to think.

Maybe Sevin had all sorts of secrets hidden in those blogs that Ben loved so much.

I sigh, saying the obvious. "So, she chose the roommate."

"Finley Sparks." Ben twirls the glass in his hand before sitting it on the bar top. "And they're still together today. Both beautiful and married happily-ever-after style with a child." Ben smirks, one side of his handsome face curling with some secret. "But from what *I* hear, happily ever after may not be so damn happy, as far as her marriage goes. And no knows why exactly it didn't work with Sevin and Kimmy."

He pats my leg. "Some say your little boyfriend might be the reason."

I roll my eyes, finishing the rest of the Riesling at the thought of Sevin, a man who rides secret service elevators and avoids putting his profile picture on public platforms being exposed on seedy blogs.

I know he must hate it.

Being pushed and prodded into a life he never wanted.

Like me.

I feel my nerve trembling under this new information. I take another sip of my Riesling. "Do you think it's true?"

"Who the hell knows?" Ben leans in even closer, lending me a whiff of his floral scent. His blue eyes twinkle in my direction. "Remember this about Chicago. It was built on the back of the mafia, ice-cold winters and brutal politicians. The city has rules. And it's important for outsiders to learn them really quickly."

"I'm slowly starting to realize that."

"Good." He slaps my knee. "Now...are you sufficiently drunk enough to screw Sevin or do you need another Riesling?"

"Is that why you agreed to have a drink with me? You're supposed to convince me to do the right thing: To tell Sevin who I am before this gets any more complicated. I thought I made that clear when you showed up."

Ben gingerly touches his chest. "Do I look like the type to tell you to do the right thing? For once in your perfectly planned life, please, *do the wrong thing.* Get laid. If you even remember what that means because it's been, what, eleven months?"

"Twelve," I mutter inside my empty drink. *And even longer than that since I've had 'good' sex.* The room swirls for a bit, and then stops. "*Shit.* I suck at this. What do I do? Do I message him on the MyNeighbor app? Do I 'Like' *his* last message? Do I send him a wink emoji?" I check my cell as if it will magically come back to life. "Dammit, this stupid phone."

By the time Ben and I have stopped talking, I realize another hour and more has passed, nearly two.

Stepping off his stool, Ben grabs his trench coat, slipping the elegant fabric over his shoulders, and I'm furious at myself for not leaving sooner. For not charging my phone when I had the chance.

Ben glances down at me with sympathy. "Clearly you can't do any of that with a dead phone. If you're brave enough, you could, you know, *act like a human being* and go meet him in person. You do live one floor below him."

He steps in for a hug, squeezing tight. "And will you call me right after you come?"

"You mean after I go?"

"No, honey. I mean, after you *come*.'" He grins. "I want all the dirty details."

I roll my eyes. "Wish me luck."

Five minutes later, I find myself practically drowning on the sidewalk after attempting to walk the several blocks home.

The rain is cold this time of year in Chicago—nearly freezing, and I wrap my thin coat tight, my collar pulled to my face as I brace my body against the quickening winds. The city is barely recognizable under the sheet of precipitation bearing down on us, and contrary to the assurance I gave Ben back in The Alchemist bar, walking the few blocks back to my apartment building is like braving a Biblical plague. My umbrella can barely block the rain.

I'm soaked to the bone and shivering before I make it half a block.

Ducking beneath a store's nearby awning, I wait for the rain to finally relent. But it doesn't.

Bad news is…the alcohol in my system won't relent either, and the wine pushes me, wet and shaking in my business skirt suit, all the way back to my apartment, fumbling and bumbling right up until the moment I reach the elevator in our over-done lobby.

Of course it's empty.

It's late again. Nearly eleven.

I step inside, pressing the button for my floor, my fingertips moving nonstop.

One thumb against the "Up" button, the other against the edge of my skirt, I stand—a dripping, sopping mess from the rain, and for the first time, I'm not grateful that the late-night elevator leaves me alone.

The metal rail is cold against my skin, and I shiver. I tell myself that's why I'm really shaking. That it's not because of Sevin.

That it's not because I'm on my way to meet my neighbor, the most mouthwatering man I've ever met. And that I absolutely, positively do *not* want to sleep with him.

That's what I tell myself. As for what I'm *thinking*, well…those two are completely different.

The small steel square rumbles around me, coming to life as it ascends. And I concentrate on anything, everything but the red display reading each floor as it passes.

Floor two. Floor four.

Then six.

I'm in full-on tremors by the time I hit eight.

Each new level leaves me shuffling worse than a cat in heat, and by the time the elevator slows, I can barely breathe.

It stops on my floor, halting with a groan, and before I can set one high heel into the hallway, I hear a small whimper just a few feet from the double doors.

I'm a ball of nerves, ready to come apart and instead of walking into the hallway, I lean forward, peering down it, finding it empty…save for one thing.

Felix.

Blinking innocently up at me, our resident cat's wide green eyes glow bright beneath a frazzled coat of beautiful black fur.

My gaze shoots from the top of his little head towards both ends of the hallway.

Poor Felix. All alone.

I head towards him, hands outstretched, when I realize that I'm not.

Something—or rather, someone else—is also running down the other end of the hall…in my direction, no less.

The quick *thump-thump-thump* of footsteps around the unseen corner make my heart beat a similar rhythm and with a few quick steps, I rush forward, scooping quiet Felix in my arms, holding the furry feline like a shield.

I wait for the footsteps to reach me.

Hiding my face behind his soft fur, I hold stance in the hallway, knees knocking, feeling instantly sober as a set of legs comes barreling around the corner.

A set of round eyes in the middle of an adorable heart-shaped face gawk upwards at me, stopping in their tracks.

I blink, my heart slowing aside Felix's.

It's a girl staring back at me. A little girl.

Sandy brown strands of hair spill down her tiny shoulders, and with eyes as expressive as Felix's and just as green, she ambles towards me, seemingly unsure of how to take in the scene, the sight of the frightened cat and the drunken lawyer holding him.

She purses her lips. "Is he your cat?

I glance down at my living breathing shield. "Depends on what you mean by 'yours.' Technically, he's nobody's cat." I shrug. "He kind of belongs to the building. No one's ever claimed him, so, yeah… I guess that might make him part mine."

I smile, maybe at the knowledge that an eight-year old—maybe nine?—could have scared me out of my wits. I inch downwards as she comes closer, meeting her eye.

"Did he hurt you?" I ask.

She shakes her head, those sandy locks swinging all over her head. She doesn't smile.

"I found him in the hallway. I tried to grab him, but he turned and ran. I followed him all this way, and I thought he disappeared. Until popped his little head up again so I…"

She shrugs, her small arms lifting a second before dropping.

Her face is so sad and yet familiar in the strangest way. I pet the back of Felix's head, closing the distance between us.

The little girl freezes and I stop.

"I—I'm sorry. I should have introduced myself to you first." I reach a hand out, hoping she'll take it. "My name is Emily." I nudge the fuzzball in my arms. "This is Felix. *Unofficially*. But I'm guessing he might have told you that since you've already met."

My fingers float in mid-air and Little Green Eyes stares at

them, never moving. I lick my dry lips, swallowing back the remnants of Riesling still there.

I take a shuddering breath. "What's your name?"

Time stretches for an awkward second. But then she reaches out. Extending her small, slender fingers, Felix's new friend wraps her hand around mine, shaking it in the most adorable way.

I grin again as she peers at me through the longest lashes I've ever seen.

So familiar. Her face is so familiar that it shocks me, though I can't place it.

"Charlie," she says at last, her voice as small as her stature.

Still mesmerized by the sense of déjà vu tap-dancing on my mind, I don't even hear my front door open until someone steps out of it.

The smoky smell of aftershave reaches me before anything else, and I turn to find an angry Olympian glaring back at me— god-like and intense.

Sevin.

And I know—with everything in me—that *this* time? He knows that I'm, well, me.

I take a deep breath and one step, bringing myself closer to him.

CHAPTER 7

$\mathcal{E}$MILY
Wednesday night

He stares at me across the small hallway space, taking my breath away.

"I thought I heard your voice out here." He motions over his shoulder. "We've been waiting for you inside."

We're?

I swear I'm going to swallow my own tongue as he nods towards the inside of my messy one-bedroom. He glances at the little girl named Charlie.

"How you doing out here, kiddo? Did you find him?"

She reaches for Felix, her green eyes shy as I hand him over. "Yup." She pets his soft fur. "You were right; he does need a friend."

"We won't be here long," he tells her, his voice softening. He glances at Kayla. "Kayla's going to keep you and Felix company for a few minutes while I talk to Emily. And then we'll make a plan to find your mom, I swear it."

Find her mom?

So many questions but I don't ask. I simply look up at Sevin, who answers all my unspoken inquiries with his eyes.

"Well, come on. We've been waiting for you."

He smiles, as smug and as arrogant as ever, and I don't know whether I want to smack or kiss his breathtaking face.

I motion to my apartment. "You might want to lead the way… since you seem to know your way around better than I do now."

He laughs lightly, turning his back to me as he walks—no, more like swaggers—inside. "Kayla let us in with her emergency key." He scoffs. "Actually, that type of thing's been happening a lot in this building these days."

"Oh, great. Remind me to choke her when I have a chance."

"Get in line. I already had my chance earlier."

Sheer attraction mingles with fear in an intoxicating mixture that is stronger than the cocktail bar's wine, and I hold in an unexpected gasp as Sevin, now standing beside me as we walk inside my apartment, allows his gaze to brush across my body.

His eyes roam my skin, touching from head to toe. And then like the arrogant bastard I'd first known, the handsome Hercules-clone walks past me, sitting on the love seat opposite my overwrought armchair where Stephan Knight's muscular body takes up space.

The senior lawyer stares as I settle on my couch, feeling like a foreigner in my own home. He leans forward in the leather chair, hands perched.

"Welcome, Emily. Glad you could make it in. You're right on time."

I inhale slowly, taking a deep breath as I process what's happening around me. My heart pitter-patters. "It's great to see you too, Stephan. I just somehow assumed I would be seeing you in the office…" I can't help but glance at Sevin. "Alone. Did I miss a call for a late-night meeting or…?"

"No," he corrects. "You did not. But Sevin called in for a meeting and I figured 'Why not'? Seemed like the perfect opportunity to get you two acquainted since you will be working on his case."

A kaleidoscope of butterflies takes flight in my tummy, and I settle a hand there. "Sevin is ready to get this blackmailing situation behind him," he continues.

I bet he is. But I don't say it.

I smile instead. "As am I. I'm ready to take care of whatever the, uh, *client* needs. But I'm sure there's a lot of paperwork we'll have to take care of first before, uh, Mr. Smith and I will have to get down to business"

I fold my hands in my lap, avoiding Sevin's stare. "When in the next few weeks would you like Sevin and I to get together to discuss?"

Stephan blinks, his dark eyebrows burrowing deep on his forehead. "Immediately." He nods at Sevin. "Kayla, Sevin and I have already discussed this. Seems this little blackmail scheme has gone a step further." He inhales. "*Deborah Jett has skipped town. And left her daughter behind. Which may have been her aim all along. Gives the name Jett a whole new meaning, doesn't it?*"

The smile on my face fades. "Well, child abandonment is illegal in the state of Illinois and I'm sure in New York where she's from. And I'm sure we can get the police to..."

"*No police.*" Stephan's voice is strained. "No police. No cameras. And not a word of this to the press. We're not going to give in to Deborah Jett's ploy. Mr. Smith wants all of this taken care of as soon as possible."

I blink. "You mean *right* now?"

"Yes, of course." Stephan's stare is unwavering and I realize with those three words how many miles of shit I'm currently buried under. I close my eyes, strengthening my stomach muscles.

"I understand." I manage to avoid Sevin's searing stare only a few feet away. "Mr. Smith and I can meet tomorrow in my office. First thing."

Stephan smiles—or makes a facial expression as close to one as he can get. "Why wait? Now's as good a time as any." He motions to the both of us, looking proud. "I can already see how this will be a perfect fit. You two, plus Kayla, will make a killer team."

Killer team.

Me and Sevin. Good God.

From the corner of my eye, I can see Sevin glance at me, his green eyes glowing. He rubs his jaw. "You know what, Stephan? I think you're right… In fact, I know you are." He stares unblinkingly at me, his gaze prodding, poking at me. The butterflies in my stomach form a fist, punching me in the solar plexus as he leans forward. "Shall we?"

A minute later, Stephan leaves, and the tension between Sevin and I grows thick enough to jump on, like a moon bounce. I glare over at him, wishing he weren't sitting so damn close, looking so damn good.

I stand to my feet, as he does the same.

I lower my voice to the depths of hell, crossing my arms across my chest.

"If you're pretending to be okay with us working together for Stephan's sake, it's not going to work, you know?"

"Oh really?" Sevin cocks a dark brow, eyeing me.

"Yes, really. Let's just get this out of the way right now, okay? I know you know that it's me. I'm the downstairs neighbor you can't stand. And you're the upstairs prick preventing me from sleeping. But tricking me into meeting you here, waiting for me in my own apartment…Well, I don't find it very neighborly. All animosity aside, this is my *life* we're talking about here."

"And this is *mine*," he retorts. "I have a baseball career to keep. And I won't let anything get in the way of it. And I do mean anything, Emily." He inches his large body forward, and I can see the new resolve in his pine-colored eyes, a closed off wall that wasn't there the first time we met.

He seems harder now. Colder. I straighten my shoulders to battle the urge to back down.

"I admit: I let my guard down with you. Before I knew who you were… Trust me: It won't happen again."

His tone is accusatory, venomous, and every inch, every centimeter, of me is shaking with indignation, quivering.

God, my will is strong. But my nerves are shit.

And even through the anxiety, even past the slivers of fear and through the haze of inexplicable hurt, I feel my backbone stiffen, strengthened by some inner confidence I didn't even know was there.

I still don't move as Sevin takes another step closer. I won't let myself.

His rugged face—bearded and angular—comes within a few inches, and I let him, smelling his heady scent, a combination of citrus, amber and cedar wood, a knee-knocking mix. One butterfly finds its way between my legs, and I squeeze them, hating how he affects me.

Hating how he makes me feel more than Jason ever did in two months.

Using every ounce of courage in my veins, I keep my feet firmly planted to the ground, chin steady, my stare focused and unblinking the entire time.

I don't know how I succeed. Especially when Sevin keeps talking, his words a husky whisper.

"At first I considered just staying away from you. But then I landed on a better plan: If you're going to be sniffing around my life—like you have already, it makes sense that now you'll be paid to do it. That way, I can ensure no more visits from Chicago PD or you taking out your misplaced outrage on someone else's love life." He grits each sentence out through tightened teeth, and I balk, that desire to smack him across his stubbled face stronger than it was even minutes ago.

Who knew a face like that could warrant such violence?

Part of me wants to mangle it.

"I can assure you, Sevin," I insist, my tone searing. "That I don't give a damn about your love life. *And I never will.* I'm not going to let you frazzle me because I called the cops on you and your, uh, *guests* for making animal noises at ungodly hours. And I'm not going to let you get in the way of doing my job because your love life—which seems largely to be devoid of *actual love*—is just one big rolodex of women whose names I'm sure you forget by sunrise."

He bristles at that part.

"You are not going to bother me, Sevin," I continue despite his rising rage. "From now on, you are going to be nothing more than my neighbor—not a particularly good one...and a job." My stare thins in his direction as I tilt my chin. "You might be the star athlete. But right now, we're playing by *my* rules. Got it?"

He doesn't blink back at me, his stare just as steady. His gaze roams from my chin to my mouth to my nose and just as I think he's not going to respond, he glances up at my eyes, making every inch of my skin shudder under his scrutiny. I stop myself from biting my lip as he watches me, not saying a word.

His face never moves until he speaks. "I got it... Loud and unbelievably clear."

"Good." I nod, the knot of butterflies in my gut finally loosening. "Now, if that's all, I think I need some sleep before our office meeting tomorrow. Not that having you as my neighbor lets me do much of that anyway..." I turn to head for the door to escort him out, and Sevin reaches for me, grabbing my arm.

His voice is low, almost inaudible even at this close range, and I stop, peering up at his green eyes pierce me. His breath is cool across my face.

"Wait a second," he says. "I never agreed to meet in any office. I have spring training in Arizona and need to be there for Friday's game."

"What?" My mouth drops as he stares at me. "But...you heard Stephan. We—*I*—need to help you figure out *all of this* craziness now."

"I know. And we will."

He glances at my lips again, his touch warming as his hand remains on my arm. He slowly lets me go, and I breathe—or at least I try to. It's hard when he's so damn close. His green eyes glint down at me.

"But," he continues, "Stephan never said *where* we needed to work this out. First things first: We need to get you a jersey and one of those foam-fingers so you'll fit in." He starts marching away, and I have to follow to keep up. I gape at his muscled back, feeling those damn butterflies again.

"I'm sorry, foam-finger? Jersey? Wait, Sevin…" I yell at his back as he walks out my door. *"Sevin!"*

CHAPTER 8

*E*MILY
Thursday afternoon

Sevin eventually gives me an answer to my question.

Too bad I was an hour too late to stop that answer from happening, and because of Ben and too much wine, I wasn't early enough to stop my boss from sending me to Arizona.

Arizona.

All to play babysitter to a client.

I should have asked for more money.

"Good afternoon passengers," the captain's voice rings out over the intercom. "This is your captain speaking. We are now beginning our descent into Sky Harbor International Airport, your final destination. The time is 3:25 pm. The weather looks good and with the tailwind on our side we are expecting to land approximately fifteen minutes ahead of schedule. Forecast in Phoenix is..."

I want to tell him the forecast is *"drunk and unbelievably outraged."*

I signed up to handle a crisis, not watch a few baseball games under the West Coast sun.

It's been over twelve hours since Sevin left my front door last night and still, two first class glasses of Chardonnay are not enough to soothe my nerves. Or make me forget that because of my boss, I am now at the beck and call of Sevin Smith—beautiful baseball player, asshole athlete, candidate for Worst Neighbor Alive.

In a first class seat built for a King, I order my third glass of wine from the nearest flight attendant as Kayla crosses her arms beside me, one hand landing on my forearm.

She peers over at me, blue eyes bright. "Still feeling weirded out?"

The flight attendant hands me my final drink, and I take it, almost inhaling it in one gulp. I sigh out loud. "How can you tell?"

"I don't know… Maybe because you've had enough wine to suck Napa Valley vineyards dry." She shoots me a sly grin. "I know this isn't exactly how you pictured your work at The Firm would be when I helped you get this job."

"No." I peer over her shoulder at the little girl sitting across the aisle, her sandy hair tucked behind her ears as she sleeps. "Hadn't known babysitting would be one of the requirements."

The real child, I could handle. No problem.

It was babysitting the athlete that would be the issue. Watching over a famous baseball pro. Keeping him away from the press. Out of any more trouble.

Making sure the blogs didn't find out about Charlie.

It's a great thing the little girl doesn't seem to be as freaked out as I am. On the flight, she barely budges.

Thankfully, the plane is quiet. But my mind is not.

The additional thought that a mother—any mother—could leave behind her daughter is driving me to drink. And I don't even want to think about the man who could be the little girl's father.

A man who's done little but drive me crazy since he's come into my life. A man I'm flying hundreds of miles to oversee.

A man who's currently messaging me right now.

And I know I shouldn't be texting before landing. I know I shouldn't.

But my cell phone pings, another notification from the MyNeighbor app, popping up on my screen.

And I'm just tipsy enough to answer.

I read Sevin's seventh text.

SEVIN:

I'm not going to stop. I'm going to keep bugging you until you answer me.

I BLOW OUT A BREATH, replying.

EMILY:

Yes, you're a pain in the ass.

SEVIN:

That's not what I asked.

I WATCH FLOATING ELLIPSES APPEAR.

DON'T MAKE me interrupt your cartoons. I know you're watching some on the flight right now.

DAMN. Why did I ever tell this man that?

I ignore my in-flight episode of Rugrats.

· · ·

EMILY:

I don't know how to answer you any differently than I did the first time you messaged me.

Yes, Charlie is fine.

No, she is not uncomfortable on the flight.

And yes, Kayla and I are very comfortable watching her.

I HESITATE a second before writing more.

IF YOU'RE SO CONCERNED, why did you take an earlier flight than us?

SEVIN:

Because my trainer threatened me with death if I didn't meet him.

EMILY:

I like your trainer already.

SEVIN:

Just wait until you meet Coach. You'll be in plenty murderous company with him around.

EMILY:

**Taking notes.

I'D WRITE MORE to press his buttons but then he texts back something unexpected that makes my stomach dip from more than just the turbulence.

SEVIN:

No, but seriously now... Is she okay? I mean, her mother just left her here. I don't know many eight-year olds who can deal with as much as she is.

I SMILE, feeling sentimental even through the wine buzz.

EMILY:

She's tough. She's a tough little girl. She's nothing like I was at the age. Just from the few hours I've spent in her company, I can tell. Charlie's a trooper.

I GRIN HARDER, writing more.

AND IT HELPS **that she has her soldier sidekick coming with us to Arizona.**

SEVIN:

God...

I IMAGINE the sigh on his lips.

I SHOULD HAVE NEVER AGREED **to drag that furball with us.**

. . .

I LAUGH OUT LOUD, ignoring Kayla's curious look.

EMILY:

You'll learn to love Felix yet.

SEVIN:

I hope so.
I'm not so good at this.

EMILY:

Good at what?

SEVIN:

Caring about other people (or animals) the way I should.

I WANT to ask what that means but the captain is back over the intercom, and what I prepare to say dies quickly.

"Ladies and gentlemen," the captain voice rings out over the intercom, "as we start our descent into Phoenix, please make sure your seat backs and tray tables are in their full upright position. Make sure your seat belt is securely fastened and all carry-on luggage is stowed underneath the seat in front of you or in the overhead bins. Thank you."

Tucking my phone away, I take a deep breath.

For as long as I've been at this job at The Firm, I've been a good employee, a serious lawyer. And somehow I've let myself be talked into taking on an assignment that crossed the line of appropriate long ago.

Hell, Sevin's paternity hasn't even been proven. And yet we're hauling a little girl across state lines to make sure no magazine or blog's the wiser. Even a hint of an issue or shift in Sevin's schedule, and the tabloid press would pounce.

I've seen them do it before.

Problem is: I want to say it isn't my fault. That I was double-teamed by Sevin and Stephan, pushed by Kayla.

But truth is: I was a goner the second I looked into that little girl's eyes. I'm sure I would have done anything Stephan asked of me.

The hopeful look in her big green eyes had captured me—not to mention the adoring way she looked at Felix and Sevin.

Caught between a cat, an athlete and an eight-year old, I was starting to think the captain was right.

I needed to make sure my seat belt was fastened and my luggage, emotional and otherwise, was stowed.

I was going to be in for a bumpy ride.

* * *

SEVIN

I finish my last MyNeighbor message to Emily, wondering if what I said was true about caring about people.

Hopping out of the black Navigator to take me back to my Scottsdale hotel is a chore as my entire body aches from today's practice, and by the time I make it to the lobby, Naomi's already calling. My finger hovers over that "Eff You" button as I sling my glove-filled bag over my shoulder, but I decide I don't need her popping out of my bathroom tub "Fatal Attraction" style just because I don't feel like hearing what she has to say.

I answer the phone, taking a deep breath before I fill her in on the last twelve hours.

As expected, she goes into nail-biting nuclear mode. Her voice is shrill.

"Holy shitballs, Deborah did *what*? And you're doing fucking what?"

"Language, Nome," I shoot back. "You never know when a kid could be around." I pause. "Hell, a kid who could be *my* kid."

"I'm sorry," my assistant mutters. "I just mean… I can't…" She drifts off into silence, echoing how I feel. "I just don't get it. What kind of mother would leave her own daughter on your doorstep?"

"Which proves my point on the sanity of this Deborah woman. She's clearly nuts."

"I mean, this is completely boggling my mind right now." I can just imagine my assistant pushing her glasses up, her index finger poking over her nose. "It makes no sense. You're a single man, Sevin."

"I'm aware of that."

"And a professional athlete."

"Kinda knew that, too."

"I mean your fan-base avatar is your basic acne-faced fifteen-year old or forty-year old man-child. Not exactly ideal for raising kids."

"Again," I grunt, "you're not getting any argument from me." I run a palm over my lips, letting my stubbled face scratch it as I head for the elevator back to my room, every inch of my body aching from head to toe.

The practice with my trainer Ivan the Terrible today was more brutal than most days, and it didn't help that the taste of vodka was still on my tongue from last night.

During today's practice, my knee was hurting, my mind was swimming, and my swing was off.

Fifty minutes later, practice is over, but the Arizona air is still dry in my throat as I cross the lobby, and when, at last, I ride up through the hotel lobby elevator, back to my suite, I'm already exhausted.

I walk right up to my hotel suite, closing the swanky door behind me, tempted to sag against it.

Right now, I need to get the baseball diamond dust washed from my shoulders and the smell of the grass off my skin. I push all of that to the back of my mind as I strip naked, needing as much downtime before tomorrow night's game as I can fit in.

I pull my baseball cap from my sweaty hair, letting it slide to the floor. I grunt through the aches and pain.

"I just didn't know what to do, you know. I mean, she had to come with me. I couldn't just leave her there. I wouldn't just leave her there."

Naomi's voice is soft. "I know you wouldn't."

"And I can be an asshole…"

"Yes, you can. No argument there." I hear her underlying smile.

"But I'm just not—I'm just not the type of person who could abandon a kid."

Naomi inhales. "I know you aren't. That's not you. Anyone who knows you knows that. You're not that type of guy." She takes a small pause, prompting me to do the same. "Makes you wonder if this Deborah Jett knows that, too." She pauses. "I'll call Kayla, and, if I have to, her boss to get to the bottom of this."

Naomi. My good old faithful.

You could always trust my adorably uptight assistant to take care of things.

Including this Deborah woman.

The mystery woman who'd come into my life that no one can get a hold of.

A phantom who'd slipped in and out of my life like a ghost, here one day and gone the next.

So far, I'd left the Deborah handling to Kayla, my ex-PR guru, but as I head towards the hotel bathroom to turn the shower on, I wonder more about who the hell this woman could be.

Who was she to me nine years ago? *And why the hell didn't I remember her?*

My thoughts are still on Deborah when I hear a knock on my

hotel suite door. Reaching to wrap the nearest towel around my waist, I answer the door, finding Sawyer standing behind it.

The big loaf grins. "Did Ivan kick your ass or what? I'm still hurting from practice today."

I let him in, pointing to my phone. But he doesn't get the message.

He falls out on my mattress. "Jeez, I could use a proper Annie right now." He closes his eyes. "Someone who can massage my bruised cheeks." He hesitates. "And I'm not talking about the ones on my face…"

"Is that Saywer?" I hear Naomi ask through my phone.

I sigh. "Yes, that's Mr. Cheeks, at your service."

"Of course it is. I can smell his BS from all the way in New York, it's so bad." I imagine her brown eyes tumbling in her head. "Not looking forward to smelling it in person tomorrow morning when I land in Arizona. But if it helps: Tell him I'll handle his cheeks."

"*You'll* handle them?"

"Sure. Free of charge. With the backside of my boot."

I snort out loud. "I'll relay the message. Talk to you later, Nome."

"Who was that?" Sawyer finally glances up. "Buzz-Kill again?"

I toss my phone to the side. "You know if Naomi ever learns that you call her that, she'll spit frisbees."

"Well, I mean, admit it, Sterling: The woman is a hitman for fun. Where there's fun, you can guarantee that Naomi will show up, sniper rifle and black mask in tow, to snuff it out. She's allergic to the shit, I'm sure. Bet she had a hell of a time shutting down our Playboy party so abruptly. I barely had a chance to put my pants on."

Jesus. The party. It feels like a million years ago.

I don't confess that it couldn't have been Naomi to kill the party, since my Type-A assistant was still in New York.

In fact, the second the police had showed with Charlie in tow, it was *me* who ended the debauched festivities, showing every partygoer and Playboy Bunny the front door as I phoned in Kayla to help me clean up the mess.

I didn't mention at the time that the biggest mess was me.

Having Kayla usher Charlie away from my madness was bad enough, especially when Kayla had called big boss Stephan Knight to tidy up loose ends. And I just sat there and let it happen.

The kid had only been around for less than an hour, and I was showing that I was a shit father.

I didn't know if she was mine or not—I'd hoped not.

Because when it came right down to it, when you looked at my life—a life filled with high-noon heaters in overcrowded stadiums, city after city, bedmate after bedmate, I wasn't built for this.

I'd never be the kind of man any kid needed. I was barely the kind any decent woman would.

The thought makes the ache in my body burn. I roll my shoulders.

"Alright, Saw." I brush the party talk. "I need a shower or stuff is going to start growing on my skin. You're welcome to reschedule the party later, but right now, I need to get my skin wet. Dry air is giving me hell."

The second baseman stands with a grunt. "Don't worry, Sterling. I get it. I just took one myself." He starts towards the door. "Well, I'm off to get something *else* of mine wet. Call me later." He checks his phone. "Well, actually, call me much later. I've got a guest in five minutes." He winks. "I'll see you later."

And then he's out the door.

The sound of silence in my hotel room is welcome, if not a little strange. I chuckle at the thought that I'm semi-getting used to hearing Sarah McLachlan music filtering through my floorboards from Emily's apartment, and I head back towards the shower, shedding my towel.

I wash with the slow deliberate manner of a man who feels like he finally has time.

The shower lasts long, well over a half hour, even as the water runs cold.

Naked and dripping wet, I slide my towel over my hair, wiping the soaked strands. Headed back towards my bedroom, I hear another knock—loud and insistent, and I can't help but groan, snatching the towel from my head to place it at the apex of my thighs.

I unlock the door, ripping the strong wood aside. "What, Sawyer?"

But it's not Sawyer who stands behind the door. Far from it.

Shocked hazel eyes stare in my direction as Emily's gaze goes directly to my face and then between my legs as my towel drops to the floor in a heap.

I wish there was a MyNeighbor app emoji for *Oh shit.*

CHAPTER 9

$\mathcal{E}$MILY

Thursday evening

Seeing Sevin at his door without his shirt on is a shock.

Seeing Sevin at his door without a stitch of clothing on is a *heart attack.*

The thick cotton towel in his hand falls to the floor, and I can't help but look, my gaze dropping to the neatly trimmed thatch of hair between his thighs.

He's huge, even semi-hard, and it takes every ounce of my will to turn away, my hands shooting to my eyes as I swing my gaze in the other direction.

"Holy wow, I am so sorry."

The words keep coming off my lips even as I hear Sevin make a grab for his towel, and I feel myself shaking, literally shaking, as he does, my hands in tremors.

"It's fine. Everything's fine. It's just a little slip, that's all," I hear him say from the doorway.

But I can't look back. Can't allow myself to mistakenly gaze at the most delicious male form I've ever seen in my life.

Good God, the man is built.

In a split second, I got an eyeful of his chiseled muscles, his lean thighs. It seemed every bit of his over six-foot frame was made out of stone, and if I had looked even a second longer, I'm sure my heart would have stopped completely.

I place a hand on it now, trying to calm it as Sevin tries to calm me.

"Emily." He calls out. "Emily, it's alright. I'm decent." I hear him chuckle. "Fully wrapped up like a pig in a blanket. You can open your eyes now."

I release my squeeze on my eyelids, one-by-one, glancing up to see him newly wrapped in the bath towel, a smug look on his handsome face.

He pulls the fabric even tighter around his waist.

"Look, see? It's practically locked around my body." He heaves a deep breath as if he needs it as much as I do. "Now, what can I do for you? Besides make the both of us super uncomfortable?"

"What…can you…do?"

My brain can't work when the thought of a naked Sevin is still in it. I tap my throat.

"Yes, that's right. I knocked on your door."

His green eyes glow. "Yes, you did."

"I came up here because I wanted to talk."

"Just you?" He glances behind him. "Where's Kayla? Where's… Charlie?" A ball of emotion seems to clog his throat.

"Both asleep." I shrug. "The flight wore them both out."

Sevin arches an eyebrow. "And what about you? Flight didn't have the same effect?"

"Takes a lot more to wear me out."

My response makes him smile, and I brush off the fact that what I said sounded like an invitation for him to do just that: Wear me out.

I shift on my feet. "We have a lot to go over…with this case and the potential tabloid blowback. Stephan wants to make sure everything is perfect."

"Stephan. Right. Of course. I'm your job… Almost forgot." His full lips frown for a second, but then he steps aside, giving me a clear shot to the inside of his hotel room. "So, come in. Let's talk."

The invitation is sweet. And yet I'm no longer sure I want to take it.

Straightening my backbone with as much fake confidence as I can muster, I walk me and my newest Armani skirt suit past Sevin, smelling his soapy fresh scent, reminding myself he's just a client…and that this? This is just a job.

Just like he said.

Problem is: It's a little harder to remember that when Sevin closes his hotel door, locking us in.

I take a seat on the far side of the suite, setting up shop at a small dining area table.

I lay out notes from the briefcase on my arm. "So, can I begin?"

"As you wish." He motions. "Would you like a drink?"

"I don't drink on the clock."

"Ah, right. You equals employee. Me equals client. You're right."

He walks over to the wet bar, pouring himself a drink. He still hasn't changed into his clothes and I watch his back muscles bunch, resisting the urge to wet my lips. I sit up straighter.

"I want to address what would happen in the worst case scenario: That is to say, if Deborah Jett actually does publish her story about your potential paternity to a blog or magazine."

I feel my hands sweating but I keep going.

"In order to file an injunction against the magazine that publishes these rumors about you, I'd have to make you aware of what your options are." I glance up to see Sevin nodding, a new glass of gin in his hand. I keep going.

"In this case, since the story about you would be in print, we may be able to pursue a case of libel, whereby a journalist or media outlet has published something false about you—a statement that has no merit. Are you staying with me here?"

I watch Sevin blink at me, blankly, his jaw ticking slowly. He puts down the glass. "I am."

"Here in the U.S., the bar for proving libel or defamation is a lot higher for a celebrity like you as opposed to any regular person…" I shrug. "Like me."

I lick my lips. "The publication will have had to demonstrate what is called a "reckless disregard for the truth"—either a lack of fact-checking, or printing the false story in spite of knowing the facts. So, not only would we have to prove that a false statement was published but that it was published with actual malice."

I pause. "Am I being clear?"

"Crystal, actually."

I notice Sevin's shoulders tense, and something in me wants to stop. "Keep going?"

His jaw pulses. *Pulse. Pulse. Pulse.* "Yes, I need to hear this."

"I'm not going to lie to you, Sevin. Winning a case like this, if Deborah does take it public, won't be easy. And in terms of the PR?" I sigh, one hand smoothing my skirt as I sit straighter. "Look, I'm no expert here. But from what I've heard from our firm employee Ben, pursing something like this might not shine the best light in your favor. Since the bar for proof is so high for a public figure, it's quite likely that we may not win."

I inhale steadily. "And *if* we do—*and that's a big if*—then a drawn-out court case can cause a slew of bad press, leaving you facing a very negative public opinion. And let's face it: Your reputation isn't exactly sterling silver."

This makes him stand more upright, his large hand pushing the glass of gin away. "Meaning what exactly? Let's get specific."

I feel my stomach tighten, apprehension gripping my gut from the inside-out. I take a deep breath, meeting his eye. "Your departure from New York hasn't exactly endeared you to all NYC fans who would have rather seen you stick out the rest of your career back in your hometown."

"Plenty of other athletes request trades."

I raise an eyebrow. "You're not exactly the most media-friendly player on the team."

"Because those blogging bastards never quit hounding me."

"And the women…"

His jaw won't stop clenching at that one. His green eyes narrow.

"I've done my research on you dating back to your college years…" I flip through his file. "And the number of women you've been connected to range from several Miss USA's to pop singers. There was once even a rumor that you were exchanging more than pleasantries with the president's wife…"

"She asked for *gum* at a press event," he interjects, his pine-colored eyes hard. "That was it."

"And last but not least…" I don't stop. "There are the persisting stories about you and your college coach's daughter."

At this, Sevin's mouth snaps shut, and I continue talking. "There was talk that you and university darling were perhaps once a 'thing.'"

"A thing?" He scoffs, leaning forward. "Is that the legal term for it these days?"

"Sevin," I warn. "I'm only telling you what's been said about you…"

"Well, I'm sorry, but I have to admit: It sounds a hell of a lot like you being my judge and jury." Crossing his large muscular arms, Sevin's palm drops to the hotel wet bar with a thud that makes the surface shake. I glance up at him, my heart starting to beat hard.

"That's not fair to say."

"Isn't it?" His dark hair falls forward as he stares at me, arms crossing, his deep voice lowering to an accusatory rumble. "It wouldn't be a stretch, Miss Armand, to say that you've judged me the moment you met me. Hell, even before… Maybe that's why you're not so great with people."

"That's not true," I retort. But my voice is trembling, my breath leaving my lips in ragged breaths. "You don't know what you're talking about."

"Oh come off it. I may not be the world's most clairvoyant man, but it's clear as hell that you have something to prove. To who or what I have no idea. And I have no idea, Emily..." He throws his hands in the air, letting them fall. "I have no idea who or what hurt you, but it wasn't me."

"I think it's time you turn that finger around and point back at yourself, Mr. Smith. You are *hardly* the most trusting man in the world, don't you think? For all the women you've been connected to in the press, you've never *once* gone public with a woman." I count on my fingers. "Not a wife. Not a fiancée. Not even as much as a girlfriend."

My anger throws my professionalism out the window, and even though I'm doing my best at playing serious-faced lawyer in my sensible high heels and Armani, my emotion gets the best of me.

"My thoughts?" I throw at him. "There's a reason. A reason why you won't so much as let yourself get comfortable with a damn hallway cat." I stand up, cross my own arms, forgetting that this is supposed to be a business meeting. That I'm practically yelling a client. And that the client is nearly naked. "I'm not the only one 'not so great with people.'"

My nerves join my anger, taking a flying leap out the window with it.

Because this *is* me doing my job.

This is me proving myself as part of my crisis management firm. This is what it takes.

It takes truth.

And I'm not going to be afraid of it any longer.

Yes, I admit to myself: I am attracted to Sevin. But that doesn't stop me from telling him, my client, exactly what he needs to hear.

I level an important question at him. The most important one, actually.

"Do you want to take a paternity test?"

He stiffens. "Take a paternity test?" He scoffs. "To prove my paternity to a mysterious woman who dropped her kid off on my doorstep for a million dollars? A woman who I wouldn't trust with an imaginary goldfish for a pet? *That* woman?" He closes his eyes, opening them with a fire blazing behind them. "You said it yourself. I'm not so great with caring about people." The blaze in his green stare sears my skin. "What do *you* think a man like that would do?"

I wet my bottom lip, my eyes flickering up to his, as I blow out a breath. "You want me to be honest?"

A hint of humor hits his bright irises. "You've been honest so far. Don't stop."

I hold his hot gaze, battling the war inside my body that keeps me stuck to the spot. I take a step closer. "I think you're a man capable of doing whatever you want, Sevin. A man capable of *more*."

I risk another step. "Fighting a paternity suit isn't all you're up against. You have to fight your case in the court of public opinion. No matter what you say or do, you will *always* be wrong in someone's eyes. Whether or not you are Charlie's father, there's a fight that you have to fight, and that's whether or not you want to be the man the papers will paint you as..."

Another step brings me nearer.

"Or whether or not you want to be the man you know you can be."

I shrug, my stomach tightening as Sevin's eyes settle on my face. "Question is: Which man do you want to be? *Do you want to be that man who doesn't know how to care about people?* You'll have to figure that out on your own before you ever take anyone's paternity test."

I inhale, and the tension between Sevin and I draws tighter

than a string. *Drawing me to him.* I finally exhale. "Because once you do, Sevin, there's no going back. There's no going back to the man you once were."

The question carries with it a ring of truth that sucker-punches even me. And the raw energy between the two of us standing there, mere feet apart, thickens enough to make the room sway.

I swear the hotel suite actually moves.

Especially when Sevin picks up his glass of gin, giving it a single swallow, his naked damp chest heaving.

I watch him, even as he sets the glass on the bar, pushing it away once more.

And I can do nothing but watch further as he crosses the length of the room, his green eyes hotly on me, his arms raising as he grabs me and kisses me, pushing the last thing—my sense—out of the window too.

CHAPTER 10

*E*MILY
Thursday night

His kiss is every bit as incredible as I thought it'd be. And I can't get my brain to slow down.

To remember that he's a client. A client that could make or break the case I'm currently on.

But I don't care.

I don't care about anything that's not Sevin's lips or hands or tongue.

My backside pressed against the hotel suite's dining room table, I let him sink his mouth onto mine, and it may be the best thing I've ever felt in my life.

Every thought in my brain is fried the second our lips meet, and I instantly wrap myself around the walking, talking wall of muscle, my fingers reaching up to dig into his naked broad shoulders.

He is one large contradiction standing before me. Soft and hard. Sensual. Rough. Infuriating and yet so damn soothing to my senses that I feel myself melt right on the spot.

For a man who claims to be good at nothing but baseball, he is a certified professional in weakening my knees with one eager kiss that erases all thought.

Deepening it with the ferocity that probably makes him unstoppable on the baseball field, he slides his tongue to smooth against mine, and I grab onto whatever brain cells are still left in my mind.

I take a step back, meeting his eyes which are hooded with enough desire to make me crumple to the floor. I lick my lips, searching for sense.

"We can't do this."

"Do what exactly?" His words are a raspy groan as his lips hover over mine.

"*This.* Kiss. We can't kiss."

"Who says?"

"Common sense, Sevin. You are my client."

"And your neighbor and an asshole according to my assistant and probably a lot of other things." He holds onto my face. "But the most important thing I am right now is a man who will literally implode if I take my hands off you."

Good grief. That common sense is sure slipping out of my fingers. I hold on for dear life.

"I could get in trouble," I say as his lips trail softly to my neck, his hands drifting to my hips.

"With who? Our doorman Hank? I'll kick his ass."

I sigh, whimpering as his wet mouth lowers. "With Stephan. My boss, Sevin."

"You're a grown woman, kitten," he whispers against my skin. "And I'm an adult. We can do what we want, you know."

I don't even know what I want.

I've never wanted anything outside of my career. Not really.

I'd wanted Jason at some point. But then again, Jason had never kissed me, touched me, stroked me like this.

And the more Sevin moves his mouth against my neck and collarbone, the more his slightly calloused hands caress my lower back and hips, the more difficult it is to remember wanting anything outside of him.

I make a final attempt. "Sevin, it's hard to talk when you're doing this."

"Then maybe you should think less about talking..." His fingers roam lower. "And more about this."

"This what?"

"*This.*"

And then his fingers find their mark.

His hand finds its way under my business skirt and he begins skimming the cotton across my pantyline. The move makes me gasp, and I won't even allow myself to think about what will happen if the half-naked athlete moves his hands any lower.

I'm already wet just from a simple stroke across my hip bone.

Sevin lifts his mouth from my skin to look at me.

"What *do* you want, Emily?"

He pecks my lips with a sensuous short kiss. "Less Led Zeppelin playing on those late work nights? I'll keep the music down."

Another kiss.

"More alone time in the elevator? I'll tell that mean old Mrs. Headley to take a hike."

He reconnects his mouth to mine, and I swoon.

"Or do you want something a little more *immediate?*"

His fingers toy with the edge of my underwear, and it is like a straight shot to my sex. I know I am soaking poor Bugs Bunny, whose face is imprinted on my crotch, but I don't care.

I don't care about anything other than what Sevin is doing to me right now. His hand dips one inch lower, and I bite my bottom lip, meeting his hot green gaze.

"I'm guessing that's a yes to my question?" He asks, even as his hand lowers to stroke my damp slit, sliding across the drenched fabric.

I nod, coming apart as my fingers dig deep indentations into his broad shoulders. My eyes flutter closed.

The sensation of Sevin stroking two fingers across my sex, slowly and deliberately, is enough to make me come, and I steady myself against that same dining room table, legs quivering as, at last, Sevin slips his hand beneath my panties, meeting me skin to skin.

I can't stop the moan that leaves my mouth.

He cups my mound, curling just two fingers over my slippery center, and just when I think I can't take enough sensation, his head lowers, bending to cover one blouse-covered nipple with his hot mouth.

I come instantly, soaking his fingers like the inexperienced lover that I am.

His name is a rough moan on my mouth, and I am powerless to stop him as he keeps sliding those two talented fingers along my heat, his teeth tugging around my sensitive nub.

"God, Sevin…" I breathe, wanting more.

I'm suddenly greedy for his touch, my body arching into his.

But the sound of a knock on the door interrupts any more I have to say, and, shocked right back to reality, I pull out of Sevin's embrace, my fingers flying to my skirt as I adjust.

"Shit, shit, shit," I mutter over and over. "Were you expecting anybody?"

"Absolutely fucking not." His deepened voice is a growl. "And I'll get rid of them right now." He glances at me, his dark hair falling over his face, like a sexy angel. "Don't you move from that spot. *Please.* Don't move."

But before I can answer, he's already heading towards the door in large steps, one hand on his towel as he unlocks the door, shoving the heavy wood aside.

I can't see who's in the doorway. But I can hear him. Clear as day.

"Glad to see you're out of the shower," the deep voice rumbles from the doorway. "Now we can really get this party started. You remember Daphne, don't you?" The voice drops even lower. "Because she sure as hell remembers you."

"Hi, Sevin," I hear, a sugary sweet southern voice chipping in. "It's good to see you again." The woman drawls. "Really good. And what lucky timing." I hear the voice come closer. "A couple of the other bunnies and I are in town for another event with the Milwaukee Bruisers. Thought you might want to pick up where we left off…"

My stomach swirls at the woman's words, and I clutch my stomach to settle it.

This is it. This is him.

This is the Sevin that I remember. This is the man man living above me, with more women than a Sheryl Crow concert.

I slide my skirt further down my hips, feeling my face enflame as Sevin speaks up.

"Yeah, Saw, now's not a good time."

"What? It's not like you couldn't use the company…"

I close the distance, stepping towards the doorway so that I can gaze over Sevin's shoulder.

Right at the busty blonde and what can only be another base-ball player. The man on the other side of the door frame looks like he just stepped out of an ESPN 'This is 30' episode.

I swallow thickly. "Actually he could use the company." I glance at Sevin's hard-lined face, searing my stare into it. "I was just leaving."

He reaches for me, scarcely missing my wrist. But I'm moving too fast.

I hear my name called out into the hallway, but it's barely a blip over the rush of blood surging in my ears and the sound of the suppressed sob on my tongue.

My brain has finally slowed down after Sevin's kiss, and remembering that the bed-breaking athlete is my client is easier than ever.

* * *

SEVIN

It takes me five minutes to get rid of Sawyer and the blonde bunny from the party in my penthouse.

But it's going to take a lot longer to get Emily to respond to me.

No amount of messaging her on the MyNeighbor app can get her to reply, and I decide after two hours of trying my luck to turn to something else.

Wrapping my head around how to get her out of the suite she shares with Kayla and Charlie? Well, that's the hard part.

Finally dressed in a t-shirt, jeans and cap, I take the elevator down the several stories to her floor, feeling like a virgin on prom night, my heart pounding.

I need Emily.

I hate to say it, but it's true. Getting a glimpse of the lawyer, the professional she is, has me convinced: She's the only person who can get me out of this paternity scheme unscathed.

And I trust her. I hate to say it.

Despite her hiding the fact that she knew we were neighbors, I can see the resilience in her hazel eyes, the absolute dedication in her job.

Not to mention the adoration she has for the little girl who may be my own.

She stared at the eight-year old with the sort of innocent appreciation of a woman who actually likes children—a rarity in my career where female hangers-on care more about breast implants than babies.

Not that anything was wrong with either.

It's just that... There was something protective in the way she hovered around the abandoned child and the hallway cat. Something sexily possessive.

She stood beside each, as if she'd shield them from harm in any way she knew how.

And I had to admit: It shocked me. Inspired me.

Racked me with guilt in ways that I'd never delved into exploring.

Would I ever be capable of that kind of caring?

It is all I can think of as I disembark the elevator on her floor, ambling down the hallway.

But that's when I see him.

That damn cat. Dawdling there. Belonging to its own category of "pain-in-the-ass."

I walk towards the small mewling beast, reaching for it when it runs.

Fuck.

I head after the scampering creature, turning the corner as he claws around the bend.

But I run into something else on the other side.

Her round green eyes peer up at me in surprise. I stop.

"Charlie," I say her name, my voice a startled croak. "What the…?" I glance over my shoulder. "What are you doing out here? And by yourself?"

The little girl points down the hallway where the black cat is bunkered down, staring at us both.

"Felix needed some space. After that small plane we flew on." Her little chin tips towards her collar with guilt. "But then he ran after I opened the door."

I walk closer, my throat closing up. "And where's Kayla? Where's Emily?"

"Kayla is still asleep. Emily went to pick up some food for us." She grins shyly but then it falls. "She's nice. I was hungry." She raises her chin. "I ate all the snacks she gave to me for the plane ride."

"But you can't just roam around here by yourself." My throat almost squeezes shut. I try to swallow around the knot there. "Something could happen to you."

She frowns up at me, a hint of anger touching those pine-like irises. She crosses her arms, her little wrists intertwining across her chest.

Looking eerily like me.

I swallow again.

"I can take care of myself, you know."

I nod. "I'm sure you can."

"I'm eight years old now. My mom says I'm more mature than other kids my age. They barely even let other kids into the sky boxes at the baseball games, but I'm so much more mature than other kids."

Sky boxes? Baseball games?

I thought Deborah was a down-on-her-luck waitress. I try to shake the sentence off, but then I notice the long-sleeved t-shirt Charlie's wearing.

It's a New York Fever baseball t-shirt. My old team.

I bend at the knee to meet her eyes. "You like baseball, don't you?"

"Softball, really." She grins, her little teeth gleaming. "I'm the best player on my team."

Her confidence makes me smile. "That right?"

"Yeah." She nods. "We're on Spring break now from school. But our last game, we creamed the other team." She pounds one little fist into the other and I can't hold back the laugh that leaves my throat.

"Of course you did. Baseball runs in your blood, grasshopper."

The laugh stops as I realize what I've said. My head feels tight and my tongue goes dry.

Without another word, I head towards Felix, huddled in the corner of the hallway, and this time the furry feline actually lets me grab him, holding him close.

I return to Charlie, putting one hand on her shoulder, knowing that tonight is not the night.

It's not the night to push this connection on Emily. *No matter how damn strong it is.*

I decide to get Charlie back to her hotel suite where she belongs…and my libido back to my own suite. Where it too belongs.

"Come on, softball champ." I motion. "Let's get you and Felix back to where you belong."

And as Charlie walks in front of me, I notice the writing on the back of her t-shirt. Writing that makes me realize I'm in much more trouble with this blackmailing-paternity case than I thought.

Because it's my name imprinted on the back of her small jersey.

CHAPTER 11

*E*MILY
Friday morning

The morning after my kiss with Sevin is no better than the sleepless night I spent last night.

After I left Sevin's room, I was trying to avoid leaving my hotel suite for little else other than Kung Pao and a mental ass-chewing.

I came back to my room last night—*post-make-out, of course*—to discover a newly awake Charlie and Kayla, noticing that the shy little girl that had come into all of our lives with this case had, in a matter of a few hours, changed since our arrival.

With a (finally awake) Kayla as a co-partner in an effort to keep the mood light after Charlie's *clearly* crazy mother's abandonment, I showed the little soldier a series of my favorite cartoons—the Tiny Toon Adventures, the Animaniacs and more, laughing with the two sleepyheads over spicy sauce and fried rice, checking in with my boss Stephan before heading to bed to what turned out to be the most fitful night of sleep I've ever had.

It was almost impossible not to think about the disturbingly sexy athlete a few floors ways.

Almost.

For the rest of the night after our kiss, I managed to avoid the elevator, taking the stairs and keeping radio silence on the MyNeighbor app.

Until this morning...

As my mind replays the devastatingly sexy way Sevin nipped his teeth at my bottom lip last night, my phone blares, signaling the start of another day.

The morning sun stretches itself in Arizona-orange colors around the edge of my heavily-curtained hotel window, and I slowly sit up in the humongous, tousled bed, imagining all the different ways I'll have to prevent myself from running into the bunny-attracting baseball pro.

But first...*the phone.*

I pick it up, hoping it will be my former boss, Violet, who still hasn't responded to my last text.

"Hello?"

"Well, hello and a happy Chicago morning to my favorite whore," Ben practically sings over the line, his voice a laugh. "How's your A.M. going?"

"Just fine," I sigh, "until you reminded me that I'm the stupidest woman on the planet."

"You are not stupid. And I oughta smack you for saying that about my best friend. What?" He presses. "Are you still freaking about this whole Sevin deal? I thought we talked about this at an unreasonable length before."

I exhale, feeling my body slump as I lay in the gigantic hotel bed. "And what if I am?"

"Then you really are stupid. And hush. I can say that about my best friend... Because she knows how much I love her. You listen to me," he warns, "there is nothing wrong with you taking a second to step out of your perfect plans. What, did he reject you?"

I groan into my pillow. "No, the very opposite."

He gasps, his voice a raspy croak coming out. "And how was it?"

"It wasn't much. Just a few kisses." I hesitate, warming at the thought. "But it was seriously incredible." I sigh. "And it can't go any further than that."

He sniffs with a sudden haughtiness. "Dammit, Ems, you should have gone for it. Free yourself from the constrains of propriety. See how good a little chaos can taste."

"No." I shake my head, knowing Ben can't see it. Knowing that he can't know how badly I've screwed up. "No, Ben, I should have known better. I mean, for Christ's sake, Sevin is a major player. I've heard his late night antics enough times to know. And in case we're forgetting, the man is a freaking client of ours."

"You're human. And Sevin is one of the hottest men on the planet. It could have happened to anyone."

"No, it couldn't have happened to anyone…because a rational person wouldn't have slipped up and forgotten that. A rational person would have stayed away."

"Are you insane? A rational person would have slipped and fell on that immaculate cock of his instead."

I scoff, covering my mouth. "You are the crudest person I know."

Ben makes kissing noises over the phone. "And you love it. But if you love your sex or love life even a little, you will do it a favor and let yourself have this—have Sevin. I mean, what man have you actually tried dating this year?" His voice sinks. "And that jerk-off Jason doesn't count."

"You know the answer to that."

"Uh huh. And before Jason?"

I think back, coming up empty. It'd been forever, actually.

I'd avoided men, choosing my career instead.

Ben expels a harsh breath, letting it reverberate over the line. "I'll take your silence as a big fat 'it's been too long.' And seriously, you can't have only a relationship with your job, Em."

"What are you talking about?"

"I'm talking about the fact that the only late-nights you pull…

are with a case file. I'm talking about the fact that you never let yourself get close to anyone. And the fact that the only 'Favorites' saved in your phone are me—a man who sleeps with other men and your boss, a man who, despite his great looks, seems *depressingly* asexual." I can hear his frown from here. "Now tell me that isn't true."

"It isn't true," I toss back. Ben sucks his teeth as I keep talking. "My mom is *also* saved as a 'Favorite,' asshole."

I chuckle, hearing Ben do the same, silently despising that what he's saying is so true. We hang up shortly after, and afterwards I lay there, starfished on the bed, not ready to start readying myself for the day.

For Sevin's game.

I have no choice. Babysitting our client of an athlete means I have to watch his, as Ben called it, perfectly formed butter pecan ass.

Sevin's a job. And I'm in a relationship with my job. A serious one.

But that's what's keeps me going.

Because a job was simple. And it was safe. And it, in no way, shape or form, would ever break my heart.

Careers couldn't do that.

They couldn't 'forget' to call. They couldn't stand me up.

A career wouldn't shred my feelings into a million shards and leave me to pick up the pieces.

Which makes my decision to avoid Sevin seem smarter and smarter with every passing second.

So, why do I feel so damn lousy?

Even stretching my limbs out in every direction on the eight-hundred count sheets doesn't help.

The silence wrapping itself around me in my empty hotel room would be complete…if it were actually silent in the room at all.

Because without a conscious thought, I perform my daily

ritual of blasting whatever nineties girl rocker I can find (at the lowest volume so as not to wake Charlie and Kayla in their own rooms), and after everything that's happened in the last week or so, Tracy Chapman's throaty trill makes the morning bearable.

The thought of Ben's words circle through my mind until, weirdly enough, my fingers float to the cotton between my legs, pushing the fabric aside.

I push the shame associated with my feelings for Sevin inside me far enough that the sound of my music overshadows it, and with a few slow swipes, I start fingering myself to the man I'm not allowed to want, a slow shudder sliding across my skin as I close my eyes, giving into sensations I'd long thought were forgotten or at least very much buried in some secret compartment I rarely saw.

I missed that compartment.

I haven't seen it since I was a lowly secretary in New York City. Better yet, I don't think I've seen the damn thing since *college*.

My once carefree love life was now stuffed between an Indigo Girls album and a Rocko's Modern Life cartoon t-shirt that was worn down to the threads.

But then again so was my love life. *Worn.*

Or rather barely used. Not in years.

Daydreaming about a man I work for should be borderline weird, but with Sevin, it's not.

And masturbating to him, imagining his face?

It's dirty in a way I've never delved before. But I guess that's what happens when you're not going according to your perfect plan.

The man living in the penthouse above me has been my neighbor for less than a month and aside from MyNeighbor app I use and the regular rounds of his late-night sex, I may not have even known he existed.

What would my life be now a week later? Without Sevin in it?

I can't even imagine it.

I was getting closer to the man behind the uniform, and it was terrifying.

I'd had an idea of who he was from the sound of his late-night antics. But experiencing them was very different.

And I was quickly learning just what kind of man Sevin Smith really was.

A man with talented fingers and an even more talented tongue. A man with deep kisses and dark stares, the kind that leave you panting in anticipation, waiting for just a hint of what's to come and a sexy smile that drove me absolutely wild.

It would be nice…if I could be that woman he used those fingers and tongue on.

And in my mind, I am that woman. The object of his loud, scream-inducing desire.

A woman temporarily free from my corporate wake-up call. A woman free to desire.

I think of the way I'd thread my fingers into the hair of my off-limits neighbor and client, and my fingertips find the folds between my legs and part them. I imagine massaging the surface of his muscles, and I whimper.

Rubbing my palm across my clit to the rhythm of the song playing in the air, I let myself indulge in the absurd fantasy of bedding the irresistible athlete, and with every quiet thud, every squeak of the bed spring, with every muffled scream and tempered whimper, my hands grow more and more bold.

Parting and stroking and sliding.

I explore nerves I'd never taken time to know, and as Tracy Chapman's warm, woodsy tones reach a peak over the radio, I push myself towards my own, climbing higher and higher.

I see his face—Sevin's—hovering over mine, his full lips connecting with my neck.

And I almost reach the brink.

Until I remember how that little scene ended with a buxom

blonde on the other end of the doorway, and suddenly, I come crashing back down to the earth, the high that Sevin takes me on obliterated as I think back to the bastard he was before this case ever got started.

Before I broke my "common sense" button and I got close to a man who belongs to no one but the magazines.

I slam my hands back down on the bed, squeezing my fist, so my eyes won't squeeze out emotion.

I won't let them.

I need to be a professional right now.

Today more than ever.

Ruining an opportunity to inject life into my sex life was one thing. *Ruining my career was entirely another.*

Because I sure as hell wasn't going to do that.

I'm tempted to call Ben back. To tell him he was right.

A rational woman might sleep with Sevin Smith. But I wasn't a rational woman.

I was a woman with a job to do. And even if it killed any shot at a sex life, that's exactly what I was going to do.

CHAPTER 12

$\mathcal{S}$EVIN

Friday evening

The lights grow hotter and brighter at Scottsdale stadium as the sun begins to set over the Arizona horizon. And the anxiousness in my body settles with it.

The smell of fresh cut grass is in the air and all around me.

Headphones in, focus on, I'm the first person to leave the locker room fully dressed, and though the Cougar team clamors around me, I can barely hear them over the sound of my own attentions.

This is the moment where I lose myself. Every time.

The twenty minutes before a game starts is always the same—like clockwork, and with my baseball cap on, music turned up, I tune myself like a machine before the umpire even hits the field, every muscle in my body relaxing as I hit the zone.

Baseball is my first love. And, in some ways, my only.

The practice swings I take before the game starts always help, but it's this time—this twenty minutes—where the real magic is made.

When I see myself there on the home plate, hands raised up.

105

The feel of the baseball bat's wood between my fingers is like finally coming home, and with every second the crowd roars, with every moment of eye contact between the pitcher and myself —a silent battle witnessed by a hundred thousand faces—I become free.

A man at peace.

It's the only place in my life where I have complete control.

And I use those twenty minutes before my first at-bat to remember that.

But not today.

Today I can't remember a thing.

Because the only thing I can think about is the woman I keep telling myself I don't want…and the little girl I'm convincing myself can't be mine.

I push my headphones farther into my ear.

The sounds of Jim Morrison and The Doors can't even help me now, my normal concentration shattered.

Out of my element, I don't even notice the brunette waiting for me in the stadium's visiting team tunnel.

Until she places a hand on my skin.

I nearly jump out of my uniform, my voice a growl. I drop the headphones.

"Jesus. Fuck." I turn. I notice the huge eyeglasses first. "Naomi?"

"Surprise, asshole." My first 'asshole' of the day, and she smiles, a wide one I can admit I missed. She reaches in for a hug. "D'ya miss me?"

"You mean have I missed being harassed and called every damn name in the book?" I hug her back. "Hell yeah. What took you so long? I thought you were coming in an hour ago."

"I was. But the snow still hadn't let up. There was a delay." She shrugs in a casual colored t-shirt and jeans, looking less worried than ever.

I'm used to the practical Naomi. The punctual Naomi. The pushy Naomi.

But this version, fresh out of New York, is more laid back than ever before, her brown eyes smiling behind her bifocals as she gazes up at me. Meanwhile, I'm a mess.

I try hard to pretend that I'm not. "You seem different."

"Do I?" She hides a smile. "Maybe it's because I have good news. Maybe it's that Stephan called and reported that The Firm found Deborah Jett."

My heart separates from my body, its beating stopped. "The Firm found what?"

"They found her, Sev. We found her." Naomi grins, tilting those dark frames up her nose. "She's staying in a hotel in New York. Under her own name, no less."

"A hotel?" My heart falls flat. "Which one?"

"You're never going to believe this."

"Give me a try."

"I'd tell you to guess…"

"But you know I'm not going to. Nome," I can barely keep myself in check. "Which hotel is she staying at?"

Naomi starts to pick at that red nail, and I know I'm not going to like the news. She sighs. "The Waldorf Astoria?"

My poor heart. It's forgotten how to work at this point. And I nearly can't breathe. I take a step forward, seeing red. "The Wal-goddamned-dorf Astoria?" I close my eyes. "How can she afford it?"

"I don't know."

"And why would she need a million dollars from me if she can?"

"Makes you think, doesn't it?"

"Alright." I manage to open my eyes. "Let's get Kayla on it. She's been doing a great job so far."

Naomi nods. "She's already all over it. Stephan's sending her to

New York to retrieve her. And make sure she doesn't slip out of sight again."

"Great. That's great." I nod, feeling numb, my body unmoving.

Naomi squints at my face. "Wait, what's wrong?"

"Nothing." I shake my head, trying to clear it. "Nothing at all."

Naomi's long lashes flutter behind her blocky frames. "I thought you'd love this kind of news. Sev," she stresses. "This is pretty much proof, isn't it? Proof that she's lying? This basically shows that this whole blackmail ordeal is a lie."

A lie.

If Naomi's right—and she *does sound* right—then I should feel great.

I should feel on top of the world that I can stay in the existence I've built for myself. Loyal to no one. Not Charlie and this case or the woman who's come into my life because of the former two —Emily.

Loyal, faithful and devoted to nothing but baseball.

So why the hell do I feel so damn shitty?

I didn't let many people into my life.

Sawyer. Lenny. Those two lugheads were always there.

My friendship and bar co-ownership with Deacon Cross and Kayla, his fiancée.

Anything more was left back in my college years. When I'd almost fell over an emotional cliff.

I'd long ago pushed my ex-girlfriend Kimmy and ex-roommate Finley's betrayal to the back of my mind. Or so it seemed.

But had Emily been right? Was my solitary life bullshit?

No wives. No fiancée's. No girlfriends.

I lived my life in the limelight, and lately, it was as if there was no room for anyone but me.

The lights are still bright in the Scottsdale baseball stadium. They always are.

But tonight?

Tonight, they are full on-blazing, blue-white fluorescent

beams of eye-frying radiation, and I consider, for the first time in my life, if living my life this way—married to my career—is actually what I want.

After a few minutes of finishing up with Naomi, I head towards the field, stuffing Jim Morrison back into my ears, feeling lonelier under the spotlight than ever before.

* * *

EMILY

I'm not a baseball girl. Far from it.

I don't like the smell of beer in the air. I don't like the loud horns. Or the foam fingers.

Or the phony attempts at doing the wave.

I don't like any of it.

But what I do like is the eight-year old beside me, having the time of her life. Little Charlie hops in her sneakered feet, taking it all in.

The excitement of the stadium is radiating through her bright eyes, and with every announcement from the loudspeakers, with every hard-thump beat through the loud surround sound, I can feel her elation amp up, a contagious energy emanating from her as she turns to me for the fortieth time, green gaze wide and full of wonder.

She pulls on my jersey like a tug on the string. "When's Sevin coming out?"

"Soon." I assure her. Again. "He's coming out soon, I promise."

But that's all I can promise.

Tonight? Tonight is for her enjoyment.

But who knows what tomorrow holds?

Maybe her mom will come back. Maybe not.

Maybe this entire blackmailing scheme will be exposed as the sham it is, and maybe this case will end in complete flames, with Sevin's career going with it.

Or maybe Sevin will step up. Prove himself to be the man he's showed glimpses of.

Maybe there's a different man, one capable of caring more than he lets on—buried beneath the singular focus and striped uniform. A man I could fall for.

Trouble is: Whatever man Sevin Smith is, someone else has definitely already fallen for him: A now rambunctious eight-year old with similar eyes.

Charlie's cheers grow to earsplitting level as the announcer chimes back in over the intercom, introducing the Chicago Cougars players one-by-one.

Starting with the league's last MVP.

Sevin himself.

He emerges from the stadium tunnel, dark cap on, stubbled jaw set on his handsome face.

But there's nothing smiling about this version of him, and I take my first glance at Sevin, the serious athlete, scared to death of what I will see.

I sit down as the first inning kicks off, the Cougars filing into their defensive positions as the Milwaukee Bruisers ready to take their at-bats.

I can barely breathe.

With my new Chicago Cougars baseball cap and jersey on, I feel like a new woman standing here watching him. Watching them all.

Denim shorts have replaced the Armani skirt suit for once, and with my ponytail slipped through the back of the cap, I barely recognize myself, catching a glimpse of my reflection in Charlie's shiny sunglasses.

I don't recognize the look on my face.

It's fun sitting there. And I'd forgotten what fun looked like.

The last Bruiser at bat is out after three strikes, and with only one run in the first inning, the team trails by the end of the second as Sevin saddles up to the batter's box to hit.

Even from this distance, he is an Adonis among men.

Dark cap on over his darker hair, broader shoulders fitted into the black and white striped uniform, he fills out the fabric as if born into it.

His strong jaw is visible from our front row seats, and through the darkened stubble, I can make out the angle of his razor-sharp jaw, remembering what the sharp dark hair there felt like between my fingers.

Against my neck. Over my collar.

He fits his helmet over his cap and I hold my breath.

The catcher gets into position as the pitcher sets up, and a pitch faster than a blink comes flying in Sevin's direction.

I barely see the swing of his bat, but I do see the baseball that comes careening off it. Over left field and halfway center, Sevin sends the white ball of yarn soaring towards the crowd.

In an arc that crashes over the fence, it lands among the crowded bleachers to a horde of screaming fans, and the billboards light up all around us, drawing a scream from my throat I didn't know I could give.

Two words. Flashed everywhere.

Home run.

He circles the bases, a smile finally back on his face, and my eyes follow him, my heart swelling to twice its size inside my chest.

Charlie tugs on my jersey. *Tug tug tug.*

"Did you see Sevin?" Charlie exclaims on the edge of her seat. "He sent that ball flying, didn't he?"

"He certainly did!" I grin back, barely hearing her over the cheers. I hug her close.

"Mommy always said he was the best player in all of baseball. Daddy used to say it, too."

The eight-year old's words are muffled against me as she clings to my side. But I hear those sentences loud and clear, glancing down at her, scarcely hiding the surprise on my face.

"Your mommy and…daddy, Charlie?"

"Yeah," she repeats, "my mommy and daddy. Sometimes when we're back at home, mommy lets me watch Sevin's games. Well, when daddy's not around." Her eyes dim. "He's not around much anymore."

"He's not?" My heart beats even harder than when I was cheering. "Why not?"

"They fight a lot nowadays. He doesn't stay much at our house anymore." A small frown imprints itself across her face, but she doesn't stop. Her face lights up again, eyes excited. "Mommy's lawyer is there a lot now. Sevin says you're a lawyer."

I nod. "I am."

"Mommy says lawyers help families out. She says when families are in trouble, they help them figure things out. That's why I want to be a lawyer. Just like you. So I can help families like mine. So I can help daddy."

The notion of this 'daddy' of hers draws me near. My negotiation skills aren't the sharpest these days, but I try them on Charlie anyway, hoping she'll tell me the truth.

Hoping she'll help me figure out her family.

Sevin's career depends on it.

"If you don't mind, Charlie," I bend towards the little human, straining to hear her, "what's your daddy's name?"

"His real name?" She thinks. "It's Finley. My dad's name is Finley."

CHAPTER 13

$\mathcal{E}$MILY
Friday night

Arms full of foam fingers, my coat pockets full of peanuts, I land on the hired driver's black leather back seat after the Cougars beat the Bruisers 5-4, jumping in beside Charlie who sports a grin so large it takes up all the space on her pretty face.

Sevin lands last, jumping towards the large truck's passenger-side seat, his breath emitting in heavy huffs as he shuts the door behind us, directing the driver to go.

If it weren't for potential onlookers who might connect Charlie and Sevin in any way, we might have stayed.

Part of me wants to.

But with Kayla missing in action, taking off to track down Charlie's mom, Charlie and Sevin are now my charges.

But tonight is the most fun I've had…hell, since I can remember. I can't recall a single day that work wasn't on my mind.

And even with Charlie's little revelation during the game, I find myself enjoying the night, putting off the thought of Sevin's case until tomorrow.

Even the thought of all that I have to do for The Firm is like a flicker in the back of my subconscious. Because the second Sevin stares at me across the seat, he snuffs that flicker out with a disarming smile, giving me that glimpse of his silly side—a side I love seeing.

I roll my eyes with a grin and the incorrigible athlete laughs softly, his full lips widening beneath his dark baseball cap, his warm voice a rumble inside the truck.

He directs his attention back to the windshield without looking at me.

"Well, at least we know how much Charlie likes baseball. So, what about you, Emily?"

I hug my elbows, still rubbing away the cold from my skin. "What *about* me?"

"Did you enjoy the game?"

"I did. And I usually don't like anything that requires balls flying at my face."

He laughs again, making Charlie giggle, the truck warming with their melodic sounds. I can't help but join in.

"The balls wouldn't be flying at your face, if you actually used your hands to catch the fly balls instead of your nose..." Sevin trails off, humor shining from his half-hooded eyes. "Isn't that right, Charlie?"

"That's right!" She chimes in beside me.

"See, even the grasshopper agrees."

Charlie sneers, tucking one side of her sandy hair behind her ear. She squirms in the seat. "Yuck. I don't want to be a grasshopper. I want to be a lawyer. Like Emily. When I grow up."

I wink in her direction. "But if I'm an animal, I want to be something else. Something cuter..." She ponders, tapping her chin with one finger. "Like Felix."

"You mean that demonic hallway cat?" Sevin shoots a glance at us while we laugh. "Oh no, unh unh, anything but that. You gotta have another animal you'd rather be, Charlie. Pick any other."

"Mmmm," the little girl hums beside me, adorable as ever.

Glancing over her shoulder out the rearview window, she bounces back down in the car's back seat, inspiration making her green eyes go wide.

"How about an ant?"

Sevin's head whirls around. "An ant?"

"Yeah, an ant," she reaffirms. "They always work on a team. Like a baseball team. Or like us. Me, you and Emily. We're like a team..." She glances up at Sevin. "Aren't we?"

I glance up to notice a rare sight: Sevin—stunned. With Charlie, he's no longer the franchise player on the field, Mr. Baseball Royalty, or Mr. Flirty MyNeighbor App, the arrogant player living upstairs or the demanding client.

He's someone different.

He's the same someone he was when we were alone in his hotel suite: A walking dichotomy. The best of two worlds.

Hard and soft. Tender and tough.

And somehow Charlie brings out every bit of both. His stare softens on his face, his jaw growing slack. He lifts his chin.

"Of course we're a team. The best team." He glances at me. "Emily?"

I nod, emotion making the words heavy in my mouth. "Yes, we definitely are."

Our gazes clash and for a second, the business-like defenses Sevin and I regularly raise against each other fall.

For just a second.

Charlie breaks the moment when she chimes in again.

"Plus, ants are really good at knowing how to play 'Follow the Leader.'" She juts a tiny thumb over her shoulder. "Just like that silver car behind us is following."

I glance back, feeling a chill down my spine when my eyes land on a silver sedan trailing twenty feet behind, its windows tinted. I don't remember seeing the silver car when we left the game...or maybe I wasn't looking.

Either way, in the next few seconds, I realize that she may be right. When we turn a corner through the rapidly falling darkness of night, there the car is again.

Behind us. Like a little ant.

Following the trail of bread crumbs.

I place a hand over my heart, finding it beating hard. I turn back around to face the car's front.

"Sevin…" I start.

But he's already looking at me, his brow furrowed. "I see him. What the hell does he think he's doing?"

"From the looks of it," I murmur, peeking behind us, "'Following the Leader.'" I swallow around a knot in my throat. "Got any idea who this guy in the sedan might be?"

He shakes his head underneath his baseball cap. "None." His voice lowers, a menacing hint underlying its tone. His stare tightens out the rearview window. "And I'm not exactly trying to find out." He glances at the driver. "Think you can go any faster? We're in a bit of a hurry."

The driver simply nods.

Stepping on the gas, the silent driver accelerates, sending the large truck speeding forward. And still the silver sedan remains behind us, no longer keeping a safe distance.

The night sky twinkle teasingly over the horizon as we sail through Scottsdale's orange-dusted streets, and still the hired driver pushes the speed limits…and some of my own limits.

I check Charlie's seatbelt making sure it's secure, and as the truck's tires screech slowly around another corner, I feel the bottom of my stomach drop out, my heart climbing up into my throat.

I croak out loud. "Are we sure we want to go this fast?"

Sevin's stare sears me. "Just until we lose the sedan. I'm not having whoever this creep is catch up to us."

I listen to the truck continue to accelerate, my pulse pounding a dangerous rhythm. "He won't have to do much to catch up to us…" I hiss, leaning forward to face him. *"If we're corpses.* It's dark out now, and the winds are picking up. It's not safe."

"Some unidentified car following us with God-knows-what intention isn't safe, either, kitten." He whispers back. "And I have Charlie to think about." He glances back at the hired driver, his stubbled jaw rigid. "There's another hundred in it for you, if you can go any faster. *Two, if you lose that car behind us.*"

My glare closes on him, my fingers gripping onto the back of his passenger-side seat. My tone sinks even lower. "I don't think you're thinking clearly about anything right now. *We need to slow down.*"

"I will be the judge of that."

"Not with three other lives in the car, you won't."

"I'm just doing what's best for all of us. I'm trying to keep us safe."

My teeth grind, my heart now hammering as the car speed ticks up by another ten miles per hour. A car honks as we barely make a red light, speeding past as the light changes color.

I hear Charlie whimper next to me, and I nearly lose it. My voice lowers to a hiss. "I'm not really feeling safe right now." I whisper lower. "And it doesn't look like Charlie is, either."

Sevin peers over my shoulder out the rearview window as the engine rumbles loudly around us, the air inside the black truck growing thin. The shadowed half of his face eclipsed by his baseball cap seems even darker somehow.

But before he can answer, the silver sedan turns a corner behind us, somewhere out of sight.

They weren't following us after all.

And less than a few minutes later, the driver pulls into the motor court of the hotel, a giant smile on his face.

Even in the absence of the silver car we thought was following us, the face-off between Sevin and I stretches on, and we stare unendingly at each other, neither of us backing down—unwilling to give the other an inch.

The driver is the first to speak.

"Uh, that will be two hundred dollars…please."

Sevin whips out his wallet without breaking eye contact with me. He grabs two large-faced bills. Finally glancing over at the driver, he lays two hundred dollars in his hand, slipping the thin wallet back in his coat.

His green eyes are hidden from my view as he looks past me.

"Come on, Charlie." He beckons to the little girl in the back seat, his expression unclear. "Let's get you inside. It's late." He pauses, his gaze roaming over me. "I'll have the hotel send up some hot cocoa before you go to sleep. Deal?"

The precocious ball of energy nods, forgetting all about ants and following sedans. "Deal."

And then he hops out. He leaves me dumbfounded in the back seat as he walks around the truck.

Opening Charlie's door, he escorts the eight-year old out of her seat, with me following stolidly. My footsteps barely create a dent in the Arizona dust on the sidewalk, and I huddle against the west coast desert's deepening cold, the chill from the now dark sky sneaking its way under my clothes.

I sigh once we make it to our floor, stopping in front of the suite door, knowing that it will be just me and Charlie tonight after Kayla took off to New York at Stephan's request.

Charlie slaps hands with Sevin, scrambling into the suite, presumably to turn on some of my favorite cartoons.

But me? I'm still dusting the long day and orange dirt from my shoes and clothes as Sevin faces me by the closed door, his face unreadable, a thin line drawn across his full mouth. He doesn't say a word.

"Look…" I amble closer. "Why don't we just call it a night? I'm tired." I motion towards him. "You're tired. I'm sure we all could use a good night's rest." I reach my hand out to shake Sevin's. "I'll see you tomorrow."

The dangerously grim baseball pro stares at my hand, but

doesn't shake it. Instead he wraps it inside his own, his touch warm and tender—soft as his fingers play against my palm.

Until the door to my hotel suite swings open, and Charlie emerges from the now open doorway, her green eyes panicked.

"Felix is gone!"

"Charlie," Sevin interjects softly, "Felix is a smart cat. I'm sure he just ran out when housekeeping came in."

"But he's out there alone."

Sevin hesitates. "In the hallways he loves so much. He'll come back soon. He'll be fine."

"But Emily said that he belongs to everyone in your apartment building." She glances up at him with moon-like eyes, her stare growing glassy. "That means he belongs to *us* a little bit, doesn't it? And it's starting to get cold outside. Really cold. I could tell. What if Felix freezes outside in the cold?"

Her melodic little voice starts to reach into panic, stabbing me with pangs of guilt.

I glance up and into Sevin's eyes, discovering the same pangs there. And though I know I should run while I have a chance, though I know I should grab onto the semblance of the serious lawyer I once was when this all began—the lawyer who once knew better than to risk her case by becoming emotionally entangled with a client, I feel myself losing my internal battle.

Especially with Charlie still gazing up at me with those weepy green eyes.

The ever-present hot and cold between Sevin and me thaws under the spell of Charlie's concern for the hallway cat and something else—*something warmer*—ignites between us.

And for the first time since last night, Sevin looks at me—really looks at me.

I want to say something smart, something snarky to break the tension, but then he reaches down, wrapping his hand around mine and Charlie's, a resigned smile working its way to his chiseled face. His eyes light up.

"I guess we've gotta got us a cat to find, don't we?"

I nod robotically at him, and he lets me go.

"But I don't care how many cat cartoons you two have watched or much you've bonded with this new little fur ball. One little incident or scratch, and I'm handing him over to mean old Mrs. Headley. Feel free to report that to the rest of the MyNeighbor app."

CHAPTER 14

*S*EVIN
Friday night

The victory over the Bruisers should still feel good to me.

The bastards have been kicking our asses all spring training season, and in the back of my mind, I know beating them should feel better than sex.

And if this were a year ago—Hell, a few months ago, after a win like this, that's exactly what I'd be doing.

Having sex. Having lots of it.

But not after last night. *Because last night changed things.*

Emily's in my goddamned head, and I can't get her out.

I thought Naomi's news about Charlie's mysterious mother would ruin whatever focus I'd found towards the game I love so much.

But it didn't.

In a matter of minutes after hearing proof that the blackmail might be a scam, that Charlie might not be mine, I should have been elated.

But my entire train of thought was turned around, flipped over front and backwards.

Any joy I might feel was tumbled and turned inside out the second I saw the two of them there—Charlie and Emily, standing in the stadium. Clad in Chicago Cougars jerseys and denim, you couldn't miss those one-hundred watt smiles anywhere.

Especially not the gorgeous, lithe, normally business-suited lawyer in the crowd, side-hugging the bright-eyed little girl beside her.

I was drawn to them inexplicably.

My damn neighbor. My current 'fixer.' And the eight-year old she was helping me with.

And it still got to me, that out of all the elevators in the world, she had to walk into mine. Or rather I walked into hers.

I'd been drawn to the strong-willed lawyer since that luck-fated elevator ride that left her on my mind for nights to come.

And then Charlie.

She'd come into my life at what should have been the worst time possible. But having her here was something I was getting used to.

Dangerously used to. Considering who the hell I was, had been all these years. *Looking out for no one but myself.*

I never had to.

I never wanted to be a father. I knew I wouldn't be good at it.

But the knowledge that I could be, the thought that the eight-year old ball of grit and fire could be mine didn't scare the goddamned dickens out of me in the moment that I saw her in the crowd—cheering and waiting for the game to start… And *that* was the scariest part of all.

And I didn't even know if I believed I was her father or not. I didn't know if I could believe a word of it.

But after Naomi dropped her little bomb on me, I did know that I needed to focus on that damn game.

Five minutes after Naomi left, ten minutes before the spring game against the Bruisers, as I tightened my grip on my lucky baseball bat harder, preparing for another practice swing, a chill of hyper-awareness ran down my neck.

Like in that lonely locker room, back in Chicago.

I was still hundreds of miles away from the Windy City, and I still felt as if someone was watching me.

Eyes on the horizon, I geared up for the game, the Scottsdale sky blurring with its light-polluted stars when I heard the crunch of grass behind me, confirming my suspicions.

I turned, facing off against a pair of cement gray eyes.

"What the fuck, man?" My old teammate Lenny Rodriguez drilled me with a daggered stare. "You mind putting that bat down?"

"Shit." Lowering the baseball bat, I slapped hands with the Milwaukee Bruiser player. "Sorry about that, bro. Just got…a lot on my mind."

"I can see that." He grinned. "Tell me: Does that 'something on your mind' come in a size six with beautiful tits?"

"You sure you and Sawyer didn't come out the same womb?"

"I'm just saying, brother," the big lug slapped me on my shoulder. "Since the cops showed up and the party ended early, I thought you might be having a small party of your own with that bunny you'd been talking to."

Oh, yeah, that's right. Daphne. The one who interrupted what could have been a fantastic night with Emily.

Sawyer's Miss Bunny of the Year'.

The night prior suddenly felt like forever ago, so much having changed in twenty-four hours.

The day before, I'd been a single athlete, nearly seeking my next conquest. Today? I was someone else.

A caretaker. Possibly, a father. And a man who couldn't keep his eyes off the woman in the crowd in some of the best seats in Bruiser stadium.

Out of her normal business blouse and skirt, fitting delectably in a Chicago Cougar shirt and cap, Emily Armand laughed out loud, one hand perched on Charlie's bouncing shoulder.

The pair were a sight to see, snuggled closely under the chilled desert night, two foam fingers fitted neatly over each hand.

The Milwaukee Bruiser mascot circled the stadium to get the fans riled up, and somehow it felt that the only one who was getting riled up…was me.

Some part of my heart that I didn't know existed warmed at the thought of the saucy-tongued brunette and the even saucier eight-year old becoming friends, and in a flash, I imagined what my life would be like if things were different.

If Emily and Charlie were waiting for me at the end of a long night. If I could come back to my penthouse to more than one-night-stands and my trainer's texts. If Emily and I were…

"Earth to Sevin." Emily waves a hand in front of my face, and the memory of the day fades just as fast. "We just lost Felix. I'm not sure I can take losing you."

I blink, bringing my focus back to the present. "Sorry. I was just…thinking of earlier."

"The game?"

I nod, continuing to walk beside the sexy attorney.

The suddenly mute lawyer and I follow Charlie to yet another floor in search of Felix, the mangy beast that has already wreaked havoc in our lives, I can't take the silence between Emily and I anymore, my anger from earlier melting with every corner we cross.

I put my hands in the pockets of my sweat pants.

"I was an asshole to you."

The sentence is a whisper behind Charlie's back, and Emily doesn't look at me.

"Excuse me?"

I gaze at Charlie's back a few feet away, trying to keep my voice low.

"I said I was an asshole to you." I inhale deeply, still walking.

"Last night. Tonight. Hell, lots of nights before. The notes I left you on the neighborhood bulletin board…" I trail off, thinking of just the last twenty minutes.

I grind my teeth. "Fuck, scratch that. I was an asshole to you in the car. I was an asshole to you at your apartment. I've *been* an asshole. My assistant Naomi can tell you better than most. I'm not good at handling most aspects of life besides a baseball bat." I scoff. "God knows how hard I try… It's just not in me."

Emily ambles beside me, her hands holding her own elbows, her arms crossed. "I wouldn't say that's true. You seem to be handling this paternity-blackmail situation pretty well. I'll give you that."

I snort out loud, the sound as pathetic as I feel. We turn another carpeted corner on the tenth floor, and I wait, making sure Charlie can't hear us, her little footsteps echoing.

"I'm doing a good job of pretending I'm fine. But in reality? I'm pretty damn freaked. Guess you could tell that at your apartment when Stephan and I showed up."

She laughs, and I like listening to it, the sound tinkling and sweet in the empty hallway. Our shoulders brush as we walk.

"I could kinda tell that you were stressed, but I figured that's normal." She hesitates before saying the rest. "Kayla filled me in on a few details about what you're going through—the trade to the Cougars, co-owning a bar with her fiancé, adjusting to a new city and team. I can't…imagine."

She shakes her head, her dark hair spilling over her shoulders —soft enough to touch. I ball my fist.

"Your team's been going through a lot. *You're* going through a lot." She lowers her voice an octave, and her tone is so sultry I almost close my eyes. I continue walking.

"And I shouldn't have said what I said on the ride here. I was out of line." She goes on talking. "I judged you, Sevin. I've *been* judging you. It's just…my 'normal.' I guess that's why I don't have many people in my life. Sometimes, I don't let people get close enough to get a chance. In the past, when I have let people get close, it's been…"

She lets the statement linger, and I'm tempted to press. She seems so open.

Outside of the elevator and MyNeighbor app, I've been dying to get the guarded brunette alone, and though Charlie is barely out of earshot, her round, wide eyes searching the halls for Felix, I can't stop myself from digging deeper, my curiosity besting me even now.

I let my eyes drift towards her face, enjoying the view.

"I'm guessing it didn't go so well? Letting people get close?"

Her shoulders hunch. "You could say that."

"I don't get it." I mock quietly. "Who wouldn't want to be around for all that cartoon trivia and bad nineties music of yours?"

Emily laughs. "Oh, fuck you very much."

"I'm serious. I only know one woman in the world who can quote ten different cartoon cats and all fifty-something members of a Lilith Fair concert from nineteen ninety-seven. Your brain holds a wealth of natural treasures."

"And what about you, Mr. Stuck in the Sixties?"

"What *about* me?"

"If I had to hear another Led Zeppelin or Jim Morrison record coming from my ceiling…"

"Were you going to sic Felix on me?"

"Worse." She glances over. "Mean old Mrs. Headley."

"Oh, I think I can handle 'The Headley.'"

Emily shakes her head, sliding strands of silky hair farther into her hat. Her shoulders shake with laughter. "You say that now, but I wouldn't be so sure. I hear things on MyNeighbor, you know. *Interesting* things. Headley's a woman who might chew you out on Monday, have you over for dinner on Tuesday and get matching tattoos with you by the weekend. And usually in some place naughty."

"Really?" I lift an eyebrow, tilting my head towards her with interest, one hand on my cap as I pull it low. I catch her eye. "How naughty are we talking here? On a scale of 'Hand in the cookie jar' naughty to 'Fifty Shades of Grey' naughty, how bad?"

'I'll say this: She's a grandmother, but I heard Old Mrs. Headley could teach Mr. Grey a thing or two."

"Well, hell. This conversation just gave the term 'grandmama's cookies' a whole new meaning."

She shakes her head with a scoff and I laugh, liking this honest side of her, my ears eager for what she'll say next. Emily doesn't disappoint.

"Oh, I'm sure she might love sharing her, uh, *'cookies'* with a good-looking, card-carrying professional athlete like you."

Her laugh comes from the heart—musical and soft. But it hits me everywhere on my body below the waist. With the soft smell of stadium peanuts and fresh-cut field grass on her skin, a tinge of red from the harried day still on her cheeks, she looks adorable underneath that dark Cougars cap and curtain of silky hair.

Innocent and absolutely fucking delectable.

I've had one goal for the last two weeks, and that's how to get my mind back to baseball and out of this blackmail mess. But with the introduction of these two new crazy women in my life—one still a girl, *the other anything but*, I can't seem to get myself back on track.

And I'm no longer sure I want to.

I want to tell Emily exactly that. A part of me is damn dying to.

But my cell phone suddenly rings, cutting me off. And I reach for it immediately, answering the second I see Naomi's name on the screen.

I wet my lips. "Nome? What's going on?"

"I've got good news and bad news, Sev. Which do you want first?"

I grunt. "Do you have to ask?"

"Okay, bad news: I just ran into Sawyer with a harem of

women coming into the hotel lobby, and yes, he's still an asshole, so my condolences for being connected to such a prick."

"Thanks for your sympathy, Nome. It's appreciated. And the good news?"

"The good news: Stephan and Kayla found your Deborah Jett. They called her NYC hotel room and she actually picked up. She'll be in Chicago by Sunday morning."

"That's two days from now. And what the hell does she want now?"

"She wants her daughter back, Sev."

The statement's like a punch to the gut.

"She wants to drop the entire case," Naomi tells me—as excited as I should be. "We're having her sign an NDA and no-contact contract. And then this crazy witch will be out of our lives forever…"

I rub the back of my neck, repeating the words back in my mind. Because it doesn't make any sense.

What *does* make sense: The thought that if Deborah Jett is out of my life forever, then that means a lot of other things too.

Means that Charlie will be out of my life forever.

Meaning that Emily might be, too.

Means that I'm getting exactly what I wanted. And I'm not even sure I want it anymore.

I hang up with Naomi, feeling sick and feeling nothing like the Sterling Sevin Smith I once thought I was.

CHAPTER 15

$\mathcal{E}$MILY
Friday night

He's back. The Sevin from before.

The minute after Sevin gets the call on his cell, that something warm, that something new that I watched grow inside the sexy baseball player, disappears right in front of my eyes.

The same cold, hard version that confronted me outside of my apartment is back, and even when we finally find Felix, letting Charlie wrap the easily scared cat in her arms, he remains frigid.

Walking back to our hotel suite, I try to make eye contact but he avoids it, and when we finally reach the suite, I usher Charlie into her room inside with all our game-time paraphernalia and goodies. All sandy hair and sleepy smiles, she hugs me quickly before heading inside.

With a small moment of hesitation, she decides to wrap her arms around Sevin too and when I glance up into his face, it's as if he's in pain, his handsome face pinched as he grabs her and lets go a few seconds later.

I wait until the bedroom door's completely closed before I

129

turn to him. But he is already heading to the bar on the other side of the suite, his hands reaching for the small bottles of alcohol.

"So?" I press as his fingers find a bottle of vodka and start pouring.

He doesn't turn. "So what?"

I start walking closer. "You want to tell me what the call was about? The one that just turned you into a corpse?"

His shoulders are rigid as he brings the glass of vodka to his lips. He pauses before taking a sip. "It's nothing."

"Oh, yeah? And is it that 'nothing' that's making you drink like a fish?"

Sevin starts pouring again. "Just a little after-game night cap." He finally turns to me, the pain from earlier still in his eyes. "Care to join me?"

I glance at the glass and at his face, stepping closer. "Sure, I guess. I mean, we're teammates, aren't we? Teammates don't let other teammates drink alone, right?"

"Damn straight." He takes the second glass of vodka to the head, tilting the entire shot into his open mouth. I resist the urge to swallow as he wets his bottom lip. "Considering everything, you're better than most teammates I've had."

I blink, my stomach tightening as I look at Sevin. "What's that supposed to mean?"

"Nothing, nothing. Not a damn thing." He scoffs on a laugh, turning back to the bar. "Just thinking of old memories for a sec."

I glance at his back, muscular and rippling beneath his long-sleeved cotton shirt.

He's dressed casually post-game, a simple t-shirt and sweats slung sexily over his chiseled frame. But there's something wrong, awfully wrong, and I can't help but think it has something to do with the phone call he got in the hallway.

The phone call he refuses to talk about.

I sip at my drink. "Care to share what those memories were, teammate?"

Sevin opens the vodka again. "Not particularly."

I take a deep breath, this time my diaphragm tightening as I gaze at a slowly simmering Sevin, his anger heating just below his well-built surface.

"Does this have anything to do with Finley?"

He turns, his baseball cap still shadowing half of his face. But I can tell he's furious.

That angular jaw of his gets to ticking, and all of that hidden anger, that slowly boiling ire, shines through his pine-green eyes. He puts down his glass for the first time since he started drinking.

"Who the hell mentioned anything about Finley?" It's not a question, but an accusation. And I won't back down.

I bite into my lip. "I read some things. Heard some things about your old teammate. You guys were roommates, weren't you?"

He laughs, but there's nothing humorous about it.

"Alright. Time's up. That's enough sharing for tonight, *teammate*." He throws the word at me like an insult. "And that's absolutely none of your business. You're my lawyer, kitten. My fixer. Not my therapist."

"Well, if you didn't hold your cards so close to the chest, I wouldn't have to try to be one. Like it or not, this *is* my business," I assert, lowering my glass. "*You're* my business. Charlie's my business. How you *act* around Charlie is my business. And you weren't acting like yourself tonight. Not at the end of it."

He takes a step forward, swiping his glass from the bar so hard it sloshes. He stares at me. "What do you want from me, Emily? What else do you need? I helped win the game tonight. Helped secured my spot." He scoffs. "Don't worry. You're doing a hell of a job at this case. Keeping it out of the spotlight. *Just like I asked.* And you and your firm will be handsomely paid. Because that's all you care about, right? Getting paid?"

I glare. "I never said that."

"You didn't have to. It was pretty clear that's all you care about the night you called me your 'job' outside your apartment." He raises his glass. "So, please: Go back to treating me like just your job. Because a job? *That*, I can handle. Because whatever *this* is," he motions back and forth, "whatever this is between us? I can't. So, please," he exhales, knocking the rest of the vodka down his throat. "Tell me again how I'm nothing but business to you."

I feel my eyebrows hit my hairline. "Would that make you feel better?"

"Yes, it would, actually." Sevin drinks from his glass. "It would help me remember where we stand."

Yup. *There he is.* The asshole side of Sevin we just spoke about.

But I see through his cover now. Unlike before.

It's the same side of me—the one I've used before to keep people at bay.

It worked when Sevin and I were just neighbors. It worked when the annoying athlete hadn't wanted a spotlight on his love-less love life.

But now?

Now I've gotten a chance to see the other side of Sevin.

The playful, caring, open side. And I'm not about to let it hide again.

I tighten my stance. "Yes, Sevin, if you are so rudely asking where you and I stand, then I will tell you again." I blow out a hard breath. "You are a job to me, of course."

Sevin toasts the air. "Well, then there you go. That's a relief." He finishes the drink, exhaling out loud. "Now I can properly see myself out."

He tries to turn, but I won't let him.

I shock myself when I grab his bicep, pulling him to a stop, and in a matter of seconds, I'm face to face with a six-foot-something wall of well-contained anger and hurt hovering over me with every inch of his muscular frame.

I inhale sharply, my words coming out stronger than I feel. I straighten my back. "You are a job to me, Sevin. Yes, that's true." I release a broken breath. "But I think I misjudged 'my job.' Just as you said."

I lean closer. "I think I was very wrong about 'my job.' And very judgmental about my job. I think that my job was right about me not trusting other, uh, *jobs* in the past." I sigh, feeling it all the way in my toes as the silence stretches. I can barely get the words out I'm shaking so hard. "And if my job would give me a chance, I'd like to prove to...*my job* that I'm not trying to see him as a job...." A knot hits the back of my throat, and I clear it. "Anymore."

The last word is like a dead weight.

And Sevin doesn't make it any easier.

His stare is hard—stony beneath his Chicago Cougars baseball cap. Stony enough to make me squirm.

But I'm not going to let him dismiss me like so many other women in his life, writing them off at the first sign of trouble.

This is me. And this—between us—is more.

I'm a woman with probably too much mouth and more cartoon-adorned underwear than the law should allow.

But I'm also a woman who is not letting go. My hand remains wrapped around his bicep, which doesn't move.

He gazes down at me, his skin hot underneath my own. "Are you done? Did you manage it?"

I relent, raising my jaw by an inch, meeting his gaze. "Manage what, Mr. Smith?"

"Convincing yourself that we haven't been way past the point of this being about our jobs a long time ago." He takes the cap off his sexily tossed hair and gives me a full view of those damning green eyes. Eyes that are stuck on my face. He bends closer. "I just needed to hear you admit it."

And then he kisses me.

SEVIN

It takes a second before she lets me in, her full lips opening for my kiss. At last.

The first time I kissed her…was a mistake. At least, she thought so.

And I knew it.

The second kiss, I would make sure was no mistake, and though I feel like I failed some test the old Sevin would have passed, though I've pushed buttons inside myself I buried long ago, I knew the pay-off would be well worth the effort.

With Emily, it always is.

The ballsy brunette has bewitched me.

I can smell the salty-sweet sweat on her skin from the long day. By the time she glances nervously up and into my eyes as I lean in, I'm already staring back at her, my body itching, skin humming as desire sweeps into Emily's gaze, clouding whatever resistance was already there.

I can't resist any longer.

I lower myself towards her, every inch of me on fucking fire. I hesitate for the smallest of seconds before touching her lips to mine as she pulls me in, wrapping her arms around my neck, giving me all the permission I need.

And I kiss her, feeling hungry as hell, exercising every ounce of restraint the universe will allow as Emily's mouth moves against mine, slow and tentative.

And we both give in.

The kiss starts off soft—even tender.

The question mark that has been in both of our minds is finally out of the way, but as each second passes, as our mouths slowly angle and passion builds, the touches grow faster—eager.

I hold back just a fraction until I feel Emily's tongue, and I stroke the smooth length of it with mine, hearing her moan, the last of my control snaps as I press my body into hers, letting the kiss take on a life of its own.

And what a life it is—full of everything I didn't know could even exist.

This woman's kisses are an instant addiction.

Her ample breasts press against my chest, her fingers tangled in my mane.

She tastes of honey and a hint of mouthwash, and the exhilarating feel of her soft body against mine—squeezing close, her soft tongue and sweet moans mewling into my mouth is enough to leave me panting for more, my pants tenting at the crotch as a steel erection comes alive underneath my boxer briefs and sweats, making itself known.

I twist my body away from hers to stop myself from rubbing it against her, but when she lifts her body towards me, her hips circling across my dick's tip for more, I rub her right back, shifting my hips to stroke my hardened cock at the center of her denim, loving the way the motion makes her squirm under my touch.

"Fuck, Emily," I find myself moaning on her lips. "It was never just a job. You were never just a job. And I should have told you from the moment we met."

She groans between licks and bites, her teeth sucking gently on my tongue as she writhes beneath my body, her words a gasp I can barely hear. "To be fair, you didn't know who I was when we *first* met..."

"Good thing I didn't. If I'd known *you* would be my lawyer, I'd have fucked you right there on the spot."

She sighs softly, whimpering as my hands inch beneath her cotton shirt, stroking her stomach. She shudders when I caress her bare ribs.

"*Goh.*" She mutters over and over, the Farsi curse falling from her lips with ease. I chuckle.

"If I can do that with just a touch there," I muse aloud. "Then I wonder what will happen when I put my thumb..." I inch higher to her breast, squeezing its edge lightly through the fabric. *"Here."*

She moans loudly, and it's enough for me to keep going, my thumbs circling the soft mound in search of her nipple. And when I find it, it is all I can do not to put my mouth there, not to slip my lips over the hardened nub and pull with my teeth.

But I can't stop kissing her. Can't tear my face away from hers long enough to pull it off.

Especially when I hear the sound of a door opening behind us.

I separate myself from Emily. Just before Charlie appears in her bedroom doorway, one hand rubbing at her eye.

"Emily?" The messy haired cherub calls from fifteen feet away.

"Yeah?" The breathless lawyer turns, her cheeks still flushed from my kiss. "Everything okay, grasshopper?"

She adopts my nickname for Charlie. And I couldn't find either of them more adorable right now.

I clear my throat. "I must have woken her up," I whisper to Emily.

She hisses back. "No, I think that was me. The last move you pulled put me over the top."

But the debate ends right then because without thinking the two of us head towards Charlie, ready to make amends and put our grasshopper and her pet cat Felix to bed...and maybe all of our cravings with it.

Tomorrow and all of the hard decisions about Emily and me and Charlie's mom can wait.

Tonight? Tonight I have to put a little girl back to sleep. And, unfortunately, for me, it may be one of my last chances to do it.

CHAPTER 16

S EVIN
The next morning

The only thing worse than wanting my lawyer is pretending I don't.

After putting Charlie back to bed, I retreat back to my hotel suite, lying awake in agony at the thought that I won't be spending the night with Emily.

And I could see it before I left.

The desire in her eyes.

I could practically smell it on her skin, and less than ten hours later, I try to beat the scent out of my head and body, heading to the hotel gym at the break of dawn to exercise the longing away.

But I'm not alone.

I enter the fitness center, neglecting to turn the lights on. I head towards the weights in the back when I hear the sound of a footstep behind me.

"Sev." The voice hisses.

I turn, finding blue eyes on me. I balk. "Saw, is that you?"

The blue eyes are wrapped in shadow until my teammate steps

forward. "Yeah, it's me, man. You were expecting the Easter Bunny?"

"Please." I rotate on my heel, picking up a few weights. I sit on the nearest bench. "The only person here concerned about bunnies is you, bro. *The Playboy type.*"

He grins, taking the bench beside me, reaching for a few weights of his own. He starts lifting. "I can't help it if I'm the quintessential carrot—wanted by bunnies the world around." He grunts, pulling a dumbbell to his chin. "Speaking of bunnies, what was that whole deal with Daphne?"

I groan, my arm straining with each bicep curl. I glare in the walled mirror at myself, feigning ignorance. "What? There was no 'deal' with Daphne."

"Exactly," he stresses. "And there should have been. The woman was damn near perfect, Sev. And for once, I was actually willing to turn over a woman to you. Doesn't get more generous than that."

"Wow. What a gentleman you are, Saw."

"That's what I'm saying." He winks with a laugh, his lightly bearded face shaking. "I don't get you these days, man. What happened to the good ol' Sterling I used to know? My favorite fellow man-whore? My partner in pussy?"

"For fuck's sake, Saw. Think you could you be anymore disgusting?"

"Sure, I could. Just ask the two women I woke up to this morning."

I shake my head, remembering Naomi's comment last night about Sawyer. The harem of women he'd brought back to bed, that he'd woken up to this morning.

Had I really been that bad?

Is that what I'd been all these years post-Kimmy? *Like Saw?*

I shudder to think.

Because if I had been, then it all made sense…

Why Emily had hated me as a neighbor. Why this Deborah Jett was now in my life. And why I didn't remember her.

Sawyer moves to the other side of the fitness center, heading for the squat rack. And I try to forget.

Forget the man I've been these last ten years.

And just when I think I've finally found the solitude I need, the chance to zone out to Pink Floyd blasting from my headphones and pound out my frustration, the echo of strange footsteps pulls me from my trance, the sight of Emily Armand in a set of skin-tight leggings and tank completely obliterating any chance of focusing from where I sit.

Her dark silky hair in a high ponytail, her hazel eyes grow to the size of full moons, her long lashes fluttering slowly as she stutters. Her gait slows.

"*Goh*," she murmurs, gazing down at me. "I…didn't know anyone was in here."

"Likewise." I set my headphones in my lap, ready to say more, but I can see Sawyer watching us with curiosity. "Did you need this bench?"

"Oh, uh…" She mutters softly, shooting a glance over her shoulder, finding Sawyer staring. "No thanks. I didn't mean to interrupt your workout. I'll just…work out over here. I'll leave you to whatever it is that you're doing. Enjoy your workout."

And then she walks off.

She heads over to the line of treadmills, firing one up. She sets a gym bag to the side, taking a second to stretch, and I watch, against better sense, as she bends over, the stretchy fabric sliding with ease over the curve of her unbelievably tight ass.

I bite down a growl that threatens to turn to a groan. I walk to the weight rack immediately, replacing my weights with the biggest dumbbells I can find.

But these smaller ones won't do. I need something to take my mind off the siren less than fifty feet away.

I start lifting.

One lift, two lift, three. And I'm in the zone.

The amount of weight uses every ounce of my muscle, making me sweat through my shirt. In just over a minute, the lifting has taken a toll on me, pushing me to the brink, and unfortunately, Pink Floyd is singing the words to Dirty Woman in my ear, sensual lyrics that make me want to get Emily all to myself.

I realize I can't when Sawyer comes sidling up beside me, his eyebrows reaching for the sky as he crouches near my bench.

"I think I'm going to take off, Sterling. Need some downtime before tonight's game."

"Why do I have the feeling this 'downtime' involves a woman?"

"Trust me: There's nothing 'down' about the time I spend with women." He glances over his shoulder at Emily. "And you're one to talk. Saw you talking to that sexy brunette over there." His eyes flicker back to my face. "You know her?"

"Nope. Never met her. I would remember." I shrug, but the lie feels wrong on my lips.

Sawyer may be the biggest man-whore in the world, but the debauched bastard is one of the best friends I have. One of the only ones there after everything went down with Kimmy, Finley and me.

But to admit that I know Emily would be admitting *how* I know her. *Why* I know her.

I'd have to admit everything about Charlie and her wayward mother, and I can't risk it. I still can't risk my career.

Not to mention Charlie...

Stephan Knight, owner of The Firm Crisis and Emergency Management, was right.

I can't afford police, cameras, or a word of this to the press.

Or my teammates.

Luckily, Sawyer shrugs, slapping hands with me, before heading out, his eyes lingering for just a second too long in Emily's direction.

The door closes behind him, and my gaze trails over to Emily's reflection, over my shoulder, on the other side of the room, still stretching.

This time, she sits on the mat, reaching for her toes, her pretty face scrunched in pain as she wiggles her fingertips towards her shoes without touching. She groans out loud.

The sight of her is mesmerizing, and damn, I can't help myself.

She groans again in pain, and I can't take it. Letting the dumbbell in my hand drop to the mat, I cross the length of the expansive gym in seconds, my stride strong as I stroll right to where she sits.

It takes a second for her to see me before she gasps, her full lips open.

"Yes?" She mimics me out loud. "Did you come over here to have a word with the 'sexy brunette'?"

I wince, grinning. "Caught that, did you?"

"Yup. I did…unfortunately." Her pretty lips pull downwards into a small frown. "But mostly I'm just glad you were quick on your feet. Stephan was clear; we can't let this blackmail scandal get any attention. And you and I being connected? Well…" she trails off. "That brings attention."

"Exactly." I nod.

"Best to pretend we don't know each other."

"My thoughts exactly." My voice lowers. "Which is exactly why I came over here to help the helpless brunette in the gym." I lean in. "Or that's what I'll tell people, if anyone else comes in and sees us talking."

"Excuse me?" She blinks, her hazel eyes wide. I keep speaking anyway.

"You're stretching all wrong, you know. And you're going to hurt yourself." I place my hands on my hips. "Correction: You're stretching all wrong. And it looks like you've *already* hurt yourself. Otherwise, you wouldn't be wincing in pain every time you try to touch your toes."

"I think I can handle my own stretching, if you don't mind."

"I don't mind," I utter out loud, staring at her. "But your muscles will, once they start turning against you. Running on a treadmill is killer on the legs, core and knees. And if you're not taking care of them, they'll go out on you. I've seen it enough times to know on the field and off. I don't think you want that."

"I don't think anyone wants that," she fires back.

"Then let me help you…unless you'd rather stay in pain."

She finally looks up at me again, giving me a glimpse at the beautiful face—bare and innocent. "And this is *just* help, correct? I mean, it's not anything more, right? Because we did talk about this last night. Us behaving. *Seriously.* It's why I booked a hotel sitter at the front desk for today. So, Charlie could behave. And I could do the same. In fact, it'd help if every Chicago Cougar affiliate in this hotel is on their best behavior. Especially us."

God, I hate it when she's right. And she's right most of the time, as much as I hate to admit it.

We did say we'd behave…as much as I don't want to.

Agreeing to stay away from each other until this entire blackmail-Charlie situation is solved *seemed* smart last night. It did.

And though we said it'd be for the best, the 'best' didn't mean 'easiest.'

Because there was nothing in this world *easy* about pretending I didn't want to spend more time with the sassy lawyer.

But I am trying my 'best' to behave. I take a deep breath.

"Let's just say I'd rather not have my workout ruined when I need it most. I was banking on having an uneventful morning after everything that happened last night. And things are going to get *plenty* eventful in this room, if I get hard while hearing your background track of groaning and moaning from all your aches."

Her hazel eyes cloud, and I know I've hit a lustful nerve. The same nerve she hits inside me all the time. I smile.

"Okay…" She stands to her feet, wiping her hands. "Mr. Smith. I'll let you help. But if you think this is going to be an excuse to misbehave," she sends me a wry smile, "then you can save your breath and overprotective instructions. I already have a father. And thankfully, you're not him."

"If it's all the same to you," I motion to the mat and Emily sits. "I'd rather not be your father, either. Otherwise, the thoughts I had just a few seconds ago would be illegal in most of the fifty states. Now, put your legs together. I'm going to show you how to get the most out of your body. Starting right now."

Her eyes widen conspicuously at me. But she obeys.

She closes her legs on the mat, connecting them almost at the knee. I direct her to put her palms on either side, and as she leans forward, I kneel behind her, pressing on her back as her chest lowers to the floor.

I listen to her moan.

Her body loosens under my touch, her limbs growing limber. The sounds she makes are no longer from pain, simply relief, and I can hear the tension leave her body as she sighs.

I stand to my feet, directing her movements once more.

Pushing and pulling at her body until she's bent from a bridge stance into child's pose, I command her to breathe through every motion, inhaling and exhaling.

The sound of her breathy sighs is enough to make me the tiniest bit semi-hard, and I struggle with every lunge, stretch and twist to keep my eyes focused on the task at hand—to help a woman who at this very moment I'm still consider strangling.

I stand up, directing her into a "downward-facing dog" and she frowns, her entire face falling into a scowl.

"You've gotta be kidding me."

"Nope," I answer, pointing to the same black mat underneath her now bare feet. "It's easy. Feet flat on the ground. Butt in the air. Palms on the ground until you form a triangle. Go."

"And then I'll be done?" She eyes me, one brow curving towards the sky.

"And then you'll be done. And properly stretched. Now, get down. Make this one good."

She does as I say—palms down, feet flat, butt high. Except for that back.

She arches the damn thing as if she's auditioning to be a question mark, and I place a hand between her shoulder blades, commanding her to keep her core tight and back flat.

As expected, she doesn't do it.

"My back *is* flat," she insists.

"I'm looking at it, kitten. And for sure, it is not flat."

"Calling me 'kitten' is not behaving, Sevin." She nearly growls, making me smile. "And for sure, my back definitely is flat. I think I'd be able to tell."

"Well, for one: You could have fooled me last night as far as being a kitten because you and that damned black cat nearly mind-melded with how close you were cuddled. And for two: you need to take a look in the mirror. Your posture would put the Hunchback of Notre Dame to shame. And that's being nice to the hunchback. Now, pose…" I wait one more second. "Please. I swear it will help."

I listen to Emily sigh. Her ponytail twists in the air as she glances at the wall-length mirror, gazing over her form. She inhales sharply, hissing in what's likely Farsi, and I suppress a chuckle, reaching over to place my palm flat between her shoulder blades, ignoring the small spark that shoots off the second I touch her skin.

The touch between us is electric, and no doubt Emily notices. She wheezes out loud.

"What are you doing?"

"I'm helping. You're going to hurt yourself."

"No, I won't. I've got this."

"I gave you a chance to correct it. And you most certainly didn't. So, let me fix your posture by just…" I move my hand and Emily flinches.

"No, don't, Sevin. I've got this. You don't have to…"

"If you'd stop being so stubborn," I interrupt as she cuts into my thoughts, "I could help you avoid…"

But the words "hurting yourself" aren't out of my mouth before that's exactly what Emily does. She twists as I lean my hand against her, sending us both tumbling down.

She lands on the mat, and I land on top of her. Or rather I catch myself before I can crush her to the floor, my hands shooting out to form kickstands as I brace my body above hers —hovering.

The fall brings us face-to-face, bodies almost touching.

And I can't help myself. Can't pretend any longer. Can't behave.

I need Emily. And I need her right now.

I bend my head to take her mouth. And just like a disobedient kitten, she lets me.

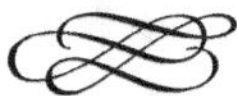

*S*EVIN
Saturday morning

I've now decided: Nothing feels as good as Emily. Nothing.

Not even keeping my career—something I know I should be trying to do.

But the minute my mouth connects with hers, something else sparks. And the third time's the charm.

This is the third time I've put my mouth on my feisty-lipped lawyer and every time is better than the last. Every time I get a taste of her cherry mouth and tongue, I want more.

And right now? After what we shared last night?

It would take the Jaws of Life to pry me off her body. To make me believe there's anywhere else on earth I'd rather be situated than in between her sensuously toned thighs.

She speaks between kisses. "Something like this is going to make it awfully hard for me to pretend I don't know you. Or hate you, in front of my coworkers."

"Hate you?" I nearly whisper, aligning the length of my body with hers. "Never. Well, at least not anymore…" I grin. "You didn't exactly make it easy, as my cop-calling neighbor. But I wouldn't blame you, if you hated me. That stunt I pulled in front of my teammate earlier wasn't exactly smooth. I'm not the best actor, if you hadn't noticed. It's why I stick to baseball. I'm shit at all else."

Emily grins, a slow smile spreading on her face. And I lick where her teeth meet her lip, loving the texture. "As long as it keeps everyone securely out of our business, I'm fine with it."

I blow out a breath from my nostrils, the snort small and angry. "Especially Sawyer. That fucker. I could already tell the bastard had a huge crush on you."

"Really?" She blinks. Her hazel eyes go wide. "I hadn't noticed. I was too busy looking at you…" Her slender arms tighten around me, never letting go. "Besides, don't you think having people believe we hate each other is much better that everyone on your team and in my firm finding out that I'm thinking of sleeping with the National League's most valuable player?"

Her honesty shocks me. And I lift a brow. "Almost as bad as my coach and PR agent finding out that I want to give my lawyer multiple orgasms on call? But that's just me."

"Multiple orgasms, did you say? Are you that confident?"

I gaze down at her. "Oh, I'm more than confident of it, kitten." My voice lowers. "Speaking of which…you need to get your script right. If it ever comes out that we do have sex, I wouldn't exactly admit to *sleeping* with you, Emily."

"You wouldn't?" Her eyebrows lift skyward.

"No." I take her chin in my hand. "I believe they call what I would do to you 'fucking your brains out.' We'll leave the finer details out for those with more sensitive ears."

I lean closer, letting my lips finally touch hers. It's electric—the charge that sparks between us the second our mouths meet, and I deepen what is a little caress into a full-fledged kiss, conquering Emily's mouth with mine in a hot wet embrace that leaves her trembling in my arms. She pulls back slowly, the slight sheen of sweat across her body making her smell good enough to eat.

And I'm tempted to try it. Even in this gym.

"You know kissing me like this, Mr. Smith, is not going to make us want to behave any sooner."

I inhale. "'Behave'? I don't know the meaning of the word when my cock is this hard, kitten. But keep going."

Her sparkling cider-like eyes glow, and I kiss her again. She clears her throat. "I have a few more rules I want to discuss."

"More?" My head tilts. "Weren't the ones we talked about in front of your apartment and then again last night *more* than enough?"

She grins. "Hardly. If we're going to do this in secret, we need to do this right. I don't need anyone knowing. It could jeopardize my career. And yours."

I nod my head softly. "I'm aware of that. Tell me more."

"Our hotel suite is not exactly Fort Knox. Sound does travel from bedroom to bedroom. I know Kayla's in New York, taking care of things with Charlie's mom. But for the rest of the day, let's cool it, okay? I don't want us taking this any further. Not while we're still in Arizona. Not while Charlie can find out. I don't want to scar her."

My stare hardens at her, my frustration getting the best of me for the first time all morning. "Neither would I. Despite not needing this shit from her mom, Charlie is a priority. And I would never be so selfish to pretend she's not right now."

"I know," she retorts immediately. "Which is going to make it all the more difficult to say the next part..." Her slanted brows crease, her pretty mouth lowering into a frown. She sighs. "Rule number three..." She hesitates. "I am *not* going to be just another number in your bed, Sevin. I don't want whatever you had or didn't have with women like Charlie's mom. It's not me." She exhales. "Look, I'm attracted to you. I'm sure you know that by now."

"Well, the feeling is *very* mutual, kitten."

"And I definitely want to do more things like this with you."

Her smile is sad. "But if I've worked hard to make a name for myself. Labored way too long to be a lawyer. I won't throw it away. Not even for this job."

Her hazel eyes flit between mine, moving fast. "Yes, you are more than just this job. And yes, I want to explore this with you. I really do." Her shoulders rise then fall. "But I will not throw my career down the toilet for a fling. No matter how badly my brains are fucked out." She graces me with a curious smile. "Got it?"

"As always. It's your rules." I have no choice but to take her seriously. And in the midst of processing everything—Emily as my neighbor, Emily as my lawyer, Emily as my lover—I'm already wondering what the hell I'm going to do when all of this is over.

When Deborah comes back to take Charlie away. When this blackmail case is over. When this tryst with Emily is done.

I don't even want to think about it.

"I understand career suicide, kitten. And trust me: This situation going wrong could lead down a trip to that path. For both of us. If this goes wrong. And I acknowledge that." My fingertips dig gently into her waist, my cock hardening as she melts between my palms. A knot hits the back of my throat. "But I also want to tell you that I won't let that happen. I'm not going to tell you that I have this all planned out. I have little to guarantee. I can't."

I lick my lips, needing to wet them. "But know this, Emily Armand: Whatever this is between us, it is not a 'cheap one-night.' And this is not a game. Trust me: I've played enough in my career. And lastly, this is not me putting you on this 'rolodex of women whose names I forget by sunrise.' For as long as we are in this fucked-up situation, that makes Charlie my primary concern. That makes you my primary concern. And letting anything else get in the way of that is not happening. *That…* I *can* guarantee."

"And how can you be so sure?"

"Because I can't stay away from you, Emily Armand… God knows I've tried." I shift my body over hers, leaning in. "I'm a baseball player. I've worked with enough catchers to read signs. And every sign in the universe has been pointing me to you." I settle my figure farther between her thighs. "And I know you know it too. This was supposed to happen." I lower my lips. "So just let it."

She moans as I recapture her mouth a second later, not holding back this time. Slanting my lips to slide against hers, I kiss Emily until she is putty beneath my touch, sighing softly, her breath a gasp as I sweep my fingers from my waist into her soft brown hair.

The feathery strands tickle just above her shoulder blades and I pull handfuls of them, my hands roaming from the nape of her neck to her slightly exposed hip and back again.

Leaning her head back at the tantalizing touch, she offers me access to the full cleavage at the apex of her damp sports bra and tank, and I take full advantage, dipping my head to play between her breasts, my tongue swiping out to sweep at the lightly salty skin between them.

A sigh turns into a sexy moan and I can no longer control the erection making itself very obvious from beneath my sweatpants.

"Jesus Christ," I mutter, lifting my mouth before it can lower to one taut nipple poking beneath the fabric of her thin shirt. "I swear to God if we weren't inside this gym right now, I'd bury myself so deep inside of you that I'd disappear completely."

Her voice is a murmur when she replies. "As much as I've complained about it, what I wouldn't give for an elevator right now."

I tease her nipple with my teeth. "If only our doorman Hank could see us right now…"

"We'd be banned from the damn elevator permanently."

But I barely hear her. I'm still internally battling with my cock as I reach one hand lower, shifting it to the side as my mouth attacks the skin at the side of her neck instead. "I know we said no hotel suite sex while here in Arizona, and I'm on board with that."

I pull back a few inches, meeting her eye. "But does putting my tongue between your thighs count? It would be like a 'walk' in baseball. Technically, it doesn't count. It's not a hit, but you're getting on the base all the same."

Emily's neck straightens slowly, while she lays on the mat, her back straightening as she lazily shifts. Her eyes grow even more glazed as she looks at me.

Or maybe it's just the heat rising from my skin.

The sensation of a slight warmth between us reminds me that Emily's skin is still glistening from her sweat and small workout.

And the look in her eyes is the very opposite of cold, making everything inside of me turn as solid as stone. Especially when she nods, a move that makes my erection diamond-like.

I kiss her lips, ready to taste her other pair when I hear a throat clear above me, sending my gaze upwards.

My eyes find the most unexpected thing…

Sawyer.

Hovering a few feet away, an amused expression on his face. I push my body away from Emily's.

"Fuck," I mutter, meeting my teammate's gaze. "Saw, what the hell are you doing back here? You came back just to bug the hell out of me some more?"

"Not at all. Came back because I need to pick up my lifting gloves. I left 'em. *Stayed* because I noticed you were doing some 'picking up' of your own." He grins, crossing his arms as Emily shuffles away from me. She pushes on my chest, crawling from underneath my body. I wait as she stands to her feet.

Sawyer simply stares.

"Oh don't mind me," he directs at Emily. "Just enjoying the show."

"Such an asshole." I start to say more.

I start to say anything to get Sawyer the hell out of here, but before I can make out a single coherent sentence, Emily rushes towards her gym bag, slapping the strap over her shoulder.

Stepping haphazardly back into her shoes, she hurries out, leaving me more frustrated than ever.

Two minutes ago, we were just in the process of solidifying her rules. And now I was breaking every single one of them.

I fall back on the black gym mat, no closer to figuring out how to juggle Charlie, Emily, my secrets and all the rest.

$\mathcal{E}$MILY
Saturday morning

I never imagined it would be this hard to be professional.

But as is the case with everything involving Sevin Smith, it's turning out to be a hell of a lot more difficult than I thought.

Adrenaline levels through the roof, I pay the hotel sitter the second I'm back in the suite, practically chasing the woman out of the door.

After scrambling out of the hotel gym like a sixteen-year old caught with her boyfriend in her room, it takes me three cold showers before I calm down.

Not to mention one glass of coffee, a shit-ton of Sheryl Crow playing in the background and one pillow to scream into to get my rage out.

And this is all before Charlie even opens her eyes.

The bouncing ball of energy is still asleep after our late-night unexpected game of Hide-and-Seek with Felix the cat last night, and as the rose-colored sun begins to stretch over the Arizona horizon outside our hotel windows, signaling the morning to come, I wonder again if I'm the right person to take Sevin's case.

I can barely keep my hands off the man.

His touch. His kisses. They're still on my mind as I emerge from my hotel bedroom barefoot over the soft beige carpet, now back in my usual Armani skirt suit—my new armor for the day.

Using every ounce of "Sevin shielding" in my arsenal—even this uncomfortable business-wear, I remind myself that I've never had a problem being the "go-to girl." That being dependable is part of my department.

Always has been.

I ignore the parts of me that know how much the irresistible athlete makes me want to throw caution to the wind. Cross lines I've never crossed. Break rules that shouldn't bend.

I remind myself that I shouldn't be bending anything.

Especially not my legs over Sevin's shoulders.

And lastly, I try to tell myself that what happened much earlier this morning—getting caught by one of Sevin's own teammates— could be worse, but as I reach for the fridge in the swanky hotel suite's quaint kitchen, grabbing the eggs, the sight of two green eyes on the countertop makes me drop everything in my hand.

Eggshells and yolk go splattering everywhere as the green eyes shift to the floor. Felix, hunched in a ball of black fur, glances up from the tile.

I scoff out loud. "Great. You're never around when we need you. And then you show up unexpectedly." I sigh, crouching to the kitchen floor, sweeping up shells. "You're like an ex-boyfriend reincarnated."

The cat simply blinks, head tilted as I scoop runny egg matter into my palms before standing. He meows behind me as I reach for the sink.

"Don't you have some hallway to sneak off into? More neighbors to scare? Besides this one?" I keep rinsing my hands and he doesn't move. I sigh.

"You know I have *you* to partly blame for all of this." I reach for the dish soap, washing my palms. The suds start to lather. "If you hadn't been such a nuisance in the apartment building... Not to mention running away and forcing Sevin and I together to look for you." I glance over my shoulder. "I mean, do you even have anything to say for yourself?"

He looks at me, big eyes wide, his pink tongue darting to lick his nose. I turn off the water. "Typical male. Silent at all the wrong times."

I start drying my hands, and Felix, apparently feeling my ire, crawls closer, his tiny ear rubbing at my ankle. He cuddles up close, and I look down.

"Jeez, you really are a male, aren't you? No answer for your bad behavior and now you want to make everything better with a snuggle?"

Felix licks his fur, his eyes still on me. And I can't stop talking. "You know I've never been the type of person to pick up strays." I crouch down just to rub Felix's fur. And to my surprise, he lets me, the wayward cat staying still for once. And it feels good.

I whisper near his fuzzy ear. "And in the last week, I've picked up two. Three, if you count Sevin. He can be such a lost pup, licking and shitting his adorable way over everything. Making it impossible to stay mad at him. Making you feel guilty for even considering it. How an attorney like me wound up running some sort of kennel, I'll never know. And I won't be able to explain to anyone who asks. I don't even recognize myself at this point."

Felix purrs beneath my palms, and I feel his skin rumble. The act of petting him is more soothing than I thought, and I realize that this might be the first time I'm getting my real feelings out.

Feelings I've kept bottled away from everyone. *Even Ben.*

I keep stroking the soft kitten's fur, hating myself a little bit.

"I guess you're not all that bad." I smile, suddenly teary-eyed. "At least you keep Charlie company. That's gotta count for something." I pause, scared to say the next part. "And she's not the only one who needs company. Felix..."

I scratch my nails under his soft ear. "Would you believe me if

I said it's *been a while*? A while since I've let anyone get close? Since I've *wanted* to? Sevin's been the first man I've 'let in' in a while. And if I have to admit it…"

I let the dark kitten sidle up to my Armani, no longer caring about the skirt suit's appearance—a rarity. The tears in my eyes start to spill. "Ben was right. He was too right. The only thing I've taken to bed in over a year is a legal brief. I'm more concerned with 'playing it safe' than 'playing it fun.' And I am married to my career, and sometimes even *that* isn't faithful to me." I sniffle, rubbing my nose. "I mean, what if Sevin is like all the rest? What if he's *worse*?" I stop, my fingers falling dead against Felix's fur. "And what if I just can't risk that?"

For the first time since I've been talking to the silent circle of fuzz, he meows, glancing up at me.

If cats could talk, I'd swear this one would, but then my phone rings, and any Dr. Dolittle the cute kitty was going to pull disappears instantly.

I reach for my cell, clearing my throat to answer. I wipe a tear. "Yes, Emily speaking?"

"Emily?" Her voice is strong even this early in the morning. And it's as if a day hasn't passed between us. I stand to my bare feet. "Violet?"

"You say my name like it's been plastered all over milk cartons. I haven't exactly risen from the dead."

"It feels like it. I thought for sure my next call from this line would be about your funeral, you've been gone so much."

I hear the sound of husky laughter over the phone, the smooth sultry voice of Violet Keats filling the kitchen around me with its warmth. My old friend (and boss) giggles, a rarity from the old version of her I once knew. She sighs.

"I'm a new mother, Em. I'm half-dead most of the time, so you're not too far off in your assessment."

I grin. "How is our little bundle of joy?"

"Big," she comments plainly. "And bad as hell. He's gotten so fussy in these last few weeks. Won't even take my nipple by mouth anymore."

"Good thing he has a father who doesn't have a problem with that." I glance at my watch, trying not to freak out over the time. "And Heath? How's Mr. Perfect doing?"

"You mean the dutiful dad? Still over the moon. You'd think eight months later that the newness of fatherhood would have worn off by now, but nope. He's just as in love with Fitz now as the day the little chubster was born."

I loved to hear Violet's new baby boy's name. Loved its Old World simplicity.

Heath's father Fitzgerald Sparrow had still been alive when they'd named the baby boy after him, and Violet's description of the look on the prestigious lawyer's face when he found out had even a serious love cynic like me swooning.

I'd been named after my own Persian, cosmic force of a grandmother Emagine—a name meaning "image" of her mother, and some days, if I concentrated hard enough in a Chicago taxi's noisy back seat, I could hear her soothing voice, rich with experience, heavy with the burden of raising her strong family.

I close my eyes, shutting back the second round of tears threatening to spring forth. The digital time in the corner of my cell phone warns me of the time.

Time I need to get ready for Sevin's afternoon game.

"Well, that's amazing to hear, Vi," I finally manage to respond to Vi on the line. "So tell me: What else is new?"

"Besides aching nipples, a sexually insatiable husband and a hungry baby? Looking for a new house. The one I'm in is covered in too many bodily fluids."

I raise an eyebrow, clutching the phone close. "From the baby or the husband?"

Violet laughs out loud. "Ugh, gross, Em. I really didn't need to hear that right now. Every time I even think about laughing, my boobs leak an extra ounce of milk."

"Saves on your grocery bill, I'm sure."

"Seriously, though." Her laughs taper to a soft sigh. "We've gotta get out of Heath's bachelor pad Manhattan apartment and into something more worthy of a family…"

I pause, wondering how the hell this phenomenal woman manages to have it all, an impossibility as far as I'm concerned.

My former boss was a walking unicorn.

A no-nonsense lawyer in post-divorce mode, she'd allowed me to stay at her pre-divorce Chicago apartment when she'd meet Heath Sparrow, the CEO of her firm and the man of her dreams, and in some ways, I'd felt as if I'd transitioned into her life. The dream life of a corporate lawyer, rising from the ranks of the lowly secretary I used to be in New York.

Living in a luxury high-rise apartment.

It had all felt like a fantasy.

But slowly the shiny facade was starting to fade.

Because unlike Violet, I certainly am no longer closer to having it all. I can barely juggle my attraction to Sevin and my job.

And the fear that I could lose either—one which was well on its way and one that hadn't really started—is enough to paralyze me to the spot.

I lean against the kitchen counter, sighing out loud. "You make it sound so easy…"

"I make *what* sound so easy?"

"Family. Friends. Love. Law. You make it sound like a walk in the park."

"Are you kidding?" Her throaty voice is incredulous, heavy with disbelief. "Taking care of all those things at once is a walk in the park all right… If the park was full of needles, covered in acid and dipped in ants." She snorts, the sound sharp against my ear. She inhales a second later. "Em, *none* of this is easy. Taking care of a family. Having a career. Running a business and a baby. It's not easy. It's not supposed to be. And I don't try to make it, either."

I frown. "But I don't get it… How do you keep your life from slipping into chaos?"

The question makes her laugh. And I don't mean giggle-cutesy-laugh. I mean, wholehearted belly laugh. Laugh from her toes, up her stomach and through her throat sort of laughter.

And I instantly feel ashamed of asking. But I press ahead. "What? What's so funny about that, Violet?"

Her laughter trails into good-natured titters, her voice a breath. "It's funny, Emily. Because it's something that all ambitious women ask…right before they enter the chaos themselves. I don't try to keep myself from slipping into chaos. *I swim in it.* There's no use in fighting against the tide, chica. Chaos is coming. Whether we women like it or not. All change is chaos. But there's beauty in it. There's beauty in embracing the madness. In letting it take you away. The key is to give yourself a freaking break. Take a break. Mess up and make mistakes. And if all else fails, surround yourself with people who will swim in the chaos beside you." Her words lapse, a hush falling over the phone. "That's assuming you're looking for someone to navigate the chaotic waters with you… And I'm guessing that you are?"

I consider for a second that maybe Vi knows the answer to that question already, and a piece of me—the piece of me that wants to (as Ben put it) "see how good a little chaos can taste"—is tempted to ask her that when my phone is interrupted by an incoming call, cutting through my thoughts.

I glance at the black screen, balking when I see the name imprinted there.

My boss. The current one.

Stephan Knight.

After saying a mouthful of goodbye's to Violet, thanking her for everything, I switch mental lanes to pick up Stephan's call, my heart skipping a dangerous beat as the line clicks over.

His voice is the first thing I hear. "Emily."

"Yeah, uh, hi, Stephan." Fear clogs my throat, and I clear it. "It's good to hear from you. What's up?"

I try to keep the call light, but I fail. And Stephan knows it.

His voice is as hard as nails.

"What's up?" He repeats after me. "What's up is that we need a meeting. As soon as you're settled back in Chicago... As in *tomorrow night*. There's been some news."

I clutch the phone closer. "In Sevin's case?" I hesitate, nearly biting my tongue. "Is it bad?"

Stephan exhales, and the sound itself is scary. But my thoughts are on Sevin. *Is everything okay?*

"News is not good or bad. It's just news. It is what it is. And we can't change it. I'll see you tomorrow, Emily. And don't be late."

Translation?

"I'm not asking you to have a meeting with me. I'm telling you. And yes, this news is bad or I would have said otherwise."

Unfortunately for me, bad news is Stephan's forte. He's built a business on it, for God's sake.

And if Violet is right, and chaos is indeed coming, then Sevin has no idea what's likely coming his way. *And he doesn't know about Finley.*

I know I have to warn him.

If only Felix's eyes weren't on me, judging me from the tiled floor.

I pick the fur ball up, getting ready for this afternoon's game and the storm that I know is on its way.

CHAPTER 19

S EVIN
Saturday afternoon

The steam from the locker room is hot on my skin. But it's nothing compared to Coach's wrath after our loss.

I can still feel his anger thirty minutes after the last pitch.

Yesterday's high is obliterated by today's lousy game and the team who beat us. The Bruisers literally put a bruising on us, and whatever momentum the Chicago Cougars had going after last night's win, whatever magic mojo actually helped us beat one of the best teams in our conference by one point, is plenty gone just twenty-four hours later.

And it's all my fault.

My head isn't in the game, and it hasn't been for a while.

Not with this paternity case on my conscience. And not with Emily on my mind.

I shed my shirt in the overheated locker room after the game, slamming it inside my locker as Sawyer walks up.

"God, I need a blowjob."

"Could you not say that so loudly?" I don't even try to open my eyes as the clothes-changing second baseman sidles up beside me.

I glance over at him. "Or maybe re-think saying it so loudly in a locker room full of men?"

"Well, can someone tell me when we can leave this bloody aftermath and find some women? My flight back to Chicago lands before yours, and I can't wait to get back." Sawyer grumbles, his voice growing louder. "Losing a game always fucks up my mood, and right now, I'm too anxious to stay still and too horny to keep moving around. I mean, a stiff breeze at the right angle would put 'little me' into full-mast at the moment, and being around so many swinging sausages with zero lady-buns to put them between is depressing me even more."

"Ladies and gentlemen," I say in my best announcer voice, eyes still on my locker. "Introducing you to Chicago Cougars' 'Pig of the Year': Sawyer Kennedy."

The baseman laughs, his deep voice artificially low. "Thank you, thank you. It's not an easy job I'll tell you, but someone has to do it."

I finally give him my full attention. "We're all smart enough to get the obvious point you're trying to make here, Saw. Most of us did get college educations."

"Pump your brakes, Sterling." He rolls his eyes, his blue irises tumbling backward. "I wouldn't say most of us. Can't vouch for Mr. Failed-Underwater-Basket-Weaving over there."

He motions towards our teammate James, who acknowledges him with the middle-finger salute.

I snort out loud, the sound mingling with the melody of Jim Morrison crooning throatily inside the singular headphone hanging out of one my ears. I slap a towel over my shoulder before fastening one around my waist. "And I know Lenny and I already schooled you on that back in college, *Captain Swine.* Having this many women on the road? Always a distraction. And not a good one." I glance around the locker room and at the few down-mouthed teammates still occupying it. "As you can tell from the shit way we played today."

Sawyer stands up straighter, a new glint in his blue eye. "Women have never been a distraction for me, thank you very much. I always play best post-orgasm."

He slips on a clean shirt from his locker, sighing as he sits on the bench beside me, his body shifting the heavy wood. I hear the framework groan under his weight.

"Besides," he blows out in one breath. "You're one to talk, Sterling." The glint in his eye turns full-on glimmer, a grin sliding across his face. "In case you're forgetting, it was only hours ago that I caught you on top of that sexy brown-haired piece." He leans forward. "Care to explain that?"

I wipe my face with the towel over my shoulder, hiding the flame that hits my face. I exhale loudly. "There's nothing to explain."

"Bull. You looked as nervous as I was in the back seat of my dad's pinto on prom night with Gina Salvatore straddling me like one of my granddad's prized stallions."

"I'm guessing this Gina chick was good enough with her mouth to warrant a trip down memory lane?"

"Not even. I never got to experience her mouth. I was so damn nervous and drunk I threw up in the back seat."

That little revelation finally removes me from my little music-filled reverie. I pull the lone headphone (and the sounds of The Doors' lead singer's raspy voice) out of my ear. "Please tell me you're not thinking of pulling a repeat right here, right now…"

"Don't worry about me. I'm not the one who looks like he's going to lose his lunch at the mention of that pretty brunette."

He keeps talking.

"Listen, man, I get it. You've got yourself a little secret…"

My mouth turns dry as I wait for Sawyer to finish that sentence.

"It isn't like I've haven't found myself in a married woman's bed a time or two." He shrugs. "I was young and reckless. And I haven't been that way in about ten…"

He glances down at the large-faced watch on his wrist.

"Hours?" I interrupt, smiling hard.

"You laugh now, but I've grown since we were in college."

I toss him a pointed look. "You've grown?"

"Sure have. My cock is much bigger now than it was then."

He grabs his Cougars gym bag, as the rest of the locker room clears out behind him. "Is that why you've been abstaining, bro? Got your mind on the secret brunette?"

He nudges me, and I shake my head, finally slamming the locker and locking it so I can head for the showers. I shrug off the chill that travels down my spine. "Nah, that's not it."

Sawyer's eyebrows rise. "But you're not screwing anyone. Clearly."

"That's because I want to keep my focus on the game. Until we meet up with the Bruisers at least. I'm going to need every bit of my focus if we want to beat those fuckers. And for your information, I don't plan on pulling a repeat of your prom night, so to speak."

The bearded player starts to nod, but then he stares out the open doorway as a few players leave the locker room, rendering it empty. He looks over at me, his voice lowering to a whisper. "You sure about that 'not repeating prom night' part?"

I glance out of the open doorway beside him, finally catching sight of what has his undivided attention.

My tongue turns to sand.

It's hard to miss the long dark hair swaying there…along with the body that's attached to it.

Two familiar faces stare out the entryway, and I have to fight as my gaze flicks from one face—Naomi's, to the other.

Emily stands in the doorway, wearing one of her famous skirt suits fitted over her curvy frame, her soft hair pulled back into a ponytail.

Eyes narrowing, I stretch to my full six-foot-three height, my headphones in one hand and towel in the other.

With the lyrics to "Break on Through" by The Doors still playing softly in my mind even without the earphones, I can barely move as several sets of eyes settle on me.

I try to walk, but find myself unable to move. So Sawyer does instead, stepping forward to greet our unexpected guests.

I watch Emily's hazels widen noticeably, her gaze sweeping to the towel around my waist and back. She crosses her hands in front of her waist with a proud lift to her chin.

"Sevin." *Just that.* Just the one word... And the sound of it coming from her full, pink lips leaves my blood pumping straight between my legs.

"Emily." I offer in response. I glance at my assistant. "What are you guys doing here, Nome?"

She raises a well-defined eyebrow. "We have to talk to you before the flight back to Chicago. And since I know you're always the last to leave the locker room, I figured it wouldn't be such a hassle to come meet you here." She peers around the empty locker room. "So? Are you going to let us in or not?"

Sawyer chimes in, giving Naomi a hard time. As usual. "Depends. What's the password?"

"Um, I don't know..." She crosses her arms across her ample cleavage. *"Move?"*

He takes a step towards her, one side of his face pulling into a half-smirk. "Guess again."

But Naomi meets him toe for toe, her hard glare challenging Sawyer behind a pair of spectacles thicker than plate-glass. She cocks her head.

"Seriously, Saw? Could you be a bigger prick right now?"

"Is that a rhetorical question or would you like me to answer honestly?"

"Please. Don't say a word. I already know the answer."

"It's a pleasure to have you know me so well."

"I wish I could say the same on my end." She smiles semi-sweetly, and Sawyer finally steps aside, smiling as he unblocks the doorway, bowing at the waist.

"You may now enter. Uptight princesses first, of course." He starts to exit, waving over his shoulder. But he notices Emily before he disappears around the corner, one steady finger pointing in my direction. "I'll see you back in Chicago, Sterling. Looks like we'll have a lot to talk about. I'll make sure of it."

And I know I haven't seen the end. Not of Sawyer's question or his badgering. I know both will be waiting for me back in the Windy City.

With Sawyer out and my spitfire assistant leading the way, the two women enter the locker room.

But my eyes aren't focused on the first woman to step inside.

No. They're on the perfect brunette ambling behind her.

And even at this distance, I smell her perfume. The sweet, understated smell of lilies and honey combined with something indiscernible that makes my formerly soft dick harden underneath my heavy towel almost to the point of pain.

I close my eyes, counting to five until she finally stops.

Luckily, prayers do work. My rising dick dies down.

I lower my hands with the other towel to cover it. Just in case.

I exhale. "So, how can I help you, ladies?"

It's not long before Naomi fills me in all the new details emerging from Deborah Jett's upcoming meeting with The Firm and me back in Chicago tomorrow. My flight back to Chicago is tonight but tomorrow is absolutely booked with this blackmail crap. Emily listens intently, making no indication that just nine hours ago, I'd been seconds away from devouring her body into ecstasy.

She nods, her face calm and collected. Even when Naomi finishes up with a sentence that puts a ball of tension in my throat.

"So it's settled then?" Naomi prods.

"What is?"

"We'll turn over Charlie to Deborah. Have you sign away any fiscal and custodial responsibility. And get Deborah to move forward with the non-disclosure agreement. No muss. No fuss."

My eyes drill Naomi. "And Deborah agreed to all this?"

"Yes." She nods. "Surprisingly."

I plant a hand against my locker. "Sounds like a trick."

"Honestly, I don't care what it sounds like," my dutiful assistant responds. "As long as we can get this crazy woman out of our lives. Kayla's met up with her in New York and she's finalizing all of the details before they meet us in Chicago tomorrow."

I inhale. "So, that's it, then?"

"Pretty much."

"And we don't want to do any paternity tests?"

"Why?" Naomi's pretty face scrunches behind her glasses, her brown bob swaying. "Did you *want* to?"

I've never known Naomi to be callous. But this entire case is so business-like, so straight to the point.

Normally, this would be what I want from her. It's why I hired her.

But now? Now, the thought of treating Charlie and this paternity suit like business is making me feel like Sawyer on his prom night.

Sick to my stomach.

I peek over at Emily, who says nothing. "And you agree with doing all of this? Just...moving forward?"

Emily's amber-green eyes burn into mine, the fire there duller than ever before. She clasps her hands. "Yes," she utters stolidly, her jaw unmoving. "That was the job, really. To get this paternity-blackmail case behind us without any affect on your personal or professional career. And if this is the way to do it..." She trails off, her voice throaty. "Then I'm on board."

A moment passes between us as we stare at each other.

But Naomi doesn't notice. She's too busy writing notes and texting Kayla to tell her that the Chicago meeting is still on.

But me?

I notice everything. I notice how uncomfortable Emily is, standing there, pretending that this—us, Charlie—is just business.

Naomi finishes tapping on her phone just as Emily breaks eye contact. My eyes pull back to Naomi reluctantly as she clucks out loud.

"Perfect. That's all I needed." She glances over her shoulder. "But now I need to get out of here. Charlie's just around the corner, making friends with the mascot. Gotta go take her to get some ice cream before she implodes. She's taking your guys' loss pretty hard."

I grunt, and the words "Like father, like daughter" die on my mouth. I swallow. "Yeah, she's pretty invested in the game."

Naomi reaches out to squeeze my arm. "And she's not the only one." She tightens her grip once. "Don't take the loss so personal, Sev. You've bounced back from worse."

She has no idea.

I nod, and Naomi turns, heading out of the empty locker room, leaving Emily and I alone.

But I can't look at her.

A rage that has nothing to do with today's loss beats inside my chest.

She calls my name, but I'm already crossing the locker room quickly, heading to the showers.

I reach one hand inside a curtain, turning the shower head on, and the stream of water barely starts spraying towards the tile before I hear her voice behind me. Closer than before.

I don't turn, don't speak, don't move until the touch of a soft palm lands against my back, making breathing impossible. I squeeze my eyes shut for a second before opening them.

"You're an excellent actor, Miss Armand," I speak, never facing her.

Her voice is strong when she replies. "Just trying to keep up with you, Mr. Smith."

"I almost believed last night that you gave a shit about Charlie."

"Don't." The word wavers, but is shockingly loud. The force of it hits my skin. "Don't say that. Don't try to pretend that I don't care. *You know I do.* But you know as much as I do that I can't change anything. I still have a career to protect. And I didn't do such a great job of it this morning. And you have a career to protect, too, Sevin. Let's not forget…" She stumbles before continuing, her tone softening. "You didn't say anything to stop this either. You're still trying to protect what matters to you."

"And what if that's changed?"

I swing around this time, slowly, shifting on my feet. My eyes cast downwards to stare into the face of what is easily the most gorgeous woman I've ever known, and the words come out thicker than I expected, my throat clogging with lust and something else I won't even admit to myself.

I haven't felt this way about someone since…

Shit. I haven't felt this way about anyone. Ever. Not even Kimmy.

The realization makes the words rush out of my mouth.

"What if what matters to me has changed, kitten?"

I'm tempted to grab her. To wrap my fingers around her neck and pull her into me. To drag her fully clothed with me into the shower and cause her to be soaking in more ways than one.

But the sound of footsteps approaching cause me to look up and I find Naomi marching towards us, her brown eyes wide.

"Okay, so ice cream has to be put on a back burner. Turns out someone is sick."

My heart drops and I step away from the shower curtain, my throat squeezing. "Charlie?"

"Uh, no. Someone named Felix?" Her brows furrow. "I have no idea who this Felix is, but apparently they're throwing up all over the place."

A moment of silence fills the air. I know there's so many items I have to cross off my checklist before tonight.

Meet with my trainer. Talk to Coach.

Get my actual shit together.

But everything that seemed like such a usual priority slides to second-place in my mind.

The time I have with Charlie is limited. And I can't afford to waste it.

Naomi presses me, her shoulders hunched. "And does anyone want to tell me who the hell Felix is?"

I peer over at Emily and find the same worried look in her eyes. I direct my gaze back to Naomi. "He's a family member. One we apparently need to take care of."

I reach around turning off the shower head. "Let's go."

CHAPTER 20

*E*MILY
Saturday evening

Who knew that bringing a sick cat aboard a flight could be such a big problem?

Using Sevin's celebrity status to smuggle Felix in an oversized purse (vomit bag included) isn't a hassle, but keeping a lid on the now noisy cat is definitely a struggle as we depart Arizona's warm spring air to head back into the semi-winter chill of Chicago in March.

My meeting with Stephan tomorrow night looms in the back of my mind even when we land. And though I know I should warn Sevin of Stephan's impromptu meeting with me and of the possible hiccups to come, I can't quite form the words.

Even when we stumble into the back of Sevin's hired driver's truck, heading to the nearest vet with speed.

I pull my coat tighter, turning to Sevin in the truck's humongous back seat.

"What do you know about this vet we're taking Felix to?"

He hisses back, his voice too low for Charlie to hear. "Practically nothing. Naomi sent a few names over. I picked whatever I saw first."

I whisper in his ear. "What a wise way of choosing. Remind me to never use you to play the lotto."

"It was the only way of choosing. In case you got any better ideas…"

But I don't.

I'm freaking out. I've never had a pet in my almost twenty-five years of living. Not even one of those pet rocks from childhood that did absolutely nothing.

Shocker.

Felix, sick as hell, cuddles inside Sevin's muscular arms, and yet I'm the one feeling like I'm going to throw up.

I'm not good in an emergency. Not this kind, anyway.

And against my better judgment, I can't stop blabbing. Can't stop rattling off random facts about shit that makes no sense.

Anything to make me feel like I have control.

I still haven't told Sevin about Charlie's actual dad, Finley. And I'm not sure how to do it.

Violet was wrong. Swimming in chaos is bullshit. *I'm drowning in it.*

I mutter to myself. "How did Sylvester the Cat handle this? I don't remember Garfield ever getting sick. And do they really have hairballs? Maybe that's why Felix can't hold anything down… A bunch of hair in my throat would make me gag, too."

Sevin leans over, giving me a whiff of his smoky scent, his voice low.

"Tell me you're not doing this," he warns.

"Doing what?"

"Freaking out while we're on our way to the vet." His green eyes are dim, muted under the Chicago sunset's light. His tone is serious and I feel like a scolded school child. I lift my chin.

"And if I am?"

"I don't think talking about cartoon cat's possible sick symptoms are going to help us."

"Got a better idea?"

Sevin scoffs, his stubbled face breaking into a curious smile. His dark hair splays across his forehead beneath his usual Chicago Cougars baseball cap and I resist the urge to touch it, to feel its texture. His deep voice lowers. "I told you already. But maybe you've forgotten: I've never taken care of a living thing in my life, either."

"That's not true." I comment, whispering in his ear.

"It's not?"

"Of course not. From what I've heard from my ceiling, you've taken care of plenty of living things. The women you entertained while in town were very lively, I might add."

He rolls his eyes. "Of course they were. They had to be lively enough to scramble out of my penthouse after the cops came knocking…" He stares. "Thanks to you."

"Just trying to do my duty to serve my neighborhood."

"Is that true? Well, if you'd really like to serve your neighborhood, how about turning that God-awful Lillith Fair music ten notches down? I hear any more music from Jewel, and I'm sure I'm going to grow breasts."

"I bet you'd grow a lovely pair."

"Show me yours and we can compare. I'd like to give you a run for your money."

He smiles, and the feeling of tossing my cookies flies away, melted under his charm.

It feels inexplicably good. Seeing the same Sevin I first met in that elevator.

But before I can thank him for the welcome distraction, the truck stops in front of the veterinarian office, and for once in my life, I'm incapable of taking over.

Luckily, Sevin does.

He holds the frightened cat in his arms, Charlie at his side.

Paying the hired driver a hundred extra bucks to wait outside for us, he motions our three man/one cat crew inside the vet's brightly lit office, leading the pack.

Rattling off symptoms to a desk clerk who's clearly smitten, he handles my anxiety, Felix's sickness and Charlie's fear like a pro, petting the sickly feline with such care, such caution, that I feel my face grow green from the jealousy.

It's only minutes before they admit Felix in, and my body sags from pure relief.

In the waiting room, the three non-animals take our seats on ugly cushioned chairs when I notice Charlie, worn down from the day, growing sleepy beside us. Her sandy head of hair spills over Sevin's shoulder as she leans into him to rest, and I hand her my phone, noticing the light in her green eyes brighten as she takes it.

Her voice is small, dragging down from fatigue. She peers up at me.

"What's this?" She grumbles groggily.

"This? It's my phone. With all my favorite cartoons for you to watch it. And it's yours. For now."

Her grin is small, slight and watery.

I beckon the drowsy eight-year old to a cushioned bench on the closest side of the room and together, we watch my favorite nineties cartoons, sitting silently as we wait for the pet doctor to decide Felix's fate.

Thirty minutes later, when the Chicago sun sets, taking all the warmth with it, Charlie's eyes finally close, her sandy head falling comatose in my lap.

I almost fall asleep myself. But before my eyes can close all the way, I notice two strong legs stop in front of my seat.

I glance up finding Sevin's face—handsome and smiling—glancing down at me. He lifts one eyebrow beneath his cap.

"Comfortable?"

"Sure." I yawn, covering my mouth. "Charlie's only as heavy

as…an anvil." I peer down at the adorable eight-year old, happy to see her so peaceful after such a long day. "But I'll be fine."

"You sure?" He presses, leaning in. "Looks like you could use a bit of help."

"Mm," I mutter, rolling the fatigue from my shoulders. I meet his eye. "And you've been pretty good with the help today so far."

He tips his baseball cap, his grin sly. "Just doing my duty, ma'am."

"You did more than your duty. You handled a sick Felix and a worried Charlie like an absolute pro." I pause. "And you handled me"

He takes the seat beside me, and the entire bench groans, shifting slightly under his weight.

He's so damn big.

Big and strong and muscular. A walking statue.

The receptionist isn't the only one who can't keep her eyes off Sevin, and even the professional parts of me know, understand with everything in me, that this man is a walking fantasy—a dream come true.

And if you had asked me to say this a week ago, I would have called him a nightmare.

But there's something disturbingly sweet beneath that baseball cap. Something almost innocent.

He's a man holding secrets, silent suffering, inside those green eyes, and I've been dying to get to the bottom of it. To reach into that hidden pain and peel those layers back.

Layers that I know lead to whatever happened with Sevin in college. To what happened with Charlie's dad, Finley. To what happened with the woman who left him, Kimmy. And to what happened to the Sevin who could have been.

There was a prince hiding inside the playboy and I stare at him now, needing answers. Wanting to ask for them. And terrified to do so.

I bite my tongue.

Sevin stares at me. "What?"

"Nothing." I shake my head, trying to clear it. "Just tired."

"You've been staring at me for the last few seconds completely silent. Now, either I'm that interesting to look at—newsflash: I'm not. Or you're not saying something." He raises his hand. "Do I have airplane peanuts in my teeth? Crumbs in the hair on my stubble?"

I laugh. "Nothing like that. I was just wondering something…"

He blinks, motioning with his hand. "Well, wonder away. I won't stop you."

I exhale, shoulders slumping. My skirt suit feels hotter than ever on my frame. "I was wondering… I was wondering how you got like this. It doesn't seem to be an accident."

"Got like what? Devastatingly handsome? Or something else? Damn, maybe those airplane peanuts weren't a good idea. Knew I shouldn't have eaten those."

I place a hand on his arm, and the air sparks, growing hot when we touch. It's as if a current runs between us, and I try to ignore it.

"I mean, like this. Like you." I inhale deeply, needing the oxygen. "One week ago, you brought enough women to your penthouse suite to fill a Victoria's Secret."

He inclines closer. "And?"

"Seven days later, you're like a different guy. I talked to your teammate Sawyer. I've seen what he's like. And I guess I thought that would be you. Swimming in women. Taking another groupie to bed with you every night but that's not the case." I inhale shakily, trying to steady myself on the bench. *I fail*, wetting the edge of my lip. "Yes, I've heard your late-night show enough times to count. I just…expected more of the same here on the road. Expected to see you surrounding yourself with women. The ones waiting in the wings after every game. But lately, you just seem to not be interested."

His green eyes glow, and I know I've hit a nerve somewhere

deep. And I can't lie: I like it. His deep voice is warm when he responds. "That's because I'm not. Interested, that is." His words are molten honey over my skin, simmering in a way that has me tingling all over. His eyes find mine, searching their depths.

"I'm never been interested in most of those women. Not enough to see any of them for more than a night. But with you here? And Charlie? It's different. I know where my priorities belong these days. And they belong right here." He points. "With the two of you. Or the three of you if we count that damn cat."

I smile. "You know there's a nineties movie with Christina Ricci called 'That Darn Cat'?"

He scoffs, his soft voice a snort—sexy as all hell. "Trust you to know a nineties movie with another cat."

"Hey, you were the one who called me a freak."

"Yeah, I guess I'd just hoped it would be in other ways..." His voice trails off. "I can't confirm anything, but I suspect that there's a lot of things 'freaky' about you, Miss Armand. If given half a chance, of course..."

"Are you asking for one? A chance?"

"Please." He touches the edge of his cap, his smile sliding off his face. His eyes go serious. "I haven't been asking for a chance, Emily. I've practically been begging for one. Since the moment I saw you in that elevator, I knew I needed you alone. And trust me: The second I get the chance, I won't waste it. Not now. Not ever."

And for once in my life, I actually care.

Care that a man *does* care.

I'd spent so much time trying to avoid that feeling for fear that it would make me look like the fool I'd become with Jason, that I'd been missing out on what was beyond the fear.

And that was Sevin.

From the moment I'd found out that the unbelievably gorgeous baseball player was my client, I knew I couldn't trust myself to be in the same room with a man who made People's

Man of the Year candidates look like amateurs, a man who smelled of sugar, spice and everything sinful.

A man who makes me feel the way no other man has made me feel in more than two years.

My tongue twists as that same man stares at me, as if incapable of doing anything else. I start to open my mouth to say something —anything. But a man in blue scrubs steps forward, breaking our eye contact.

Sevin stands, as I continue sitting with Charlie's head in my lap. My heart freezes in my chest as blue-scrub boy crosses his hands in front of me, a furrow decorating his low brow.

His eyes remain on Sevin before turning to me. He takes a deep breath.

"Are you the owners of Felix?"

"Yes." Sevin answers before I get a word. "Yes, we are." The 'we' makes me weak in the knees, but he keeps going. "Is something wrong? Do we need to come back there or something?"

"Nothing's wrong." The man in scrubs waves, a shy shrug pulling at his sloped shoulders. He places his hands on his hips. "We just need you to monitor Felix's progress tonight. Make sure it doesn't get any worse. We think he has a stomach bug, really. But in case it's not. We need someone to ensure that he gets his meds, that his condition doesn't take a turn for the worse. Now," he glances between us, but his stare lingers on Sevin, his head tilting as he sizes him up.

Scrub-man's eyes widen to three times their size. "I'm sorry, but...you're... Are you...?"

"Sevin Smith." Sevin points at the clipboard in the guy's hand. "Seeing as how that's how I signed my name in earlier, than yeah, that's me.

"Holy hell." Scrub-dude's practically wetting his pants. He licks his lips, his eyes practically bulging out of his head, his grip tight. "Bro, I'm, like, a huge fan."

Sevin smirks. "Could have fooled me."

"I've seen every game you've played in, every single inning from when you played with the Fever. I cried. Cried real tears when they traded you to Chicago. Dumbest move a management team has ever made."

Sevin's stare goes to the floor, an actual flush flashing across his chiseled face. It's adorable.

And the veterinarian fan takes advantage, stepping in closer to his idol.

"I heard you requested the change from New York to Chicago."

Sevin nods, a begrudging look in his shaded eyes. "Sometimes a man just needs a change of scenery."

"From what? New York women? I've only been there a handful of times, but man." He whistles. "That city is crawling with supermodels and gorgeous women from top to bottom." He snaps his fingers, some realization ringing in his saucer-like eyes. He points at Sevin. "Like that Kimmy Wallace they say you were dating… Christ on a cracker, that woman was easy on the eyes."

Sevin's jaw starts to tick. That familiar facial spasm giving away his discomfort. He shifts on his feet, his hands leading to his pockets. His chin raises. "Damn, you *really* are a fan, aren't you?"

"The biggest." Scrub-guy doesn't seem to understand sarcasm well. He keeps talking. "If I had a woman like that, dude…"

"But you don't."

The words are like a whip, snapping through the air. And the room falls silent, tension tearing my insides to shred. I can do nothing but watch in horror.

Señor Scrubs deflates, the air going out of his enthusiasm. He backs off the line he's crossed.

"Oh, of course. My bad, bro. I just… I assumed…" He glances over at me, seemingly aware of me for the first time. He takes a step closer, offering his hand.

"I'm Dr. Owen's veterinarian assistant." He smiles. "Dean."

I nod back, taking his palm. "It's nice to meet you, Dean."

"It's nice to meet *you*. I mean, I'm so sorry I didn't see you there at first. I should have. I mean, enough about Kimmy Wallace. It's more of an honor to meet the woman who's landed Sevin Smith now. Wow." He glances at Charlie asleep in my lap before staring back at Sevin. "That's awesome. And the kid… Whoa, she looks just like you." He pauses. "Can I just…" He grabs for his phone, raising it to take a pic. "No one will ever believe you came in here."

But Sevin snatches the phone.

His hulking figure looms taller than ever as he steps into the over-eager assistant who peers up at him in fear first. And then defiance.

"You're right." Sevin growls between clenched teeth. "No one will ever know. Because you're not going to take a picture without our permission."

"Sevin," I warn. But I get the feeling that he doesn't hear me.

He moves to face Mr. Scrubs. "I'll always appreciate a fan. But this isn't fandom. This is being invasive. And I'm going to ask that you stop trying to take pics immediately."

Dean reaches for his phone, his face beet-red. "Who the hell do you think you are?"

"A person." Sevin glares. "And I'd appreciate it, if you treat me like one."

The assistant raises the phone again, taunting Sevin with the black square, the camera pointed in his face.

"Who do you think made you who you are? Huh? You wouldn't have this career if it weren't for the fans."

"Okay," I pipe in from the bench, Charlie still comatose on my lap. "Let's calm it down before…"

"Before what?" Dean pushes. "Before what? Before Sevin Smith proves himself to be a prick?"

"Now, wait a minute…" I interject.

But then Dean makes the biggest mistake, swinging the phone towards Charlie.

Sevin turns into the Hulk, snatching the phone and sending it flying across the room, the screen shattered in pieces. It lands with a crash that echoes in the empty lobby.

And in seconds I realize that we've broken career rule number two...

Don't keep a digital record of bad behavior.

Because if Dean's indicator on his phone was any sign, then that little interaction just went live.

The entire case of Sevin's paternity is supposed to be wrapped in secrecy and we just unveiled it. Maybe to the world.

And now Sevin's career (and mine) are definitely on the line.

CHAPTER 21

SEVIN
Saturday night

Leaving the vet is harder than arriving there.

With Felix, Charlie and Emily in tow, I herd the crew into my local driver's Navigator truck and from less than four feet away, I can feel Emily's anger.

Felix was released into our care with instructions to keep a careful eye. But the veterinarian assistant was already long gone.

At the end of his shift, he'd taken the phone he used to record me, Charlie and Emily, disappearing into the Chicago night with me threatening to wring his neck.

The only person who stopped me from doing it?

Emily.

The look of disappointment in her hazel eyes was enough to keep me from committing murder. And less than a half an hour later, those eyes are still filled with irritation, a cold chill that I can feel from the front seat.

I glance in the rearview mirror beside my driver Julio, finding her, sitting prim and proper in that same prim and proper skirt suit, her dark locks pulled off her face, Charlie's head in her lap.

The hour is late, nearing midnight.

And I imagine how different things were just a week ago. How, even just a year ago, on a night like tonight, I'd be seconds away from slipping the nearest blonde into my sheets, trying desperately to forget all my faults.

Instead I'm here. Bound. Tied. Torn up by the three other creatures in the car with me.

None more than complex than the petite lawyer sitting two feet away.

But she doesn't stare back.

When Julio pulls up and parks outside of the Millennium Gardens apartment building where we live, I'm the first out of the car.

A surprisingly calm Felix tucked inside my elbow, I open the back seat door, motioning to Emily to hand me Charlie, and even with a subdued fire in her stare, she obeys.

We swap sleeping beasts. Furry Felix for the spirited eight-year old.

And with a handful of bills to Julio, we make our ascent up to my penthouse.

The ride in the elevator is icy between us all the way up, and when I finally push my way into the penthouse apartment door, dragging our Arizona luggage inside, I glance back to find her dawdling in the doorway.

I turn, staring. "I'm sorry. Did you turn into a vampire in the last few days or so?"

Emily's face scrunches, her pretty brows furrowing. "Not last time I checked. Why?"

"Because you're behaving as if you need an invitation to come in. The apartment's yours."

She nods, but I can see the wariness in her face.

Robotically, I carry Charlie all the way to the guest bedroom, setting her out-cold form on the sheets.

Unfamiliar with the protocol of putting a kid to sleep by

myself, I try my best.

I remove her light-up shoes, placing them at the foot of the bed. I forego any pajama changing, slipping a quilt over her tiny body instead.

Sweeping the sandy strands of hair away from her eyes, I prepare to leave her to the bedroom by herself. But I can't help myself.

I lean in, tapping a quick kiss to her forehead, fighting back a ball of emotion that lodges in my throat.

I close the bedroom door behind me when I leave, the click soft as I shut it slowly.

But the voice from behind me when I shut it is even softer, barely louder than a breath.

"The vampire has decided to enter," she declares, cradling Felix in her arms. She gazes out my living room's floor to ceiling windows, taking the Chicago horizon in. And I watch her.

All soft lines and slender curves.

But the look she's throwing is anything but soft.

I lean against my wall. "You seem like you want to say something."

She gazes up, catching my eye. "If I did, would it make a difference?"

"Of course it would."

"Okay, well, then, I just wanted to say you were a complete dickhead back there in that veterinarian's office."

I remove myself from the wall. "Excuse me?"

"Pretty sure I didn't stutter, Sevin," she breathes, glancing at the furry feline in her hands. She lowers her voice. "You could have jeopardized everything. Yourself. Charlie. Your career. My career. Until this thing is wrapped with Charlie's mom, we have to avoid any and all microscopes. And what you did, arguing with that guy, it put us under one."

I take a step closer, feeling my head heat under my baseball cap. My footsteps sound loud to my own ears as they land over the hardwood.

"Better that I let the asshole act like complete scum?"

"Yes, actually." She blinks, her slickened ponytail swinging, soft enough to grab with my whole fist. She closes her eyes before opening them. "You overreacted. Which will cause people to wonder why you overreacted."

My pulse picks up. "I'm just protecting me and my mine."

"Like you did back in the car in Arizona?"

The memory makes my teeth grin. Emily keeps speaking.

"You react too quickly. Too fast. You don't think things through. Or consider the consequences before you make a move."

"Oh, you mean the way that you do? Overthinking every single step before you make it without a single thought of spontaneity in your brain?" I scoff, crossing the room. I reach the bar on the opposite end, but I no longer have the desire to remove any of the bottles.

I turn. "You're the most tightly wound woman I've ever met in my entire life."

Emily navigates to the huge sectional couch taking up space a few feet away. She deposits a sluggish Felix there, standing to face me.

"And you're the most impulsive man I've ever known."

"Why?" I incline forward. "Because I won't follow your imaginary book of rules?" I snort, planting my hands behind me on the bar. "Excuse me for being honest, but sounds stifling as hell to me. I can't imagine a life like that."

She glowers. "Good thing you don't have to. Because it *is* my life, Sevin. And that's how I like it."

"Really?" I glance up, finding Emily shifting on her feet, the fight in her eyes making her face flushed. "You like being bound to nothing but your career?"

"I could ask you the same thing. With your focus on nothing

but baseball, it's no wonder a man you hate wound up raising your daughter."

The statement makes me stop, and I face Emily, finding myself gazing into a mirror I don't want to see. My throat mimics the Sahara, completely sucked dry, and shock plants me to the floor, keeping me there as Emily just stands there, severing my brain's synapses with each step as her face flushes.

It hurts to swallow. But I manage anyway, forming words. "What did you say?"

She sighs, and the flush on her face is in her eyes. She wipes at one corner. "Your ex-roommate Finley… I should have told you when Charlie confessed." Her shoulders lift and fall. "He's the man who's being raising Charlie. He's the man who's been raising her as her dad."

There are some secrets that you share with your closest bros. Secrets you take to the grave.

And then there are others, *like sleeping with your coach's only daughter*, that you never tell a soul.

I'd told my ex-best friend. And paid for it.

He'd stolen my girl.

But a piece of me has been paying ever since. Because while most of my own soul belonged to baseball, there was still this other part, however small, that still belonged to both Kimmy and Finley.

I was a slave to my mistrust.

I'd filled my nights with music and sex because risking another heartbreak was something I wasn't willing to do.

But I wasn't alone. Because Emily was doing it too.

Even now I can see the terror in her eyes. Taste it.

So, Finley was setting me up to take a fall in some twisted scheme of his. What else was new?

But I can see that Emily was a person who weaponized the truth. Clearly she'd been burned in the past like me.

But blackmail scheme or not, I wasn't throwing away the last week or so.

Not when it'd been the best of my life.

I push away from the bar, strolling near, my hands at my sides, realizing that I don't give a fuck. Not about Kimmy. And definitely not Finley.

I close the distance between Emily and me drawing a deep breath. And it's as if she can feel it.

I watch her sigh.

"So what?" I utter out loud. "What does it matter?"

She blinks. "What does it... What do you mean, Sevin? It matters. It matters a whole lot." She uncrosses her arms, her back straightening. "Doesn't it?"

"No. No, it doesn't. I won't let some asshole stop me from living my life. Not even one like Finley. I can choose to never trust again. Stay exactly the same: A workaholic. Career-obsessed."

I take a few more steps, shrinking the space, and Emily watches me, her breathing picking up pace as I amble nearer. The air grows thick.

"It's time I took that finger you talked about before and point it right back at myself, don't you think? I've *hardly* been the most trusting man in the world. And those were your words."

I keep walking and talking, never missing a beat. "For all the women I've been connected to in the press, I've never once come public with a woman. Never once claimed one for my own." I count on my fingers. "Not a wife. Not a fiancée. Not even as much as a girlfriend.

"You see, there's a reason I've been this way, Emily. A reason why I won't so much as let myself get comfortable with a damn hallway cat."

I cross my own arms, forgetting that I'm supposed to be professional. I couldn't be if I wanted to. Not when Emily looks so damn delectable. Good enough to taste. I practically can.

"See, kitten, I know I haven't been so great with people this past decade or so. But I'm not the only one."

I slow down just a foot away. "I'm not the only one terrified of tying myself to another. Afraid of being abandoned. Because I can see the same in you." I hesitate just before reaching her. "Are you saying that you like living this life? This fit-in-a-box existence? Days full of sameness and nights alone?"

I inch closer, staring at her beneath my Cougars baseball cap, watching her squirm in her sensible high heels.

And she lets me. She doesn't move.

I reach a hand to her chin, tracing its line, taking my time.

Stroking her satiny skin, I catch the slightest hint of her arousal, my mouth watering at the thought. The sexy scent of it was present in my Arizona hotel room during the hot as hell kiss, but now it's full-force, making everything below my waist a beacon of steel.

I'm knee-deep in needing. Wanting. Waiting for the chance to slip my equally sensible little lawyer right out of those heels and into my arms.

And all I need is one hint, one nod to let me know that I'm not alone in this. In wanting to step outside of myself.

To trust again.

The light in my apartment is so muted, so low I can barely see her expression. But I can tell she knows I'm right.

But in order to get her to give in, I know I have to push her buttons. Prod her to the brink.

I do so with my touch, tearing down her guard. Silky inch by inch.

"Are you telling me that you like your life exactly this way? That there's nothing you would change? Because if I had my way, kitten, there's a lot I would change…"

She breathes against my hand, and it is the sexiest thing I've ever experienced. Her jaw lifts. "And what's that?"

"Off the record?" I tease.

She nods, and my tone goes serious. I swallow.

"I'd change into a man more worthy of you. I'd change into a man not scared shitless of what's happening between us. I'd change into a man who could say that kissing you, touching you, wanting to take you to bed won't change a thing. I'd change into a man who could and would play by your rules. But right now, the best I've got is to be a man who wants to make you break at least one of them..." My eyes sink to her lips, and I brush a thumb there. "Starting right the hell now."

If I did have an imaginary book of rules, it'd be out the window the moment I capture Emily's mouth with mine.

And she tastes better than I remember.

Her chin still in my hand, her tongue against mine, I explore the wet cavern of her delicious mouth, wondering how I lasted the last eighteen hours without it.

There is nothing normal about the connection we have every time we touch.

We match each other perfectly. Touch for touch. Taste for taste. Lick for lick.

Her small tongue reaches out to brush against mine, and I suck its pink tip, eliciting a small moan that makes my very skin vibrate. Our bodies move into one another, joining. And nothing has ever felt more natural.

I'm breaking every barrier I've put up with women for Gods knows how long with Emily. And damn, it feels good watching all the pieces crash at my feet, my guard annihilated, surrounded all to willingly to this woman.

And I have no regrets.

Somehow in the span of a week and a half, she's awoken a side of me I thought I'd lost. Taught me more about myself than I've ever cared to explore.

She's opened up my world to more than my career. And so has Charlie.

I've already decided that even when Deborah, Charlie's

mother, comes calling I'm not going to be so willing to let Charlie go. I can barely let Emily go.

And as I wrap my arms around her, tugging the tiny attorney close, I can only wonder if she knows it.

I break our kiss, stepping back to find unadulterated passion in her hooded hazel eyes. I gaze down at her.

"Which rule did that kiss just break?"

She huffs out a hurried breath, her amber eyes glowing under the moonlight. "Uh, every single one of them?"

"The Homeowner's Association is going to be so disappointed in us."

She shrugs. "There's no telling what Hank the doorman will do when he finds out."

"The MyNeighbor app will be buzzing by morning."

"Not if we stop this now..." She trails off, biting her bottom lip. "We technically haven't gone too far yet, Sevin. I mean, we could stop this right now. No harm. No foul."

I run my fingertips across her hairline, tracing where the moonlight hits her face, committing the feel of her skin to memory. I reach for the edge of my baseball cap, removing it to toss it across the room.

I let it land on the nearby sofa before focusing my gaze back on Emily. Her kiss-swollen lips are still slightly damp. And holding back from kissing them again literally hurts.

I chuckle, the sound echoing low in my empty penthouse. "'No harm'? You've gotta be kidding me..." I hesitate, desire gripping my throat tight. "Kitten, we passed the point of 'no harm' a long time ago. Neither one of us is walking away from this without harm." Tilting my head to get a better view of her, I at last touch the edge of one fingertip to her soft mouth, wanting to delve further.

"So what do you say?"

It's a request. An act of asking for permission.

And the second time I've put the call in Emily's hands. Something a superstar athlete never gets used to doing.

But if I'm being honest with myself, giving in to Emily is reclaiming a piece of myself I thought I'd lost nine long years ago. A piece I thought I didn't need.

It feels surreal. To want a woman like this.

To need her so viscerally.

I wait for the sexy brunette to say something—anything, and I can feel her fighting with her decision. The soft light in the penthouse, the midnight sky outside the windows and Sears Tower gleaming in the distance do nothing to make the mood lighter.

Her delicate face furrows under the living room's softened light, and the sensation of *déjà* vu takes root inside my body, my skin vibrating as the air grows silent around us.

That familiar urge to take fight or flight.

And goddammit, it's hard realizing that the remnants of fear from Kimmy aren't behind me, aren't buried in the past where they belong.

As a man, a baseball player known the world over, it's hard as hell to admit: My body is strong. But my will, my resolve, is weak.

And nine years later, here I am. In the same position.

Caught between my career and a soft Emily, I have to make another decision between a woman and baseball. Knowing I can't have both.

But I know what I choose.

I choose her.

The thought is killing me that maybe she doesn't feel the same.

Emily says nothing for several tortuous seconds before lifting her face to mine. Her voice is soft, her words slow and measured as her eyes raise to look at my face.

She sighs. "I say yes…if you answer one question for me." She inhales, blowing out just as quick. "Le Perla lingerie or Bugs Bunny bikini briefs?"

"Is this a serious question?" I raise a brow. "Depends on which fabric I can take off faster."

She smiles. "That was the right answer."

She finishes her reply by kissing me, and the fear I felt, a decades' worth, goes flying out the window. I kiss her back, ready to make good on all my unspoken promises.

CHAPTER 22

E MILY

Saturday night

The Chicago night sky outside of Sevin's floor-to-ceiling windows reminds me of all the rules I made back in Arizona.

And how great it feels breaking each one of them.

Ben and Violet were right; chaos does taste good.

Fortunately, for me, Sevin tastes even better. And when I wrap my arms around his neck, fingers intertwined into his dark hair, I sample as much of him as I can take, letting his mouth slant against mine to the rhythm of my racing heart.

His kisses are ravenous. And I'm insatiable.

He backs my body towards his wide windows overlooking the city, and I am a mess by the time my backside presses into the glass, our embrace on display for all of Chicago and the over-looked Lake Michigan to see.

I'm breathless by the time the kiss breaks. "How sturdy is this glass?"

"Sturdy enough to hold you, kitten," Sevin whispers against my mouth. "I only sprung for the best in this penthouse."

I shudder. "Fancy."

I don't tell him I've dreamed of being in this very penthouse. *If only to kill him.*

I'd secretly fantasized in the few weeks of Sevin's and my fiery feud about setting flames to this place. Of watching it burn.

But now the only thing on fire in this grandiose apartment is me. And I'm only too relieved when Sevin strips me of my blazer, his mouth connecting to my collarbone as his fingers make their coordinated way to my blouse.

He pulls on the first button and I whimper, squirming in my heels. "Am I stupid for thinking of how many other women have been in this apartment?"

"Crazy?" He keeps unbuttoning. "Yes. Stupid? Never. If I were you, I might have the same thoughts." His eyes meet mine, and they're on fire, burning in emerald tones like never before— almost an entirely different color. They frighten me. And excite me. "But I don't bring women to my apartment. I never have."

I pause. "But I've heard you. In the ceiling above me. I heard the moaning."

Sevin shoves off my shirt, letting it slide to the floor. "I'm sure you did hear moaning. But it wasn't from anyone that I was with." He inclines closer. "Sawyer's been staying in that guest bedroom while his own place is being renovated. Can't say I've been the biggest fan of his guests, but I stay on other side of the apartment." He points. "*Over there.* And I did tell you back outside of your apartment that you were taking your outrage on someone else's love life." He grins. "I just never said that sex life was mine. And you never asked."

I feel foolish enough as it is, and my face flushes. But Sevin soothes my exposed ego with an open-mouthed kiss, and I know all of our animosity, all of the neighborly anger and tension is in the past, buried beneath the passion we have for each other.

A passion that won't burn out.

Especially when Sevin lifts his hands up my skirt, exposing my half-naked ass.

A red flame fans down my skin as the ridiculously sexy baseball player drops to his knees. And me? I'm shaking on mine.

I'm barely able to keep standing as Sevin reaches for my high heels, removing each solitary one from my feet, his fingers sliding over my ankle.

I bite into my lip as his slightly rough palms rise first to my calves then to my knees. I'm wetter than I ever imagined when he puts each calloused hand on my thighs, positioning them against glass.

Prying them open for the view, his voice is a raspy caress. As tenderly rough as his touch, it brushes against the softness at my hip as he lifts my skirt.

He takes a bite of the exposed skin, and I swear I come, the combination of his voice and fingertip strokes driving me insane.

A sound I don't recognize comes out of my mouth, my need turning my words to mush. I can barely speak as Sevin talks to me, showering my very skin with every tantalizing thought in his sexy mind.

He mutters between my thighs, soaking me further.

"There is no one but you, Emily. There will be no one but you. I need you to know that." His deep voice rumbles across the cloth of my disheveled skirt. "Your awful music is the one I want to suffer through. Your loud laughter is the one I want to hear."

His fingers reach my panties, revealing the emblem printed there. "It's your Bugs Bunny underwear I want to put in my mouth, kitten. And only yours."

He reaches his hands up to my bra, unclasping it. I lift my shoulders, watching the cotton and lace fall, and in seconds, I am nearly naked before Sevin's touch, my nipples hard and red as I stare down at him, on his knees, his stare washing and worshiping over my body.

And I've never felt so sexy.

So wanted. So cared for.

"I wish you could feel what you do to me, kitten. I wish you could feel my hardness right now." He pushes up farther on my skirt, unveiling more of my panties. "But right now I'll settle for showing you how you make me feel." He hesitates. "Poor Bugs Bunny." He runs a finger over my wet slit. "Poor fucker never knew what he had coming the second I saw you in these."

And then he plunges his tongue over it, taking the fabric and my sex into his mouth.

I explode right on the spot.

I should feel ashamed. Every ounce of me knows it.

But there's no shame in Sevin's ministrations, no slowing of his tongue's strokes.

The man doesn't know the meaning of embarrassment. And in seconds neither do I, as I thrust my palms against the wall's glass, attempting to stay upright.

Sevin devours me through my underwear as if it weren't even there, and I don't hesitate to wonder what damage he could do if they weren't.

His tongue is just as insistent, prodding through the thin cotton. His mouth moves with playful pressure, and in a matter of moments, I am reaching towards my peak again, ignoring the unbelievable amount of wetness visible through my panties.

I pull at Sevin's hair, trying to get him to stop. I inexplicably fail as his fingers join the fray.

He dips them under the Bunny fabric before removing my underwear completely, flinging the tiny garment across the floor.

"I don't believe I said I was done with you yet, kitten." He removes his mouth, scolding me. "At least not yet. There's plenty more orgasms where the first one came from, and if you don't let me finish this second one, I can't promise that I'll be any kinder with the third or fourth."

He chuckles as I shift on my feet, needing release.

"There won't be a third or fourth orgasm," I pant. *"Not if I slip into a coma.* I can barely stand while you're doing that, and if you don't get me off my feet, I am really going to give you a bad review on the MyNeighbor app."

He glances up at me, his green eyes hard. "You wouldn't dare."

"I would. I'd even get Mrs. Headley involved."

"You mean that mean old neighbor who makes grandma's cookies sound dirty?" He snorts. "Hell, 'The Headley' would probably be proud of you if you report this to the rest of the building. Sounds like the sort of sex that's right up her alley."

"Please." I manage to laugh at last. "I'd rather not hear about *anything* that 'goes up her alley.' I'd be scarred for life."

And Sevin chuckles.

Even in the midst of sex, he's still the man I love to laugh with. And when he rises to his feet again, all dark hair and muscles and full, sensuous mouth, I almost beg him to drop to his knees again.

He's a little less dangerous, kneeling below my level. But at this height, towering over me, tall enough to cover his entire body over mine, I'm overwhelmed by his sheer sex appeal, the effortlessly cool confidence that comes with being one of the most famous athletes in the world.

And he's all mine.

At least for the foreseeable future.

He wraps his hands around to my bare ass, hoisting me up. Naked with the exception of my skirt-lined waist, I cling to every inch of Sevin, wrapping my legs around him.

The jokes are gone as we walk to the bedroom, and even in the near-dark, I can see the emotion in his pine-green eyes, the utter adulation as he spreads me on top of his cool thousand-thread sheets, his stare meeting mine.

He watches me for several long seconds, before reaching for his own clothes.

He removes his shirt, tossing it to the floor, and I marvel at his marble-like body, swallowing roughly as his jeans join the shirt along with his shoes.

I can barely keep myself from shaking, gazing at the erection underneath his perfectly fitted black boxer-briefs. I sink my nails into the sheets to regain control.

"Wow," I breathe, knowing no other word for him.

"What?"

"You are perfect. Literally perfect. How are you not made out of clay?"

"A week and a half ago, I wasn't made out of anything but 'asshole and arrogance.' I saw the public messages on the MyNeighbor app."

I smirk. "You were spying on me?"

"I like to call it 'doing research.' I was trying to figure out why the woman I'd met in the elevator wouldn't respond to my own messages. What I found was some pretty damning evidence…that I hadn't tried hard enough to get in your Bugs Bunny panties." He walks closer. "My apologies."

My smile widens at he reaches the edge of his ginormous mattress, his green eyes fixing me to the spot. I sit up. "After that performance against the glass in your living room, trust me: You're forgiven. Now, get over here, please."

The plea is more than enough. Sevin doesn't hesitate to join me on the bed.

But the pace at which he positions himself over my body is maddening, and I can't stop squirming on the bed, eager to have all of him inside me as soon as possible.

My breath is heavy by the time he reaches me, his arms over mine, his handsome face close.

"Are you trying to drive me crazy at this rate? I'm having a little trouble here waiting."

"Patience." He smiles, reaching over to the nightstand. "Patience, my delectable little kitten. You're worse than Charlie."

"Always nice to be compared to an eight-year old." I roll my eyes as his hand makes it to the top drawer. He opens it painstakingly slow.

"I've been waiting to make you mine for longer than I thought I can stand. I just want to relish in this moment for a little while longer, knowing that every minute was worth the wait." He grabs a foil packet from inside. "I always knew you were worth it."

The admission makes me melt. I finally fall silent.

No longer eager to have Sevin erase my anxiousness with hurried speed, I allow myself to enjoy this moment. To enjoy the addicting sensation of sealing a deal with Sevin in a very different way than I have with any client before.

We were going to make love. And it was going to mean something.

All the jerk-offs and Jason's of the world had brought me to this moment, and I know with everything in my buzzing body, with every fiber of my sexually inexperienced being, that I am totally and wholeheartedly falling in love with this man.

An athlete. A neighbor. A client.

Maybe even a single father.

I've broken too many of my rules to give a damn. And though the thought brings tears to my eyes, I manage to hold them back just as my fingers find the edge of Sevin's expensive boxer briefs, ready to sink my hands beneath.

I gaze up at him, my eyes questioning. Sevin only smiles back, his amused expression his answer to everything passing between us unsaid.

He lifts a dark eyebrow. "My, my, you turned out to be much more than just a cartoon freak after all, Miss Armand."

"You have no idea."

I pull at Sevin's sexy underwear, and he helps me send them sailing across the room. Tearing at the foil packet with his teeth, he positions himself over my mostly naked body before sheathing himself.

He stares into my eyes, asking permission, and when I nod, he plunges into me, showering me with the sweetest ecstasy a noodle-loving, nineties-music head has ever known.

And I'm convinced: If Sevin Smith is chaos, then I've just become an anarchy convert.

I cling to his shoulders.

CHAPTER 23

*S*EVIN
Saturday night

I was right; no rock record I have on vinyl can compare to a night with Emily Armand.

And it's not even close.

I can't remember the last time I've "made love." It's been years.

Following in my fellow teammates' footsteps, I had once lost myself to the destruction of life in the limelight. Used booze, baseball and women to forget the heartache that had plagued my soul the moment the woman I loved proved she didn't want to be with me.

I was lost then.

I've been lost ever since.

But with just a week and a half with the gorgeous brunette, you could consider me found.

Taking the pretty little lawyer to bed was one thing. But the moments we shared, the private messages, the small touches and big revelations have only shown me that it was never just about conquering the woman in the elevator.

If anything…she had conquered me.

And even now splayed against my pristine white sheets, her body pressed beneath mine on the soft bed, I know, without a doubt in my mind, that she is still the one in control.

My guard is down again. With Charlie. With Emily. Completely.

And for once in my life, it's not scary as hell anymore. In fact, it's fucking invigorating.

Almost as invigorating as when I slide my hardened cock into the recesses of Emily's tight body, sheathing myself in her soaking sex. She gasps the second her body gives way, fitting around me in a way so perfect it seems unreal.

I close my eyes from the sheer pleasure, loving nothing more than the sensation of being inside Emily's pussy.

I kiss the edge of her neck as I stroke, hoping I haven't hurt her. She's so fucking tight.

"Fuck, kitten, are you okay?"

"I'm a lot of things…" she pants, as I pump. "But 'just okay' isn't one of them."

I bite her skin. "Is that good or bad?"

"Please. Don't make me say it. Speaking…" she huffs, her eyes clenched in ecstasy. "Is very hard right now." Her defenses break, and a whimper so needy falls from her full mouth that I can't stop myself from capturing it. I kiss her lips.

"I'll take that as a 'very good.'" I smile as she nods her head emphatically.

Her dark hair is still in that tight sophisticated ponytail, remnants of her business side. I reach down to pull the ponytail tie loose when I have a better idea, lifting my body from hers mid-stroke.

A moan escapes off her tongue, and before I can break down and suck on its pink tip, I pull Emily up on the mattress, positioning her to flip on all fours.

Like the obedient kitten she's suddenly become, she lets me, sighing as I situate myself behind her, my hand wrapped around her ponytail tightly enough to tug.

I kiss the middle of her back, wrapping the other hand around her middle, my cock poised at her soaking entrance.

"Hold on, kitten. This is going to be a different type of ride."

And it is. From the moment I stroke into her.

Emily cries out loud, a sexy sound that's more music to my ears than any Jim Morrison. Her pussy walls grip me.

I slide her bare ass back and over my cock, and as I pump her, pulling on that silky ponytail, I revel in the symphony of her moans.

Those little noises she makes when I hit the right spots. The guttural groans she gives when I swirl my hips.

God, she feels amazing.

And I don't hesitate to tell her.

"I've never felt anything better than you, babe. God, Emily, you are so fucking amazing."

She whimpers in response, a chorus of "Oh fuck's" spinning off her tongue in hushed tones. My name is a prayer and a curse on her mouth.

"*Sevin,*" she breathes, as her face sinks towards the mattress. "You...Ohhh. God..."

I continue stroking, tugging harder on her hair, loving the feel of it between my fingers. "Careful, kitten. I might like being in the same breath as God a little too much."

But she's too busy moaning to respond, and through the strokes and tugging and teeth and tongue and love bites on the small of her back, I can feel Emily's pussy tighten around me, clenching to signal her coming climax.

And just as she begins to come, I stroke a hand over her delectably tight backside, touching the pucker between her cheeks, and her orgasm hits us both with the intensity of a tidal wave, pulsing with an exquisite pressure that pulls my own climax out of me.

I come inside Emily seconds later, bringing my adorable brunette to tears. She slumps to the bed.

I'd join her. But I'm still hard.

Even after coming in the most intense orgasm of my life, just the sight of her spent on my mattress keeps my cock as rigid as chiseled stone.

Her hair is messy, all over her head, her business skirt still wrapped around her waist.

Her legs are slightly parted and the vision of the slick skin between them is enough to make me want to take her again.

Stalking over her, I press a chaste kiss to the back of her damp neck and she groans into the sheets, her skin humming as I hover over her sated form.

Her voice is muffled.

"I wasn't prepared for that," she comments. "*Nothing* could have prepared me for that."

I grin. "I told you I wouldn't be any kinder with the third orgasm." I pull on her legs propping them up.

I shift back on my heels. "Now let me show you how unkind the fourth one can be."

Emily can barely make out another word before I bury my face under her backside. Opening her pussy lips for my view, I take my time this go-around.

With no Bugs Bunny as a barrier, I show my little Emily the meaning of being a freak. Fortunately, for the both of us, the fur fits.

I plunge my tongue into her pussy, sucking to my heart's delight until finally she falls asleep, entangled in my arms.

* * *

EMILY

Sunday morning

The morning light is bright when I wake up in Sevin's arms.

I've never felt so warm and comfortable in my life, and though the man easily outweighs me by nearly a hundred pounds, I relish in the feel of waking up with his limbs draped over mine.

His pelvis is solid, pressed into my backside. And as I start to shift under the sheets, I catch the sexiest hint of his natural scent. That cedar-like smoky scent that emanates flawlessly from his skin, reminding me once again that the man is perfect.

But then again, so was the sex.

It's on my mind from the second I open my eyes. But so is my post-coital "confession time" with Sevin last night, where we laid —well into the wee hours of the morning—in his gigantic King-sized bed discussing Kimmy, Finley, our careers and everything that led us to this point.

We bared it all.

It broke my heart to hear him recount their betrayal. *It broke my heart to have been part of it.*

Even last night, my Charlie-Finley secret was still scorching a scarlet "A" on my chest for being such an asshole.

And despite my guilt after everything, Sevin forgave me, offering me a peek at the sainted soul beneath the baseball jersey, opening himself up and unearthing the deepest parts of himself underneath his luxury bedroom sheets.

He shared the memories he'd once believed were best buried, the bad decisions that had tainted his youth.

Sevin was right...

Last night, he buried himself so deep inside of me that he had disappeared completely.

Mr. Elevator Man—the arguably self-centered, emotionally unsure, former playboy athlete I'd met inside those steel double doors—was dead.

And this morning, I wiggle awake to the completely new Sevin —the unsheathed and open one. The one who showed me how to trust again.

I wonder to myself if the reborn Sevin sleeping quietly beside me knows that he's sexed me—the old me—back to life and love. But I don't have to wonder for long.

I'm made aware of the answer to the question on my mind when I feel the sensation of circling around my nipples.

I look down to find his lengthy digits drawing spirals around my areolas, slow, tickling touches that make me wet all over again.

I don't even turn to look at him when I speak, a smile creeping its way onto my face.

"Well, good morning to you, too, Mr. Smith."

"Miss Armand." His voice is sleepy and rough, raspy still from fading fatigue, and I wish I could see his face. "How are you this morning?"

"Fantastically sore." I glance over my shoulder. "And loving it. I lost sensation in my legs that fifth go-around, but I really recovered some strength after the sixth." I grin. "And how are you?" I gaze into his handsome face. "Morning treating you any better than the night?"

"Nothing was better than last night." His green eyes twinkle under the rising sunlight, showing their sparkling depths. His returning smile is similarly sparkling. "But I think I could give the last six hours a run for their money, if you give me..." He winces, seemingly thinking. "Six more minutes to convince you."

"Six minutes?" I gape. "Is that all you need?"

"Six months straight of you in my bed wouldn't be enough, kitten." He stares at me pointedly. "And you know that. But if I recall, on the plane back to the city, you mentioned a meeting with Stephan. And I've gotta get ready myself. I have some training to do before tomorrow's game back in Arizona. Before that, of course..." His voice deepens. "I'd like to make you come at least two more times. As much as the six minutes will allow, at least."

This time, I spin the entire way around, escaping from Sevin's spooning to meet his gaze. "Make it seven, and I'll add in something extra."

"Oh? What did you have in mind?"

I smile. "Only returning one of your many favors." I slide beneath the sheets, heading southward. "I'm not only a receiver, Mr. Smith. I can be a giver. And right now, I want to give you a reason for the extra minute."

He exhales. "As if I need one." He chuckles. "But I won't stop you, kitten. Give away."

And that's exactly what I do.

It's been a long time. But I hope it's like riding a bike.

Pressing my lips to the edge of Sevin's semi-hard cock gives me more pleasure than any case brief, and within seconds, his beautiful pink erection comes alive, standing at attention in full salute.

The damn thing is beautiful.

Like the man it belongs to, it's amazingly unreal.

Long and thick and magnificent, it turns to steel under my slight touch, and I can't believe I can do this to Sevin. That I'm capable of making him this hard.

I wrap my tongue around his wide head, unsure of myself for a second. But the groan that leaves Sevin's lips when I do it is all the affirmation I need.

Soon, I am licking and sucking and stroking with the fervor of a fever. The fever that Sevin has ignited inside my body in the last few days we've been together.

I'm more *me*. More confident than ever before.

Especially when Sevin's hands sink into my hair.

"That's it, baby. Oh, fuck, you feel so good."

His utterances are an *insta-turn-on*.

I swirl my tongue along his underside, sucking with my mouth. My lips slide across the length of his cock, squeezing hard, and with each pull of my lips, with every extra ounce of pressure I apply as I stroke Sevin up and down with my wet tongue and mouth and hands, I witness the game-winning baseball player fall apart.

He pulls the sheets back, revealing his face and when I get the vision of him, lying there, attempting desperately to control himself, his eyes and teeth clenched, I pick up the pace, wanting him to fully lose control and release himself immediately into my mouth.

I get what I want.

Sevin climaxes under my touch.

I milk him with my lips, sucking him down. Even the taste of him is perfect, and I swallow with glee, loving that I'm not the only one at someone else's mercy. Savoring the not-so-small fact that I drive the unattainable athlete just as crazy as he drives me.

It feels good to know it.

When he opens his eyes, his pine-colored irises are alight, shining with lust. He reaches for me, tugging me towards him, and seizes my mouth in a savage kiss, one that makes all of my effort more than worth it.

I smile in triumph when he pulls back, locking me with his stare. "You are a crazy woman, you know that?"

I shrug. "If the fur fits…"

"Remember when I said I wanted to bury myself inside you so deeply that I disappeared?"

I'm breathless when I reply. "Yes."

"Well, I haven't quite managed that yet, and now's as good a time as any. We'll call Stephan. Push back this meeting with Charlie's mom until later tonight." He kisses me quick and hard. "I'm going to call my trainer. Find a way out of this morning's session."

"What about tomorrow's game?"

"Tomorrow's game is tomorrow." His gaze brightens in my direction. "But I need *you* all today and tonight." He pauses. "How about spending as much time as possible in bed before Charlie wakes up, then spending the day all together and going to dinner tonight?"

"And afterwards?" My chest tightens, filled with tendrils of fear. "Are we just going to give up Charlie? Let Deborah take her back to New York or wherever?"

Sevin stares. "Not without a fight. Definitely not without her father. And I don't need any paternity test to confirm it. *I know.* Charlie's my daughter...no matter who Finley has been to her. And I'm not letting her go yet."

The grip around my throat loosens with his words, and I tilt my head to him, my lips tugging upward as I gaze into his gorgeous face. "As long as the dinner is some type of noodle. I'm partial to Kung Pao."

"Kitten." Sevin sits up in bed. "You can eat whatever the hell you'd like. As long as you know that *I'll* be eating whatever I like the second we get back."

I perk up. "You've got a deal."

The words are no sooner out of my mouth before the penthouse intercom buzzes, breaking my momentary nirvana. I glance around the spacious room.

I have no idea where most of my belongings are. My guess: They're still in the living room.

But the buzzing doesn't stop, and within seconds, Sevin reaches for his discarded jeans, picking them off the floor and placing them on. He kisses me quickly, heading out to the living room, his voice the poster child for impatience when he picks up the intercom, his words a hushed snap around the corner.

"It's six o'clock in the morning. This better be important, Hank."

I want to answer that it can't possibly be. But I let Sevin talk.

The impatient tones turn into panicked ones, and though I can't hear the entire conversation, I recognize the alarm in it. A few short seconds later, Sevin's footsteps come marching around the corner.

The furrow in his dark brows deepens as he appears in the bedroom doorway, his face carved with confusion. But it's not the tone of Sevin's voice that scares me or his eerie silence right after. It's the look of terror teeming in those dark green eyes.

He looks up.

"That was Hank buzzing in."

I sit forward, gripping the sheets to my chest. "We made too much noise last night, didn't we? Dammit."

"No." Sevin shakes his head, barely able to get the words out. His speech is gritty, his teeth grinding together. "He noticed someone leaving the building about an hour ago. He had just left the desk for a minute, he said." Sevin exhales, a sharp huff that leaves his lungs in a rush. He pushes one hand through his hair. "A little girl."

He steps forward, his body so hunched I fear he might fall forward. His eyes are pained when they clash with mine.

"And I just checked the spare bedroom. And she's not there."

"What...?" I choke on my own voice. "You mean, Charlie's not...?"

"Charlie's not there." Sevin interrupts. "I think... I think that Charlie just ran away."

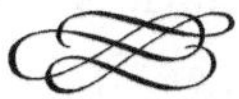

CHAPTER 24

EVIN

Sunday

I've never felt sheer terror in all of my life.

Until the second I realize Charlie is missing.

All bets are off the minute I start breathing again after my convo with Hank, and I call in my re-enforcements, my feet nearly boring a hole in the hardwood as I pace the length of my penthouse.

It's time.

I know it's time. It's *past* time.

And maybe I waited too late.

It's time to reveal my secret to *all* of the people who care about me. *As in everything.*

The press will spill it all, anyway.

Might as well beat them to the punch.

To be honest, beaten and punched is exactly how I feel right now. At least, until the women I care about come back.

Emily is the first. She retreats to my built-for-seven bathroom, quickly showering and dressing in her leftover clothes from Arizona, taking her discarded suitcase in with her. Twenty minutes later, she reappears, draped sexily in a pair of jeans and a white tight t-shirt, her hair loose—a departure from her more demure business skirt suits.

But as for the second, much tinier, much younger little woman?

Well, she's still missing.

And even though I'm ecstatic seeing Emily's gorgeous face, I kick myself with the knowledge that if this were any other day, I'd be able to sweep her into my arms, dig my hands into that shiny hair and kiss the hell out of her.

But this isn't any normal day.

This is Hell.

And Emily can tell. She approaches me, wrapping her arms around me, as she pulls me in for a quick hug. Her lips brush the edge of my jaw.

"I'm so fucking sorry."

I exhale, rubbing a hand over my forehead. "I know you are. I am, too. But there's nothing for you to be sorry about, kitten. This wasn't your fault."

"Isn't it?" Her voice is soft, and the guilt is written in her pretty face. Her hazel eyes fill with unshed tears, and she turns away, her small nose pointed towards the Chicago horizon outside of my living room windows. She sniffs. "If I weren't here, distracting you…"

I extend a hand towards her, grabbing her wrist. "Don't."

"I should have been focused on doing my job. And I wasn't." Her footsteps are stilted as I tug her towards me. "I dropped the ball."

"*I* dropped the ball," I correct.

"But this wasn't your job. I'm the professional here." Her loose hair hangs in waves, and she threads her fingers through it, tugging at the roots. "You and Charlie and this case are my responsibility. Not yours."

"Isn't it, though?" My eyes narrow at her furrowed face, and I can't hold back the rage that heats under my skin. "Charlie is my responsibility. She's… I'm…" I can't even say it.

Can't even admit what I've known all along.

From the moment I saw Charlie's face outside my penthouse apartment. From the second I took in her pine-green eyes and sandy hair and stone-faced resemblance.

Before she'd even revealed her stringent love of baseball, I'd known.

Known that she was mine.

My daughter.

There was no DNA test needed. Charlie Jett was my child. And more than anyone else on Earth, even Emily, it was my responsibility to get her back.

I'm still stuck, stumbling over my explanations to Emily when my penthouse door swings open.

Naomi bursts through the doorway, brown bob pinned off her shoulders, her eyes wide behind her usual spectacles, as she comes storming through, her head on a swivel.

"Where is she?" She demands. "Charlie!" She calls out. "Charlie!"

"Nome." Her name is stern on my lips. "I already told you: She's not here. Hank showed us the videotape." I swallow roughly, the gulp going down like sandpaper. "She took off."

"Dammit." Her perpetually red nails gather under her bottom lip, ready to be bitten into oblivion.

My assistant's clearly been around me too much. Because her movements mimic mine as she stalks back and forth, her feet pitter-pattering quickly across the dark cherry hardwood floors.

She glances up at me. "Deborah is on her way here. You know that, right?"

"Yes, I was aware the first *thousand* times you told me before, Nome. I didn't expect this."

Emily steps forward. "It was my fault, really, Naomi. I, uh…" Her gaze peruses my body before flitting back to my nervous assistant. "I distracted Sevin last night." Her voice lowers. "And this morning."

"Oh." Naomi's eyes circle like teacup saucers, and just like the organized machine she is, she starts spouting solutions, her passionate mind working a way out of this issue. "Okay, okay, let's brainstorm here. This is Chicago. It's a big city. A new one for Charlie. There's only so many places an eight-year old could go."

"Yeah," I sigh. "Like anywhere. You don't know what's she capable of, Nome. That grasshopper is one tough cookie."

"Tough enough to handle the Windy City?"

I stare. "Tougher. She can do anything she puts her mind to. Whatever she's putting her mind to right now. I'm sure our grasshopper is on some mission." I straighten, sticking my hands on my hips. "I just have no idea what that mission is."

"Huh." Naomi huffs, beginning her torture on one perfect nail. "Like father, like daughter."

I want to respond to that. But then the apartment door opens again, and in comes Sawyer, messy dark strands all over his head, his beard full-blown as he scratches it, his stare flitting everywhere around the penthouse.

"Where is he? Who the fuck do I have to kill?"

"Oh, look," Naomi comments dryly, one finger fiddling with her glasses. "It's the infamous Neanderthal coming to save the day."

"Sawyer," I interject before my teammate can start swinging on furniture. "Calm down. Charlie wasn't kidnapped." I blow out a breath, struggling to keep the words from shaking. "She ran away."

Sawyer's eyes bulge out of his chiseled face. "She ran away?"

"Or rather snuck away. Slipped out the door and down the stairs before taking off."

Sawyer's brow knits, forming a "V" on his face. "So why haven't we called the cops?"

Naomi jumps in. "Because we're not freaking crazy, Caveman.

Even Chicago PD is on the paparazzi's payroll. One whiff of this and the press will go to town on Sevin, Charlie and the whole sordid blackmail ordeal."

Sawyer leans against the wall, sizing Naomi up. "You mean you think that crazy Deborah chick will still pursue this insane case against Sevin? Jeez, this woman has balls the size of the Millennium Park bean." He crosses his arms. "Sevin called me this morning. *Told me everything.* And if I had been back in the penthouse instead of spending the night in some jersey-chaser's pink, fluffed mattress, I might have been able to talk reason into him. *Seriously.* I'm more experienced with groupies than Sterling will ever be."

"Ah, and you just wanted to dispense some advice, Mr. Groupie Guru?" Naomi questions.

"Of course." He turns to me. "I mean, we all know this Deborah woman's claims are complete bullshit..." The room falls silent. "Well, aren't they?"

His accusations hit the floor with a dull thud, as no one says anything. Blue eyes disbelieving, his stare falls on every sullen face around him, his frown deepening.

I don't know how to break it to him. How to confess.

How to tell one of my best friends since college that the nights of partying with Playboy Bunnies would soon be replaced by Bugs Bunny ones. And that the toys I'd be talking about in the near future would be the PG-kind.

I step forward. "Um, Saw..."

The second baseman raises his hand, his blue eyes squeezing in pain as he backs away. "Oh, no. No, no, no. Don't tell me, Sterling. Tell me it isn't true." He opens his eyes again, and this time his stare is softer, almost tender on the gentle giant. "Are you—Are you trying to say that you're actually a father, Sevin?"

Those few seconds before I answer are the longest of my life. I take a breath tainted with fire. It burns my chest going down. But I'm stronger than the fire.

I know that now. Because of Emily.

Because of Charlie.

I lift my chin, my stare steady. "Yeah, Saw. I am. I'm a father."

It's my first time saying the words. It's my first time admitting it to myself.

There's no doubt anymore in my mind…

Charlie is mine. My daughter.

Sawyer pauses, his gaze perusing mine then Naomi's and Emily's before swinging back. His eyebrows arch over his forehead. And then he walks forward, arms outstretched.

"Why the hell didn't you tell me, man?" He beckons. "Give me a goddamned hug, for fuck's sake."

I snort on a small laugh, wrapping my arms for a bro-hug around the muscular bear of a man. He chuckles, low and heartily, nearly picking me up off my feet.

Clapping his hand on my back, he grips hard before letting go, taking a step back to survey my face.

"Congrat-fucking-lations, Sterling."

I shake my head, my hand still wrapped in his. "I don't think anyone can confidently call me Sterling again."

He scoffs, looking at me with eyes anew, a different appreciation shining through them. "Who are you telling? Looks like that old Sterling is dead."

I nod. Because he is.

And for once, I'm not sad to see him go.

Sawyer grins. "We'll give him a proper burial when this is all over. But for now? Let's just focus on getting your kid back safely, huh?"

I let his hand go, slapping his shoulder. "Sounds like the best advice you've given me in a long time." I glance at Naomi and Emily's faces in the background—now more fortified than ever before. "Let's go."

* * *

EMILY

We all should be preparing for a trip back to Arizona. We all have careers to protect.

But Charlie comes first.

Minutes after Sawyer and Sevin have their sentimental bros face-off, the four of us take off, scouring the city, covering every inch of sidewalk we can find. Every subway. Every bus station.

Every inch of space in the wide Windy City.

I've never circled Chicago so fast.

The early spring weather is cloudy, thunderstorms on the horizon—half-cold, half-warm. We search under a Chicago sky as sullen as our moods, and a sheet of fog falls over the cemented sidewalks and buildings like the soft prelude to a sentimental symphony.

Only there's nothing sentimental about the Chicago crowds.

The noise-filled streets of downtown are alive with early spring and incoming baseball fever. People in brightly colored summer outfits swarm around the plazas and infamous Cloud Gate bean, filling the streets with color and even when we split up into two's—Sevin and me, Sawyer and Naomi, the ground still feels too large to cover.

My walking shoes are run-through, feet killing me by the time Sevin and I hail a taxi.

I relish in the momentary relief as we settle into the yellow taxi's back seat.

The air is vibrating with lively activity. Outside my window, I take notice of a slew of walking Chicago Cougars caps, and I glance over at Sevin, finding his handsome face furrowed with utter frustration.

I place my hand on his knee, squeezing tight.

"You alright?"

"If 'alright' means 'losing my mind,' then yeah, I'm alright." His smile is sad. "How are you?"

"Hanging in there." I clamp my fingers. "More worried about you. More worried about Charlie."

"I know." His face is half-hidden by his Cougars baseball cap as he stares out of the taxi's windshield, and I fight the urge to take his hat off. To get him to look at me. To get a glimpse of those green eyes and reassure him. He places his hand over mine. "I am, too. Deborah," he pronounces her name like a curse, "Charlie's mom is on her way back from New York, Kayla in tow. And I don't know what I'm going to say to her. I don't know how to tell her… I've lost our child."

"I don't think a woman who *abandoned* her child should be in the position to judge anyone. And I don't think you should judge yourself." I offer up a watery smile, biting into my bottom lip. "I've done enough judging you in the past for the both of us. And we could use a break."

"A break…" he muses, jaw ticking as he considers his words. *Tick. Tick. Tick.* "I'm sure a break is exactly what Charlie was trying to get when she took off." He hesitates, and even with the flurry of Chicago city-traffic outside our windows, the taxi air hums, the silence heavy enough to cut with a knife. Sevin lets out a ragged breath that I feel in my soul. He doesn't look at me. "She knows, doesn't she? She must have heard us talking last night. Before she… Before we…"

"Don't," I interrupt, hand tracing his knee. "Don't do that."

"Do what?"

"Play the blame game anymore. It doesn't help. Sevin," I lick my lips, needing to say this. "You are miles away from the man I first met, so don't pretend you aren't. You're a good dad. And you have a good daughter. And Charlie's strong. A complete trooper. *Like you.*"

I move closer. "Wherever she is, I am sure our little soldier is just fine. And we are absolutely, positively going to find her." I lean in, peeking under his protective cap. "*We will.* We're making the right choice, heading back to the apartment building. *Seriously.*

Charlie's probably back in front of the apartment as we speak, secretly scolding us for 'breaking up the team.'"

I notice Sevin smile, a shy curve carving itself on his gorgeous face. His head bows. "Yeah, I almost forgot. 'The team of ants.'"

I smile, thinking of the eight-year old. "Amazing, isn't it? We actually wound up 'Following the Leader' just like she said. Except she's the one doing the leading, and we're just trying to keep up. She's a natural one, you know..."

Sevin turns to look at me. "A natural what?"

"Leader. She follows the beat of her own drum. She's certainly better at it than I was at that age. Smart. Resolved. Full of spunk. Head of the pack..." I shake my head at myself. "That's Charlie. A perfect Emagine."

"Emagine?"

"My grandmother." I answer, staring at the sea of people outside our windows, wondering if one of them is Charlie. I exhale. "A woman who followed her own rules. And knew when to break them."

Sevin's thumb caresses over my skin, circling my knuckles. "Guessing your grandmother Emagine was a 'queen bee,' then?"

I laugh. "She was *the* 'queen bee.' She turned calamity into calm. Anarchy into order. She was..." My eyes water thinking of her. "Amazing."

"Like grandmother, like granddaughter, I see. A veritable force. Agent of chaos."

There it is. That notion of chaos.

I realize it was in my grandmother Emagine and all around her. The same chaos is in Charlie, too. And even me.

But I'd been too afraid of embracing it. Too afraid to lose myself to it. And now I can't think of any other way of living.

Especially when our cabbie slows to a stop by our apartment building, giving us a peek of what's around the corner...

Pure pandemonium.

There's a gaggle of cops surrounding the doorway to the

luxury Millennium Gardens apartment building, flanking a sea of photogs, cameras poised.

There's no doubt they're there for Sevin; they call out his name to any male who exits.

And two weeks ago, this would have freaked the hell out of me, thrown a wrench into my plans.

But two weeks ago, I was a woman who couldn't function without a plan. And now? I was coming closer to being the woman Violet Keats was. A woman like my grandmother.

A woman Ben encouraged me to be.

Gazing at the quietly clamoring paparazzi, I realize I can slip into chaos. Drown in it.

Or I can swim in it.

The swimming part sounds a hell of a lot better than drowning and before the cabbie can put the taxi in Park, I'm already ordering him to take off, handing him the address from the card in my wallet before Sevin can make a move.

The sports superstar gazes at me, green eyes ablaze. His voice is a low growl inside the car, rumbling soft.

"Em, what the hell are you doing? We just can't run away. We've got Charlie to find remember. I don't give a damn about those paparazzi right now."

"I don't either. But I have a plan. If we're going to get Charlie back and get her to stay, then we need to do something we're both familiar with. Something makes sense. We need to work as a team."

"I thought we were already doing that."

I shake my head. "Not without the other ants. And I'm taking us back to the anthill."

CHAPTER 25

*S*EVIN

Arriving to Stephan Knight's infamous Chicago Firm domain is one thing.

Sneaking in is another.

The Firm's offices are tucked away, barely visible from the street. Enfolded in the same building as an old Chicago cinema, there's nothing ostentatious about the place where Stephan Knight and his crew solve most of the city elite's scandals, and as Emily and I walk the short gray block from the cab to the entrance, I can feel the anticipation tugging at me from the inside out.

So many secrets to let go of. So little time.

Two weeks ago, I was a broken man not open to sharing either. But with Emily's hand wrapped in mine, I know I'm more of a "man" than I've ever been.

As a famous baseball player, I'd been caught in a perpetual boyhood, a slave to life's choices. As a dad, I'm making decisions.

Decisions that could cost me my career. Decisions that could obliterate everything I once thought I cared about.

I tug on Emily's arm, just as she stops on the sidewalk, her keycard posed over a clandestine sensor. I hold her tight.

"Are we sure you want to do this?"

The clouds from the Chicago sky are in her eyes, but she nods. "I want to do this. I have to do this. It's going to be okay."

I lift a brow. "Okay, and if Stephan fires you? I know what this job means to you. And I don't want to be the reason you screw it up. Not even now."

The city sky deepens, darkens over us even now as spring thunderclouds roll in.

With the cinema awning hovering over us in hues of dusty red and white—remnants of an old Chicago past, I can make out the new Emily in front of me, the fire in her hazel irises. A flame and determination swirls in their amber depths that makes me damn proud to be at her side.

To see the transformation of the woman once too timid to step out of her own rules.

I'm in awe of her. Especially when she squeezes my hand.

She smiles. "Someone once told me to think about career suicide. To know the path that could lead me down to it is not guaranteed. But someone also told me to read the signs. To understand when the universe is pointing me to roads that lead to somewhere great." Her eyes water. "And this road led us here."

She points at the sky. Or rather she points at the red letters above our heads, printed atop the cinema.

The featured film on the marquee sign is "The Game Plan," a sports film from years ago I vaguely remember with Dwayne 'The Rock' Johnson. But I can't recall it all.

Luckily, Emily does it for me.

"It's a movie about an arrogant playboy star who changes his ways when his daughter comes into his life."

"And is that arrogant playboy star supposed to be me?"

"There are striking similarities."

"And you expect me to be any less arrogant by pointing out the similarities between me and Dwayne 'The Rock' Johnson?"

I tug her into me, brushing my lips against hers at the thought of how lucky I am to have found her. Even amidst all the madness.

A few minutes later, I find myself alone in an elevator with Emily for the second time since I've met her.

Only this time we're entering and leaving together.

Our lives have come full circle. And now the only piece to complete it is finding Charlie. Something I know we're close to doing when we step out of the creaking Firm elevator to the 'team of ants' waiting for us on the other side.

Sawyer grins the second the doors part, his smile wide underneath his beard. "Bout time you two showed up. Everyone came after you called. They're waiting in the office."

Emily and I move forward. As one. Hand in hand.

Breaking every rule we set for ourselves. Setting fire to our old expectations.

And it feels good as hell.

Emily introduces me to her own 'teammates,' firm employees, Ben, Bowen and Sabrina who welcome us with warmth. Ben, in particular, smiles at the hand-holding between us, nudging near Emily.

Kayla and Stephan will be the last two firm employees to be present, and with one on her way and the other in the dark, we begin our impromptu meeting.

Each member of our little friend group turned family, including Naomi, takes a seat at the long oak table at the center of the offices, and one by one, we all fall silent, a silent anxiety squeezing the air out of the room as we prepare to handle our biggest problem yet.

Emily stays standing, looking regal, positively royal, her dark hair tumbling down her shoulders. She clears her throat. "Thank you all for showing up. You guys have no idea how much we appreciate it." She pauses, still holding my hand. I kiss the back of her knuckles.

"We know you all could get fired for even *considering* what we're asking you to do. But this isn't about keeping and upholding The Firm's reputation anymore. *This is about Charlie.* We need to make sure she's brought home as safely as possible and in order to do that, we're going to need to break some firm rules. And maybe even some of our own. Naomi?"

My assistant, ready as always, stands to her feet next. All eyes, especially Sawyer's, land on her pretty face, captivated by her commanding presence. The tiny powerhouse spreads her hands, talking quickly, her voice echoing in the open room.

"First things first: We need to figure out how to mitigate the story first. Figure out how to contain it. A salacious one like Sevin Smith's daughter running away can spread like wildfire when unchecked, and it's our job as the team on this case to keep the fire in one place. Make sure the other publications don't pick the rumors up as well. We wouldn't want to do this magazine any favors by adding any fuel to their fire." She pauses. "Does everyone get what I'm saying?"

The table answers with a hushed chorus of a few "sure's" and Naomi keeps speaking, addressing the room.

"That means keeping that 'cool' The Firm is so famous for."

"Of course."

"That means no speaking to the public. No answering questions." She stands taller. "And absolutely no scandals to add gasoline to this inferno. This one story's enough. That means nothing that will draw the attention of law enforcement. Nothing that would make The Firm seem sleazy. Nothing that the Pope wouldn't approve of. If the Dalai Lama wouldn't do it, neither should you. At least until..." She trails off ominously.

"Until what?" Sawyer's the first to speak.

"Or..." she drawls knowingly. "We can address the rumors head-on. Face the fire. See if we can test the heat." She sighs as the room says nothing in return. "Do you need me to sketch you a map of what I'm trying to say, Saw?"

I interject. "Thanks, professor, but I have a feeling no more markers or crayons will be needed to make your next point."

Naomi wets the edge of her red bottom lip, the skin tender from the nail-chewing. She drops her hand. "We need to take our time to process this new news."

"Oh yeah?" Sawyer grumbles, scratching his beard. "Tell that to the ten paparazzi stationed outside Sevin's apartment at this very moment. Because they certainly won't give us time. I, uh, don't mean to add another bucket of water to the rain on this shit-parade. More than what's already been added." His dilated pupils bounce from my face to Naomi's. "But we might want to consider who tipped the press off in the first place. And we might want to do it now. Before Sevin and I have to get on a plane back to Arizona tomorrow."

"There won't be a flight back to Arizona. Not if I can help it." My heart does a double-tap in my chest. I cup the brim of my baseball cap, my eyes lifting to Naomi once more.

And I know where I stand. Finally.

As with Emily, I have to make a decision.

Love or career.

Making a decision, knowing I can't have both, has never been easier. And I face my two best friends, my gaze steering between both the beard and glasses on either, standing firmly inside of my choice.

"I admit: I should have told you. One of you, at least. But Nome, I'm not going back to Arizona for tomorrow's game. Not now. Not with Charlie missing." I manage to finish. "No matter what it could mean."

Naomi lifts one finger to her spectacles. "Are you serious?"

"As a fucking heart attack."

"I hate to be a bitch right now, Sev…but a heart attack is exactly what your trainer and coach will have, if you don't show up for tomorrow's game against the Fever. And if I didn't love you so damn much…" She slaps my arms, smirking. "I'd tell you that breaking the news to those guys would cost you extra. You don't pay me enough to start whacking people."

I glare over at my rightfully mouthy assistant, resisting a smile. "Really? Because every time Sawyer's near, you threaten his life."

She smiles. "That's because I'd do that job *for free.*"

I grunt, trying to push the negative thoughts away, the notion that, right now, paparazzi are clamoring outside my apartment.

All because of my secrets.

I was still holding onto a few from some of the most important people in my life.

Having the confidence of your team was priority number one. A lesson I learned from baseball.

Keeping secrets from them was worse than lying to your own parents, and once trust was lost, it could ruin your position on a team.

Like me.

I sigh into my hand, rubbing my palm across my lips. Expelling a ragged breath as I stand to my feet, unable to sit any longer, I notice Naomi's eyes follow, her frown deepening with every second that I don't speak.

I spin on my heel to face her before I lose my nerve.

"And you won't have to look much further for whoever tipped off the press to Charlie's disappearance. Because the person responsible is right here." I take a deep breath, letting it out. "The person you're looking for is me."

The room rumbles with surprise. Only the shock isn't at me.

In fact, the rumbling isn't coming from the rest of the others looking at me. No. The rumbling comes from the sound of The Firm's elevator stopping just outside the oval room's door.

And through the glass walls, I can see exactly who's coming out of the lift onto our floor without hesitation.

Not that she's ever hesitated at anything.

Not even in these last nine years.

Pushing away from the table, I make a beeline for the exit door.

The sounds of my own heart beating shoves out all sense from my overworked mind. Because even reason isn't enough to calm me down.

Several sets of eyes settle on me as I clamp a fist at my side, bottom lip twisting as I come to a stop steps away from where Kayla and Stephan stand.

But it's not the two firm employees who have my attention.

It's the blonde behind them who does. And I watch with wary eyes as the sophisticated socialite's brown irises rest on my body, taking me in.

She hasn't changed in almost a decade. Except for her eyes.

The pair before me are redder than they've ever been. Fresh with tears. And with one timid step forward and one word, she pushes me back into my sordid past, leaving me gasping for air, the time travel sapping my body of all breath as I blink to fix my vision.

But it's not imaginary. She's real.

I can tell because it's *my* name coming off her usual full lips. She mouths it softly.

"Sevin."

I grip the fist at my side harder, my words gritty, responding to her unexpected greeting with nothing but disbelief. I say her name back.

"Kimmy."

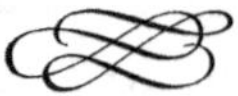

CHAPTER 26

MILY

Sunday

I *hate* everything about this woman. And I've never met her.

I hate her gorgeous face. Her sly smile. I hate how she walks across the hallway in The Firm office as if she owns it. And I hate that the adoring world allows it.

In fact, I don't think there's a thing about this woman I don't hate.

Especially the fact that she's here.

I'm not supposed to give a shit. But I do.

And I wish I could help it.

I'm also not supposed to be like one of those insecure women, wishing she could hold onto her man. And if anyone asks, this is water in the cup that Ben is now pouring me, not vodka.

I stare into the same six ounces of clear liquid as Kayla, Stephan, Sevin and Kimmy Wallace disappear behind Stephan's solid office door.

I glance again at the wood, as if the very act will make Sevin walk through it.

Anger makes me take another gulp of my now-lukewarm

liquor and as the oval room begins buzzing around me—Naomi, Sawyer, Bowen and Sabrina speaking in hushed whispers, the wait is killing me to find out what the hell is going on.

What the hell are they talking about?

I'm guessing Charlie. Then why was Kimmy staring at Sevin like that?

The question of what Sevin is doing behind those doors with his ex won't leave me alone. But neither will Ben.

He sidles up beside me against the wall, his breath puffing on the back of my shoulders as he leans in, his voice a sharp hiss.

He lowers his own Solo cup and turns.

"You think Kimmy came to get him back?"

"Say it a little louder, Ben. Don't think the people living down the block heard you. You don't even need a bullhorn at this point."

"I'm sure one couldn't hurt right now, you know? This sort of scandal needs an announcement. 'Caution,'" he motions in the air. "'*Child-abandoning bitch on the prowl.*' The headline would sell papers for days."

"She sounds like the type who wouldn't mind. As long as her face was on the front…"

And I know I'm being petty. I know I'm being insecure.

I know I should be leaning on Ben—to complain, to cry or maybe even do both—instead of taking jabs at the woman Sevin once loved.

But truth is: I guess it's because I'm scared. Because funnily enough, my upstairs neighbor, distraction he is and all, is the only man who's made me feel something—anything—since I can remember.

And I wasn't about to lose him or his daughter.

At least, not yet.

I can't tell if Ben is pulling me back from the emotional ledge. Or pushing me to it.

My closest co-worker reads my thoughts as always, chiming in before I can choke down another swallow of vodka, his words low.

"You know Sevin cares about you now, don't you?" He waits but I don't respond, still staring into the cup of vodka in my hands. I say nothing. "I've never seen a man look at anyone the way he looked at you. Sort of the way I look at Stephan when he's not watching. But I digress."

Ben huffs, twirling his Solo cop, hovering near. He nudges my arm. "The man looks at you like he's in love with you…which means he is. I heard Naomi and Sawyer speaking earlier, and it was clear. You've made Sevin fall for you. Made his daughter want to be like you. This isn't a Jason situation; you don't walk away from this one. And if you do…" He shakes his head, standing firm. "It's not without a hell of a fight. I mean, I've seen you on that MyNeighbor app initiating a few 'play ones' with Sevin, so I know you're capable of it."

The MyNeighbor app.

I'd forgotten all about it.

Since the last time I'd spoken on it with Sevin, I haven't used it. Not for days.

I was thinking about needing a team, almost forgetting one of the most important ones.

I fish inside my back jean pocket, finding my cell. Swiping up on the app, I open it to the public message forum and start typing to my neighbors immediately.

Go team.

* * *

SEVIN

I'm half the man I can be without my team.

Without Sawyer and Naomi and Emily beside me. Not to mention Charlie.

The past catches up with me. From the second I sit down with Kimmy.

It all comes rushing back in a flurry of memories I'd rather forget, and, alone, I face the demons that drag me back to nine years ago. Back to college.

Back to the night that changed my life forever. And the people who changed it.

Draft night was one for the history books. But the night before was a shitshow. And I remember it like it was yesterday.

"Fuck, I could use a blowjob right now."

"I hate it when you tell me things like that, Sawyer. It's as if your cock is my responsibility."

"It is, when you're my wingman." He swings an arm over my shoulder, pulling me close. *"Tatiana has me in blue-ball hell. Sarah only gives hand-jobs. Natalia's been teasing me for months, and if I don't get my dick wet at this party, I swear: I'm humping one of you before the night is over."*

"If this act comes down to a vote, I vote for Lenny. Most of the time, he's a walking prick anyway."

Sawyer laughs. "What the hell are you doing over here? Trying to recover from last night? I heard you had three sorority sisters clinging to your bedroom curtains last night." He leans in as if telling a secret. As if he were capable of that. His voice is still too loud.

"I heard Victoria Salvatore called first dibs on you in her sorority tonight. Janice Planko brought condoms with your name Sharpie-ed on them. And the best part..." He chuckles beside me. "Vivian Green isn't wearing any underwear. Told her roommate that's easy access for when she takes you into the bathroom. Now, what do you think of that?"

I want to say I don't think shit of that. I want to say that Vivian Green can slip her thong back on. That I'm waiting for someone else.

But the rounded shape of his drunken eyes tells me that I can't. Every teammate's eyes on me tells me that I can't.

Not now. Not on the night before the Major League draft.

Because those eyes tell me I'm the team captain. Tell me I'm a hero.

Those eyes tell me to be the 'Sterling Silvered Cock' they call me. They tell me to be the number one draft pick I'm sure to be picked in t-minus ten hours.

And I've never said no to those eyes before. Until now.

I shake my head. "Well, then you tell Vivian Green to re-think the bathroom idea." I grin. "I'm just as good in the kitchen."

Sawyer slaps me on the back, ever the proud purveyor of pussy. But as soon as he leaves, the grin slips from my face replaced with a frown, just as sorority princess Victoria "Very Good Head" Salvatore slides in his abandoned space, her cherry-glossed lips spread wide.

She glances up at me and smiles.

I fight the urge to straighten against the wall, lifting my cup. "Victoria."

"Vicky," she corrects. "You know, you never did call me by my nick-name, Mr. Baseball Big Shot. And now it's almost too late since you'll be a big superstar come tomorrow. Has a girl wondering if maybe she waited too long to get, uh, acquainted with you."

She touches my collar. The skin there is hot, heated from staring in anger at the door, and if this were a few months ago, I'd tell her to move those fingers lower.

If only my heart didn't wish she were someone else. Someone with whom I plan on leaving all of this behind come tomorrow night.

It's hard to keep Kimmy off every single thought in my mind. But I try.

"It really is a shame we didn't get to know each better, Vicky." I shrug. "Better luck next lifetime."

"Well, who says we can't make the most out of tonight? My calendar is free. I've got a clean set of sheets at home with your name on them, and if you're lucky..." She trails off, and it looks like I'm going to be. "You can put something other than your name on them, in the form of a naked me."

She flicks dark hair over her shoulder, daring me with her eyes.

I can't will my cock to react, even when I want it to.

And even as Vicky's teasing turns to whispers, even as she pushes her breasts against my chest and hisses seductively in my ear, her fingers playing along the hair at my nape, I can't find the will to get excited.

Leaving behind this version of Sevin Smith is a million times harder than I thought it would be, and I'm seconds away, inches really, from stepping out of Victoria's grasp when the famed sorority house BJ Queen plants me against the wall, grabbing my face.

With more intensity than a second inning heater, she plants those talked-about lips against me, plunging her tongue deep, stealing every ounce of my breath away. My body stiffens.

Tasting of dark cherries and unbelievable fuckability, Victoria angles her mouth against mine, lining her body along my length, doing what she does best.

And I know this kiss should be enough. She should be enough.

Hell, this life should be enough.

But it never has been. Or I wouldn't be leaving it.

I prepare to tell Vicky exactly this when I finally break the kiss, taking that long-awaited step back. But the sensation of eyes on my skin stops everything, and I turn towards the door to find Kimmy standing there, watching me, her brown eyes wide with shock.

But then again, so are mine. Especially when I see who she's with.

My roommate and best friend Finley saunters in through the door I've grown to hate, wrapped around her arm. As if he belongs there.

Her blonde hair loose around her shoulders, Kimmy's wearing the smile that I normally put on her face and a mini-skirt.

The number-one draft pick doesn't give a shit. Neither does the man they call "Sterling Silvered Cock."

But the nineteen-year old baseball player who's supposed to be running away with his girlfriend sure as hell does.

And while my pride tries to decide between which version he will be in the next few seconds, I grit my teeth and decide for him.

Nine entire years later, I'm still deciding for that nineteen-year old. Especially when Kayla stops talking, finishing her excuse.

"I had to keep my client's privacy foremost as her PR agent. I never meant to lie to you, Sevin." The brunette meets my eye.

"Kimmy was in the middle of a public relations nightmare with her divorce from her husband. The custody battle was still in the air, and to protect Charlie, she sent her to the only other man on the earth she felt she could trust."

I don't look at Kimmy, fighting to rein in the rage coursing its way through my veins. I barely succeed. "I'm guessing that man was me."

"Kimmy talked to Charlie for years about you, sharing you as her special friend. She knew you'd do the right thing, taking in Charlie, but we needed to keep it a secret. Hence, the alias and 'blackmail scandal.' Sevin," Kayla's voice lowers, settling in the air like a weight. "If we thought there was any other way to protect Charlie, we would have done it. We never thought it would turn out this way. Never thought Charlie would find out and run."

"Clearly, Kayla, you underestimate your own client. Fortunately, I do not. I've already called the cops." I cross my arms. "You see, I figured Kimmy was behind this. Especially when I found out Finley was Charlie's 'father.' And only one woman on earth would use a name like Deborah Jett. The only woman I know who would come up with an alias that's a mash of my favorite female artists from the seventies: Deborah Harry and Joan Jett... And yes, women made damn good rock music too. Even when I don't act like it."

"The press and police outside of my apartment are there because of me. And because I know Charlie and my mind is clear, I think I know exactly where Charlie is..."

I stand to my feet.

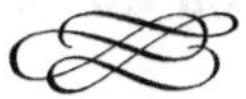

CHAPTER 27

MILY

Sunday

My taxi pulls up to my apartment building, leaving me hopping out of the back seat.

The rain has picked up, leaving the press and police scattering, and huddling in a hastily grabbed blazer, Chicago Cougars cap secured tight, I scramble inside and out of the Chicago rain and wind, making my way into Millennium Gardens.

I sigh once in the lobby, letting myself breathe.

Shaking the dampness from my bones, I inhale the warm central air for another twenty seconds before heading up to the elevator.

Once inside, I soak in the solace. But not before typing quickly back in the MyNeighbor app, my fingers moving quickly over the keys as I finish my last post.

I end with a period.

EMILY:

Thank you for your help, Miss Headley. And I promise next time I'll take out the trash a little sooner.

Gratefully yours,

Your neighbor, Emily

P.S. Thanks for always keeping on an eye on things in the building. It really helped this time. And I owe you one.

How's about dibs on the elevator?

IT's the only play I've got.

In a world full of chaos, I'm finally figuring out that life's not about plans anymore. It's about the plays you make.

The team you build around you. The signs you choose to see.

The nosy neighbor is just what I needed. Only I didn't see it before.

Overlooking the blessings in front of me have been a long time burden. But no longer.

Not going back to my apartment after finding out that Charlie ran away was a mistake. I see that now.

I'd changed into clothes from my suitcases at Sevin's, panicking about time. Never thinking things through.

Over thirty floors up, I pray that me and Mrs. Headley are right, and when I step outside of the opening elevator, I realize I might be when I hear a small voice cry out quietly behind me, stopping me in my tracks.

I spin.

For a second, I almost don't recognize her—the little girl. But there's no mistaking those big, beautiful green eyes, and as she walks towards me in her jeans and jersey-like t-shirt, a small smile hidden behind a curtain of sandy hair, I struggle not to gasp out loud.

She reaches her hand out for me to shake, a knowing look in her pine-colored irises. "Good morning, Emily. Nice to see you here today." Her tone is straight-laced, an attempt at sounding business-like.

I feel my eyes widen on my face. I grab her hand and shake it. "Charlie…" Her name is a sigh on my mouth. "What are you doing here?"

"I'm here for an appointment, of course." She gazes up at me like only an eight-year old could, seemingly questioning how I could ask something so simple. "Isn't that what people do at law places before they can see someone? They make an appointment?"

"Yes, they do." I glance around the hallway, hoping I can find some answers around the carpet. I shrug out of my coat. "But… you left the apartment. Alone this morning. Where'd you go?"

"I figured Felix needed milk for his stomach. Since he was so sick." She points at the fur ball on the floor. "But when I came back to Sevin's apartment, no one was there. So, I came back here. Where we first met. Looking for you. I think I need a lawyer."

"What for?"

"To fix my family. If Sevin's going to be my second dad, then we need to discuss some things. Starting right now."

I manage to smile through the tears. "You heard us in Sevin's apartment last night, didn't you?"

She shrugs. "Of course I did."

I pick Felix off the floor, wrapping the cat in one arm, and Charlie in the other. Leading both back to the elevator, I lick my dry lips, looking for words that won't get me in any more mischief than I'm already in.

"Um, Charlie, how *much* did you hear from me and Sevin last night? Hopefully not much…"

The eight-year old smiles. The elevator opens as we stand there in the hallway, and the resounding double doors part to reveal a pair of surprised green eyes just inside.

Just as gorgeous as Charlie's.

And I never get my fill of them—of looking at them. Sevin is so handsome it hurts.

Especially when he bends down towards Charlie, wrapping her in a hug. The motion is natural, fluid as if he's done this a million times before, and I know with every bone in my weepy body that Sevin will make the greatest "second father" on the planet.

In my eyes, he'll always be "first."

And I'm not the only who appears to know it.

Over the threshold to the elevator, Charlie swings her tiny arms around Sevin's neck, holding tight.

The gentle giant and his favorite grasshopper stay that way for several long seconds before finally parting, their identical pair of pine-like eyes coming face-to-face.

I bite my lip to keep the tears from flowing as Charlie pokes at Sevin's jaw.

"So, you're my dad, too, huh?"

Sevin blinks, his eyes glossy with unshed emotion. He nods at the little girl who, in another life, could be his twin, confirming what we should have all known since the beginning.

His jaw holds steady as she traces the lines of his face, and when he reaches up to trace hers, the tears in my eyes fall freely. I don't even try to hide the wet trails forming over my cheeks as I watch them, filled with joy, as they explore one another anew.

Friend to friend. Grasshopper to grown-up.

Father to daughter.

For the first time.

And I know that no career win could match this moment for the new Sevin. He stands to his feet, extending a hand to Charlie who takes it.

"How else do you think you became such a good softball player, huh, grasshopper? You inherited your skills from the best."

He presses the button for the elevator, calling the small lift. His gaze roving over to mine, he reaches for me, pulling me into their embrace, and the four of us—three freaks and one feline—head into the elevator, ready to face the music of what the future holds.

Only this time? With Charlie?

Sevin and I are marching to the beat of very different drums.

No Led Zeppelin. No Sheryl Crow.

Just love. Lots of it.

With a just hint of mischief and good ol' affection on the bass.

* * *

Monday

We never make it to Sevin's game the next day.

It's the first game (spring season or otherwise) the MVP misses in his nine year professional career, and not a tear is shed at the thought.

Well, maybe not many.

I do admit: A few tears leave my right eye. Especially after that last pitch.

I drop my batting helmet to the ground as I stumble out of the cage. My arms hurt from all the swinging, and I hand over my bat to Sevin, vision blinded as our fingers touch one another's in the exchange.

The gorgeous player smiles. "Too much wood for you, Miss Armand? I'm surprised."

I huff. "I told you: I don't like balls flying at my face. And the only time I'll make an exception is on a special night." I plant my hands on my hips. "After a *lot* of tequila. So, don't get any ideas."

Sevin leans forward, kissing my forehead, and I grin. The expression widens when Charlie steps forward, and, passing a nearby helmet, sends Sevin on his way to the gauntlet.

"It's your turn!" She shouts. "Good luck! But you won't be as good as me."

He winks before walking away.

The line of his body is perfect, poised as he heads inside the batting cage. I imagine it looked similarly when he walked away from Kimmy yesterday, leaving her tongue hanging, shock settling into her perfectly made-up face.

She deserved it.

Especially when she came to pick Charlie up at the apartment building.

The rain let up and the lines of press were back, bombarding her over every inch. Every Chicago paparazzo couldn't wait to rake the socialite over the coals about her crumbling marriage, and if it weren't for Sevin calling off the dogs, she would have never made it into Millennium Gardens.

Seems me calling the cops on Sevin so many times did him good.

He'd built a bond with Chicago's Finest, calling them in to shoo away the cameras.

The trade-off? One entire day more with Charlie at one of her favorite places on earth.

The batting cages.

In the offices of The Firm, we're all prepared for the inevitable onslaught of media attention that will come once Kimmy releases the news of Sevin's paternity to take the heat off her own "press mess."

But for the next twenty-four hours, we keep our focus on the tiny burgeoning softball star, and with my job surprisingly still intact *despite breaking the rules*, Stephan offers me the day off for my "hard work."

And I feel guilty. Because there's not a single thing "hard" about having fun with Charlie on her last day in the city.

Her eyes are glowing, bright as Sevin saunters up to the makeshift batting-cage base. The pitching machine kicks into gear, and with the city's most successful shortstop at bat, helmet on, the baseballs don't stand a chance.

The crack of his bat during his swing is loud—deafening. He sends the first pitch soaring, and Charlie cheers, her whoops almost as loud as my own.

We high-five, feeling the fever. The fever of watching one of the greats doing what he does best.

Playing the sport he loves.

I feel honored to be one of those who knows that's not all the Chicago superstar does best. And after he sends the tenth baseball flying into oblivion, he removes his helmet from his dark hair, sweat sticking the errant strands to his face as he flashes us a huge smile.

And we can't help but love him. Especially after he offers us his "best girls" a round of peanuts.

We head to the nearby concession stand, filling our arms and hands with the salty treats. Charlie dumps a whole set of them into her mouth, walking ahead, and outside of Chicago Cougar Park, in the shadow of the infamous Windy City stadium, the sun breaks through for the first time all day, slowly setting on the horizon.

It's hard not to watch it.

Chicago shows off, giving us its best hues of purple, pink and gold, and I know I've never felt more content than in this moment. Never knew love and trust and flying balls could make me feel the way I feel with these two people in my life.

I watch Charlie as she skips ahead, her mood light, despite her flight in the morning. I can feel the sadness on Sevin's skin as we amble the area.

"She'll be back before you know it. Kimmy can't keep her away."

"I know." He nods, not meeting my eye.

"Besides, her second dad is so much cooler than the first. I bet he can't even lift a pitch off the ground after all these years."

Sevin grins. "The only thing Finley's picked up in the past nine years is fifty pounds. Sad to say." His gait slows. "You know I don't hate the guy. I really don't. He saw what he wanted and went after it. And at the time, I thought that's what I wanted to, and now I realize all I wanted to do was win. And my ego couldn't take it."

I gaze at him, committing the lines of his face into my mind. He's so damn beautiful. I lean closer. "And now?"

"Now, I have what I want. And that's you and Charlie."

Without his usual baseball cap on, I can see the real Sevin. No longer hiding behind baseball or his buried emotions, today he's let me get a glimpse into something greater than his green eyes.

He's letting me into his soul.

Throwing an arm around me while gazing down, I know what he's going to say. But I press a finger to his lips instead.

"You don't have to tell me how much I mean to you. I no longer have to wonder. I *know* I do." I wrap an arm around his waist while walking, loving the feel of him. "But after this case, if you ever interfere with another job of mine, I can promise you won't be receiving any more 'jobs' from me." I glance up, my grin growing wide as I face him. "Got it?"

"I got it… Loud and unbelievably clear, Miss Armand. With only one condition."

"And what's that?"

"You wear those pair of Felix the Cat underwear hiding some-where in your drawers." He stares. "*And I know you have one.* Once the regular season starts, we're going to be responsible for the little despot, and I don't want that black fur ball to be the only pussy I'm allowed to scratch. Those are my rules."

"Rules were made for breaking," I comment.

"But not this one."

"I'll tell you what: I'll wear the Garfield the Cat ones next time. How about that? That way, when we're alone, you can have access to more than just one 'fat cat.'" I wink. "Deal?"

He stares, sealing our bond with a quick kiss. A promise of things to come. And I can't wait.

"You're on."

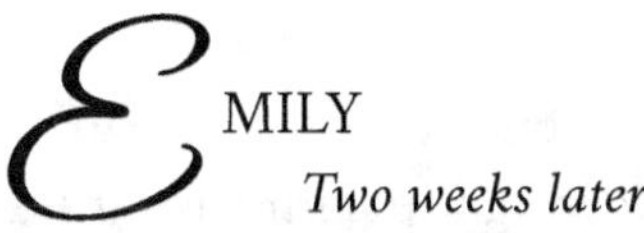

MILY

Two weeks later

Sevin was right.

I think my neighbors wait for me to arrive to the building elevator from my apartment floor so they can stack like Legos™.

Like a game of Tetris™, I squeeze my briefcase and a cup of the world's hottest coffee into my apartment building's elevator right before the heavy, silver-plated doors close.

Briefcase strap over my shoulder, phone in hand, caramel macchiato in the other, I try to swipe away from the trusty MyNeighbor app on my screen, where I've spent the last ten minutes complaining about the faulty stairs, and five floors later, after people have already started to pile on, a voice behind me in the elevator hisses over my shoulder.

I nearly give myself third degree burns as I jump.

"Ems!"

I somehow manage to not roll my eyes as I turn. "Nina." I squeeze out a stifled smile to the only other woman with me in the elevator. "Hi. Good morning."

"It is, isn't it?" The overly peppy neighbor living a few floors below inhales loudly as I attempt to juggle my entire life in my hands. "Sun is shining. Birds are singing. Or they will be once we get past this spring storm that's sweeping in tomorrow." She peers at me over a set of brown sunglasses that match the silky bob brushing her shoulders. "And I finally met that new neighbor of ours..."

I frown. "What new neighbor?"

Her small shoulders slump as she crosses her arms. "You know what new neighbor... The guy above you. Mr. Hotshot. That newly hot single dad. Or as you once called him 'the devil incarnate.'"

"Ah." I nod. "That one."

The one I'm now living with.

Slipping my phone into my briefcase, I take a premature sip of the macchiato that is still too hot. Swallowing the familiar burn, I try to hide the secret of being Sevin Smith's girlfriend on my face, rotating towards the elevator's buttons, my skin tingling at just the thought of him.

Just the thought of my sexy-as-hell boyfriend.

Until the elevator stops.

Mrs. Headley, our neighbor from downstairs, enters.

A customary scowl on her wizened face, she grunts—her usual greeting as she steps onto the small lift, her gray hair curled around her elf-like ears.

Even after our exchange that helped find Charlie, we're no closer than we were. But I do my neighborly duty, smiling sweetly as the older woman approaches.

I'm met with an even deeper scowl in return.

"Hi, Mrs. Headley." *Clearly, Nina never learns.*

The old woman grunts in response.

"Lovely weather we're...not going to be having." Nina's effort at making conversation with our miserly neighbor falls flat.

A few more floors later, and I am silently begging to be off this elevator, but my building's neighbors pile on and off until I'm eagerly shifting in my low high heels.

And the only topic each neighbor seems to be concerned about is Sevin.

The man whose bed I've been sleeping in every night.

With the regular season started, he doesn't get to join me in it as often as we'd both like.

But with no one but me to call the cops, the noise nuisance has made Sevin popular among the other tenants.

Only this time?

I'm the screamer.

My baseball-playing boyfriend and his newfound daughter are today's hot topic since the news broke. And inside the Lego™-like space, I'm forced to listen to the inane chatter all the way down.

Nina, of course, is first to kick off the conversation.

"I hear he's slated to be my MVP this year."

"I hear he's thinking of petitioning for a trade back to the New York Fever."

"I hear he's hung like a horse."

Only, the last statement comes from me…in my own head.

What could I say? The man was packing some serious size inside his boxer briefs—a fact I can't exactly share with the MyNeighbor app.

So, I'm only too relieved when my co-worker Ben, seemingly the only sane neighbor I have at the moment, walks in on the ninth floor, the smell of his slightly floral scent filling the air.

He nudges me. "How's my favorite new neighbor this morning?"

"Likely at risk of pissing Stephan off again. But what's new?" I elbow him lightly. "But how are you?"

"Oh no, we're back onto you, Miss Armand. Don't change the subject. I know that *someone* is very excited about her two favorite people coming into town today. I don't even know why you're going to work."

"Um, pretty much so Stephan doesn't fire me?"

"Huh. That's actually a good point."

I elbow his arm. "Relax. I don't plan on getting fired from The Firm any time soon, and Charlie's visitation is only for the weekend. That's only what her mother will allow."

A lie, if I ever heard one.

Kimmy has only been too eager to give Sevin more visitation days to celebrate her newly found freedom from her marriage to Finley. But for the meantime, keeping Charlie's life as normal as possible is priority number one.

At least, until Sevin gets joint custody.

I keep that little secret to myself and away from our little elevator audience. *Along with a few others...*

The Firm's newest client, Sawyer Kennedy, deserves our undivided attention (and privacy), and talking about his teammate and his daughter doesn't help.

The Lobby floor can't come fast enough as everyone continues speculating about Sevin. Even Ben.

I can't sprint out of that steel contraption fast enough. But just as I exit, I realize I've left my damn files for Stephan's meeting.

Turning the elevator back around to my floor, I'm almost there.

That is, until the lift stops on the fourteenth floor and in walks a face I haven't seen in thirteen days. A face I've been missing for what feels like forever.

Sevin smiles at me. And it's like it's the first time.

I try to hide the squeal that strangles out of my throat, but I'm too late. I'm full-on fan-girling like the rest of my building when he walks in.

He drops a brown box in his large hands, wrapping his muscular arms around me and squeezing tight. Smelling just as sexy as he did the day I last saw him, he sends my body humming from his smoky scent, every inch of my skin pulsating as his fingers linger on my skin.

He kisses my lips.

"Going down?"

There's a glint in his green eyes when he pulls back to look at my face, his scruffed face grinning.

There's no baseball cap on his head this time—as he's been long done with that defense mechanism. And I gaze at him openly, admiring him as the double doors close behind him, locking us in.

I touch his chin. "Actually, I'm going up. And you?"

"Same as ever. Retrieving a package delivered to the wrong floor. You'd think they figured out which 'S. Smith' is the right one by now, but no. According to Hank, there are about five of us S. Smith's in the building. I'm doomed to do this over and over again for all eternity."

"Yeah. But getting you in the elevator all to myself isn't so bad so excuse me for not exactly boo-hoo-ing." I hug him closer. "I've missed you so much."

"I've missed you too," he whispers. "And so has Charlie. She's already in the apartment, probably tearing it apart, chasing Felix all over the new floors."

"That should keep her busy for another hour." I giggle.

"I hope so."

The levity from the air is gone, replaced by lust. The elevator's still ascending, but within seconds, the light in Sevin's deepened green eyes goes entirely dim, darkened by desire.

He steps over, pressing one finger to the "Stop" button.

The entire elevator shudders to a halt, and my skin trembles with it, my skirt-suit suddenly feeling extremely hot as Sevin's stare skims over my body.

Down my blazer, it goes. Over my bra.

His appreciative gaze slides over my belly and against my hips, and by the time it concentrates between my thighs, I have to stop myself from shaking, steadying myself as I drop the briefcase and macchiato to the floor, preparing for the onslaught to come.

I brace myself against the metal railing behind my hands, holding on tight. I peer up into Sevin's serious eyes.

"You wouldn't dare, Mr. Smith."

"If you think I wouldn't, kitten, then you really don't know me." He takes a step towards me, closing the space. "But fortunately for both of us, you know me better than anyone else on this planet. And you know when I say 'I'm going to fuck you so damn good right now'…that I mean it." He hovers over my lips. "I can't tell you how long I've waited for this moment for us again. Waited for you."

"Thirteen days. Ten hours. And six seconds," I hiss back near his mouth. "Just to be exact."

"Actually, it's been thirteen days. Ten hours and three seconds. But who's counting?" He reaches for my skirt. "The only thing I plan on counting for the next two days is how many times I make you 'come.'"

"That's going to be a little harder to keep count of."

"Oh, I'm counting on that." His lips curve upward. "I'm counting that we lose count by the time the next forty-eight hours is over." He reaches for his belt buckle, slinging the thick strap to the floor. He unzips his zipper. "Starting right the hell now."

Nothing is more natural than when Sevin and I come together. Not even breathing.

We're in sync in everything we do. Including sex.

And when Sevin hikes up my skirt, exposing my panties, when he lifts me in his arms, stroking one deft hand over my skirt, it's as if we've done this very act a million times before.

And I'm not so sure we haven't.

Sevin finds me wet in seconds, groaning out loud.

His fingers slip over the bits of lace covering my sex, and I can tell his shock by the way he stops. He pulls back from our frenzied kiss, gawking down at me.

"What happened to the Bugs Bunny? I liked his furry ass. I almost miss him."

"Sorry, Mr. Smith. I replaced him with something a little more worthy of a *homecoming*."

He smirks, and soon the only object in the elevator coming…is me.

Sevin releases his thick cock from his jeans, letting it jut against my hip. Slipping the black lace under my skirt to the side, he thrusts inside of me so skillfully that I almost orgasm immediately.

My ass cheeks in his hands, my nails against the railing, Sevin pumps into me at the sight of our first encounter.

Except everything is sweeter about this rendezvous. Ten times better.

Specifically when he tells me he loves me, murmuring in my ear.

My name is a prayer on his gorgeous lips. Full of worship.

Bouncing my body along his, my handsome man takes me to the brink of a naughty nirvana—some sacred heaven, and lets me tumble over it. My ecstasy in the tiny compartment is sweeter than it ever was, our stars aligning full circle, and as Sevin pushes me to my second climax, my pussy walls pulsing against his throbbing length, the stars find their destination at last.

In Sevin's dangerous eyes.

My body milks his, taking everything he has to give, and I cling to him, my limbs spent, body splayed over his as he holds me, our bodies still connected in the most sensual way.

I lean my head onto his shoulder, struggling for breath. "That was more of a welcome than I intended."

"Same here."

With a minute to recover, we attempt to straighten ourselves before seeing Charlie, starting the elevator up again.

Sevin adjusts my skirt. I fasten his fly.

But when we land on the penthouse level, there's no Charlie to greet us from the hall. In fact, she seems to be missing.

We open the penthouse doors, exploring beyond them for her. But still, no sight of the precocious kid anywhere.

A familiar panic starts to set in, but then she appears in the apartment door. Same sandy hair. Same playful wide smile.

Same green eyes as Sevin.

Only these ones are held wide in disgust, her pretty nose wrinkled as she stares up at us, seeming so much older than her eight years. She cocks her hands on her tiny hips before petting the fur ball at her feet.

"I went to the fourteenth floor to check out the laundry room. I heard it had a vending machine with sweets." Her brows lower. "But then the elevator opened. And then basically stopped." She stares. "I think I heard your voices on it. And this was so much worse than last time."

I swear… I hear my bottom lip hit the floor. My mouth gapes.

"Next time you guys want to do gross things," Charlie continues, "can you get a hotel? You're scaring poor Felix. Which is probably why he was sick the first time."

She spins away, and Sevin and I have no choice but to gape at each other.

My gorgeous boyfriend shrugs, saying the only sentence you can in this situation. "My daughter's better at games than I am."

I agree, nodding as I reach for him, knowing we'll never be able to keep up with her. Not in a million years of regulation and rules. I grin. "Well played."

* * *

There's more scandals, secrets and steam to dive into.

Are you ready to spend another night in Chicago?

*

Read on to FIND OUT what happens when Sevin's best friend and teammate Sawyer Kennedy find himself in a **salacious scandal of his own**…and the only person he can rely on to help him get out of it is **his favorite enemy** (and tempting new assistant), Naomi in THE PACT.

Flip the page to read a **Sneak Peek** from THE PACT now!

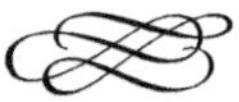

S AWYER
Four weeks later

Theoretically, the blonde in my newly renovated bedroom is damn near perfect. Too bad this liquor isn't.

The gin burns my tongue more than I thought it would. The taste of the vodka twist and the lips of tonight's bedroom treat compete for space on my tongue, and for the four hundredth time since my entire world turned upside down, I wonder just how the hell I've allowed myself to get here.

To this point of drunkenness. To hanging on the cusp of becoming that has-been athlete I'd never wanted to be.

And if it weren't for Naomi Silva, I can't say that any of this would ever happened.

But I'm one week too late for that. Not to mention minus one set of clothes.

The anti-Naomi I picked up earlier coos towards me in a molasses-like drawl. She's sugar, spice and everything sinful, but on a night like tonight, when my shoulder hurts, and I'm still feeling particularly sorry for myself, everything that normally would make my cock shoot due-north does absolutely squat.

I feel nothing. Nothing but the alcohol in my system, as she stalks towards me in barely-there lingerie, her bubble-gum pink lips pressing into a smile. She gazes down at me.

"I've never been with a celebrity before." She purrs in a strong Southern accent, her words like syrup.

"Oh yeah?" I ask, not particularly interested in her answer.

"Yeah." She crawls over the mattress, moving slow. "I've seen you on TV before. And you looked so. Damn. Strong," she emphasizes, nearing my comatose figure on the bed. "Dribbling that basketball in your great, big hands."

I want to correct her. But I'd have to care first.

My mind is still stuck on this morning's doctor's appointment, when all I've been trying to do is forget.

Forget that my career just might be finished. Forget that my shoulder—the best weapon in baseball—is almost blown to bits.

Forget that only several hours ago, my doctor, in all his infinite wisdom, just told me the worst news an MVP could ever get. An athlete's death sentence, if I ever heard one.

I hung my head.

"And to think, I came here for your help."

Dr. Semenal's dark eyes bore into mine. "No. You didn't."

"I didn't?"

"No," he repeated, his chest inflating by just the smallest fraction. The famed physician inclined forward in his seat. "You came here for me to give you good news, Mr. Kennedy. You came here for me to give you a magic cure. Unfortunately, the world doesn't work like that." Those agile fingers of his steeple again, mimicking a perfect diamond, and I feel the air vibrate ominously around us.

The man who diagnosed my SLAP tear never broke eye contact. His stare is dark. "There is no magic cure, Mr. Kennedy. No easy way out. No shortcuts. Not for the things that matter, anyway. You should know that better than most." His eyelids flicker for a second. "So now you have a choice..."

His deep voice was like an anvil wrapped in silk, weighing heavily on my ears with each word. He continued talking. "Four weeks. Four weeks of rehab with my facilities. Four weeks for us to help you recover the right way. The proper way. Or..." He shrugs, leaning back into his seat. "You can try unsuccessfully to take the easy way out, Mr. Kennedy...at what I'm sure will be an additional cost."

A fire worked its way into my chest, spreading into my extremities. Every inch of my body filled with unfueled frustration, and I knew that it would only take one match to light me into a veritable explosion.

The doctor's words, his orders, build inside of me, like a bomb waiting precariously to go off, but before I can utter a word, before I can take my Led Zeppelin-like animosity with life out on the straight-talking sports medicine pro, I heard his office door open.

I half-expected Naomi to walk through that door. Since she still was listed as my "In case of an emergency" person...

Lord knows I must have been out of my mind when I put her there...

Which isn't the case anymore.

Because right now? I do have someone here, company I need to entertain. If only for the night.

I try to smile up at my expecting guest, but the damn expression cracks on my face. Finishing what's left in my glass, I set it on the nearby nightstand, and I prepare myself to put on a performance. The same performance I've been putting on every night in the hopes of numbing more synapses.

The numbness has threatened to consume me since I collided with the opposite team's catcher over home base four short weeks ago, and secretly I'd known this day would come.

I *had* known that much. Known the second I heard my shoulder give that singular sickening pop.

The solution?

Well, that was easy. What else was there to do but screw your brains out when the rest of you was already fucked?

Luckily, for me, this southern seductress in my sheets looks up to the task. And she grabs my zipper, sliding it slowly with a firm tug, her smile bright, white teeth flashing as she eyes my unzipping fly with interest. My name is like a moan on her lips.

"How do you like it, Sawyer, baby?"

I close my eyes, the back of my hand hitting my eyelids. I breathe out a deep sigh. "Silent for the most part…if you don't mind."

"I can be silent," she chuckles with a low growl. "But I'm not sure you will be."

That'd be a first. Most women I'd brought with me to bed turned out to be screamers.

They'd try to hold out a for a while. Show some restraint, of course.

And once I was bored with whatever ministrations my new pickup tried to put on me, I'd turn the tables as my buzz from the bar wore off.

Delivering multiple orgasms—straight up, no twist, climaxing and leaving each woman deliciously limping out of my front door.

It wasn't a habit I was always proud of. But I didn't hear the women complaining.

At least…any women but the one texting me now.

The thought of Naomi cursing me to high heavens—enraged, is the first thought that brings a genuine smile to my face all night. I grin.

"Oh good." Miss Southern Belle giggles as she climbs atop my body. "That's only the second sign of interest I've gotten from you all night."

I sit up, finally intrigued. "You think? That's interesting…" I clutch the Antebellum Annie in my lap. "Because I've got a whole lot of other ways of showing you interest other than a smile."

And just like that, "Mini Kennedy" is finally hard, rigid despite the liquid haze that makes my head—the one that isn't in my pants—extremely light.

I grab Miss Georgia Peach, flipping her to all floors. Grabbing the foil wrapped condom from my jeans pocket, I set it between my teeth before sending the denim wrapped around my legs to the floor.

Next to go are t-shirt and boxer briefs, followed by the foil as I rip it apart.

There's nothing sweet about my nights like this—nothing sentimental. I stroke two fingers over the peach's panties, pulling the lacy threads aside.

She's already wet for me. And the knowledge that she's not wet for me and instead the "Celebrity Sawyer" makes me hate myself just a little bit more.

I grab for the gin, swigging it.

"Come on." She begs, her elbows pressing into the mattress. "Give it to me, Big Daddy. Play me like you play that basketball."

Reason number two to hate myself a little bit more? I can't even fuck women who know what sport I play.

But like the fraud I know I've become, I do it, anyway.

I fuck her.

I circle my twenty-four karat cock to her slick entrance and with a gin-fueled thrust tinged with self-loathing, I bury myself in the southern Barbie, my strokes soon picking up speed as my cell phone starts humming again, Naomi's text playing a tune on the nightstand.

And I can't stop the smile that spreads on my face.

It might be the only time I feel something other than anger over these past two weeks. My new assistant's anger gives me some sick sort of amusement kick, and as my bubblegum southern sweetheart reaches for her first climax, I swirl my hips to the vision of Naomi.

Brown eyes glaring at me through her sexy glasses. Wavy hair bouncing.

The thought of the annoyed enigma writhing beneath me has me stroking harder than before, pumping harder with each slickened, subsequent thrust.

Miss Gone with the Wind is on her fourth orgasm, screaming

louder than the music by the time I finish. And when I do, I climax to the inner-vision of Naomi. Of clamping down on her ire with my mouth.

I could answer her frosty texts in person, arriving at her apartment. The notion of knocking on her door and giving her a reason to rage makes me come harder than I ever have.

I'm spent by the time my orgasm's ripples stop.

I slump to the mattress just as the phone buzzing stops, the deep-seated self-hatred finally fading from my conscience as I catch my breath.

That is, until my own version of Blondie bolts upright, her blue eyes wild as she gazes down at me in awe.

"That was more 'interest' than I've ever had..." She licks her lips. "Can we do it again?"

I laugh out loud, a light sound that finally has humor in it.

Thank God.

I've reached the point of drunkenness and distraction to forget that my career might be ending. To forget that I should be more sad.

I imagine my doe-eyed assistant balking at the blonde's prospect, and funnily enough, it's thinking of her—and not the blonde in my bed—that actually makes me feel more than I've felt in what feels like forever.

* * *

Make sure you don't miss THE PACT, coming Summer 2020!

And if you're in the mood for **more sexy city nights**, be sure to skip on over to NYC in the Manhattan Nights series.

The first book in the steamy steamy contemporary THE VOW is FREE now on all platforms!

FREE BOOK

Reviews are so important to authors, and every single one I receive from a reader is such a gift. (It's better than getting a bottle of red wine. And I LOVE red wine)

If you loved **The Play**, I would love it if you could take thirty seconds to write a short review for Emily + Sevin's story! Just one or two lines would make all the difference in the world!

Thank you so much for reading their story!

And if you haven't joined my VIP list to receive an exclusive steamy suspense from me, tap the link to claim yours! ➜ http://bit.ly/NatalieReaders

THE GAFANELLI MOB SERIES

The Bodyguard

The Investigator

The Imposter

The Enforcer

—

The Gafanelli Mob Series: Novels 1-3

THE HATING HIM SERIES

Hating The Boss

Hating The Best Man

Hating The Player

—

The Hating Him Box Set

THE MANHATTAN NIGHTS SERIES

The Vow

The Bet

The Deal

The Kiss

The Note

—

Manhattan Nights (Volume 1): Novels 1-3

CONNECT WITH NATALIE WRYE

I love talking to fellow readers. I also love tequila.
And carbs. And all things books.

Connect and get weird with me anytime here:
Facebook & FB Reader Group
Instagram
Pinterest

Join my VIP list to receive an exclusive steamy suspense from me
and get even more bonuses!

ABOUT THE AUTHOR

Natalie Wrye is a reader, writer and tequila lover best known for writing heart-of-gold alpha males, suspenseful big city romance and characters you'll love rooting for.

A notebook hoarder whose books have been featured on USA Today's HEA and PopSugar, when she's not watching Netflix re-runs or yelling at college basketball games on TV, she's usually crafting sexy suspenseful stories about hard-bodied, take-charge heroes and the strong-willed women who crave them.

She loves it when people get weird with her on Facebook, NatalieWrye.com or NatalieWrites@NatalieWrye.com.

www.ingramcontent.com/pod-product-compliance
Lightning Source LLC
Chambersburg PA
CBHW071927150726
47999CB00001B/124